TONY HAD IT ALL—
AND HE WANTED MORE.

As a producer, his fantasies had come true. Women swarmed around him. There was BB, his live-in girl of the moment; his loyal secretary and sometime bedmate; two ex-wives; an endless parade of willing starlets whenever he wanted them. Yet there was only one woman —lovely, mysterious Deirdre—who didn't want something from him.

In the studio power game he'd been a quick learner, a ruthless competitor, a wily survivor. It was a no-holds-barred game of money, sex and deal making—and the action was everything. A game where nothing was ever enough. And once you were in, you couldn't get out. Ever.

Studio

Thomas Maremaa

PLAYBOY PRESS
PAPERBACKS

TO MOLLYANNE.

FOR JOEL KURTZMAN,
WHO KNOWS,
AND JAMES LANDIS,
WHO UNDERSTANDS KNOWING.

STUDIO

Copyright © 1978 by Thomas Maremaa

Cover photography by Morgan Kane: Copyright © 1979 by Playboy

Published simultaneously in the United States and Canada by Playboy Press, Chicago, Illinois. Printed in the United States of America.
Library of Congress Catalog Card Number: 79-88837. Reprinted
by arrangement with William Morrow and Company, Inc.

Books are available at quantity discounts for promotional and
industrial use. For further information, write our sales promotion
agency: Ventura Associates, 40 East 49th Street, New York, New
York 10017.

ISBN: 0-872-16528-0

First published by Playboy Press Paperbacks January 1980.

It is a sleepy language, and thou speak'st
Out of thy sleep. What is it thou didst say?
This is a strange repose, to be asleep
With eyes wide-open—and standing, speaking, moving,
And yet so fast asleep.

> —Shakespeare, *The Tempest*

"What is the scene? Where am I?"

> —Norma Desmond, in
> *Sunset Boulevard*

PART 1

I got to be three people this week.

Even when it's dark like this, and the sun hasn't come up yet, I can see them from my window. They're converging on the Box, disappearing inside. I'm in the building right next to the Box, so I can see them. Only a handful at first, then more, then hundreds, then . . . *thousands* of people by the time the sun is over the Hill and they're all safely inside.

They don't quite look human at this hour, all these bodies in uniforms of black, with clean white shirts, spiffy and polished, their faces like masks. I see a dance of suits and briefcases, long legs and short skirts, bottoms shaking. I don't see Jake or Mark, but doubtless they're in there, on the top floor, pressing buttons. . . .

One of their boys sees me. He's a tall, powerful man (who thinks like a boy), with a long deep scar running down his left cheek. And bulging, buggy eyes. He frightens me, even from a distance. I'm afraid Jake or Mark may order him to work me over, straighten me out. I hate those eyes of his, glassy and impenetrable; they see too much.

The other boys who work for Jake and Mark I'm less afraid of. I know them and they know me, because I've worked here for a number of years, even if I don't work on the same projects they do. They glance at me, smile and act friendly. And sometimes wave. I wave back. When I meet with them, they ask questions.

"How *are* you?"

"How's the wife and kids?"

"Kids doing well in school?"

"You happy in the new house?"

What they really want to know is . . . if I'm making more money than they are, if I've put together any hot deals, if my house truly belongs to me or if it's just rented (same with my two cars), if I'm getting laid by somebody they know, and if the sex is kinky. And, ultimately, if I can be useful to *them*—indeed, if I'm really a person they *need* to know, if it's to their advantage to know me. . . .

They disappear inside the Box each morning, as I say. And repeat the process day after day, year after year . . . and it changes them. Whatever they were outside the Box (happy, adventuresome, free) is somehow lost. . . .

There's a man I know on the top floor who keeps a snake in his office. He keeps it in a glass-and-metal box, this six-foot snake, long as a man is tall, and next to the box is another box—with mice in it that he feeds to the snake. The mice are alive —you see them peering through cracks in the box, you see their tiny eyes and long pointy noses and whiskers. He kills the mice and feeds them to the snake. But sometimes . . . he tosses the mice *alive* into the snake box and just watches . . . for the sport of it, the thrill. . . . His name is Mark. He's the favorite son around here—and a lover of the Box.

The Box was recently automated. They've got wiring and cables and circuits in there now. They've got people calling you on the phone who sound pleasingly automated. Their voices are honed for telephonic transmission; voices that speak at the rate of one hundred and fifty words per minute —across oceans, if necessary, speak to you no matter where you're hiding. The voices are designed to listen, react, sympathize, charm, persuade, soothe, plead, cajole, apologize, needle, explore, inform, explain—whatever it takes to "solve your problem," or close the deal.

When these voices all talk at once—which happens about the time the sun is directly overhead—it's as if they're synthesized into one person, nerves and circuitry becoming one mind . . . that hears all, sees all, knows all. . . . This one mind encased in this huge black Box that runs the whole show, the whole world.

I'm afraid of this mind, I'm afraid of the men and women who run it—because they control what I see in a darkened room on a white screen at twenty-four frames per second. They control what "truth" I see at that speed. They control the output of one of the most marvelous machines of the century. They really control what I dream.

At night they tell their stories and talk to each other in their sleep. And decide the future. At night *we* live in their other glass box. We don't go out when it's dark because we're all afraid of the dark. We're a nation of shut-ins, living in fear. Our heroes on the glass box are mechanical men, with mirror eyes and plastic shells for bodies. They run fast and stop bullets. But Mark and his boys tell them what to think and what to do.

Mornings I see billboards on the Strip with men standing thirty feet tall, smiling blandly "I like the Box."

If you work in the Box—as most of us do—they

want you to look a certain way, wear certain clothes, affect certain manners. "Grooming" is what they call it. I'm "groomed" on the job, and when they feel I've been groomed enough, they reward me with a promotion. And keep grooming me, promoting me until . . .

They want you to compete with the other people who've also been groomed. And get *results*. So in order to compete, I have to sublimate my sex into my work (actually their work). The more I sublimate, the better the chances of my competing against the other boys who've been groomed—and getting results.

They want you to be punctual and "report on time." They want you to be without emotion. I can't laugh or cry or feel anything (feelings mean vulnerability, and vulnerability is always exploited), if I am to get the results they want.

They want you to worry about what others think of you. Do you smell right, look right, talk right? Not to worry, I'll do whatever is "socially acceptable."

They want you to sign your name in initials, rather than as a signature.

They want you to be *smooth*, with no rough edges.

They want you to eat and eat and eat—and then watch your diet like a hawk.

They want you to have an ulcer, or work on having one.

They want you to always fall behind in your work, so you'll try like hell to catch up.

They want you to be white, even if you're black or red or brown.

They want you to be sexless—not male or female, or male *and* female.

They want you to be afraid of the people at the top because they know that fear will "motivate" you to perform.

They want me—Tony Schwartz—to be this way so I'll repeat the past, over and over again, repeat what's been done before—so we'll have continuity and make money, so they'll have power and perpetuate themselves.

"They, they, they—who *are* they?" My second wife Sandra wants to know.

"I don't know."

"You must know."

"I don't."

I remember a time when I didn't have to be so many different people, when I could laugh and cry and never worry about what other people would think. I remember my mother and father allowing me to do whatever I wanted. . . . Now I belong to everybody and nobody, certainly not to myself. The studio where I work owns a large piece of me; they control what I can and cannot do, though I try to convince myself that I'm freer than most. The studio demands things from me all the time, and whenever I meet those demands, they think of new ones for me. Performance is everything. So either I measure up, or I'm out. I'm replaceable, like everybody else. My two ex-wives own and control a large portion of the money I make. More than that, they own a good piece of my past and control the very things I value most—my two kids, one from each marriage, my daughter from the first, my boy from the second. She's nine, he's six. Although I see my kids, and they come to see me as often as our legal settlements allow, and love them as my own flesh and blood, they belong more to my ex-wives (who are both lovely yet possessive) than to me. My house and two cars belong to the bank and to the studio (which leases me my German cars, which are identical in year, make, and appearance). And whatever else I own in the way of property (some land up north), stock, and savings, belongs as much to the bank as to me, and often causes me more trouble than it's worth. (My land is dry because of the drought and therefore vulnerable to fire; I pay exorbitant property taxes and my stocks keep losing their value, diminishing way beyond what I paid for them originally.) I don't have a lot, just enough to create problems and run up bills to tax lawyers and accountants. I keep thinking, of course, that just a little bit more, a small jump in salary, or maybe an increase in the value of my stocks, will put me over the top, give me enough so that I won't have to worry all the time, worry and grow scared at night of losing what little I have. (By most standards, I know I have more than other Americans, yet other Americans are probably not as vulnerable as I am—at least I don't think they are—because of the nature of my work.) So most of what I own belongs to the banks and the government (taxes) and the company that runs the studio that runs me.

I remember a time growing up back East when I had very little and didn't have to worry so much about belonging to other people. I remember not being particularly aware of how poor we were, though I do recall my mother hating my father for it, hating him because we lived in a one-room apartment with no furniture ("boneless," I used to say), hating him because he sold junk and was going bald. Probably like most kids, I was unwanted. "Goddam

you, Tony, shut up!" Dad screamed at me whenever I cried or laughed or raised my voice. Why
did he do that? I had no brothers and sisters.
Mother said I was the "hope of the family"; she
never allowed me to forget *that*. One day I would
have all the things they didn't. One day I would
succeed where Dad had so miserably failed. I
would serve my family proud. Mother *whispered*,
"You leave, okay? Before it too late, Tony boy."
One day . . . I came out West.

If nothing of what I own truly belongs to me,
then I'm ashamed to admit that not much of what
I think belongs to me, either. I hear something, a
good idea from somebody, and immediately I steal
it, copy it, and try to make money from it. This
part of the West—this land of billboards and freeways and eternal sunshine—was founded (I'm told)
by people who did pretty much the same thing.
They borrowed, copied, and stole whatever they
pleased from other American cities and made it
work here. I'm thinking of our drive-ins, shopping
centers, and period architecture (houses imitating
houses imitating houses that were successful elsewhere), all of which sprawl out over hundreds of
square miles, with great logic and not randomly
at all. . . . They built a whole culture around the
Borrowed, a culture devoted to amusement and
escape. At the studio where I work we've done
what the city has done: We've taken the dreams of
people in other parts of the country and turned
them into moving pictures, into commodities that
can be rented, bought and sold on the market, also
for amusement and escape.

*   *   *

I remember thinking there used to be a "West" and everybody knew where it was, but now all I hear are people talking about the "Coast."

My thoughts belong to the people I work for. If they say I ought to be happy, I think I am. If they say I'm not aggressive enough, I think so, too. If they think conservatively, so do I. If they want change, I want change, though I'm beginning to discover that change is the one thing the people I work for don't want. So I find it hard after all these years in the business to think for myself. I have trouble winnowing out what thoughts truly belong to me and what thoughts I'm supposed to think.

The way I talk, my speech and vocabulary, my tone and inflection, is the way the people around me talk. My voice is flat, hollow, like theirs. (Over the years I've tried to preserve some of my own speech—the street talk and obscenity I learned growing up in the East—but it's been extremely difficult.) I say the word "entertainment" in every other sentence (last year's code word was "relevant" and the year before that "viable"), but it's more out of habit than anything else. I say entertainment (along with the new code word "integrity" which is just starting to catch on) because that's what I think people in my business want to hear. In fact, it must be, it must be *exactly* what they want to hear because they nod in agreement with me and echo the same words in their every other sentence. Entertainment and integrity.

My clothes are imitations of what everybody is wearing and what is fashionable to wear. If I have on an outfit of faded jeans and faded denim jacket with a faded western shirt and a cowboy belt, it's because everybody has started wearing it. I go with the trend. But the trend doesn't always suit me; wearing shirts open at the throat exposes the wrinkles on my neck. And I make mistakes: For a long time I thought you were supposed to have your jeans cleaned and pressed and *creased* down the middle. When I had a beard and long hair (admittedly when it was the rage), I looked fake and unreal, like one of those people in the cigarette advertisements who announce, in bold letters, "I know my taste."

I don't feel I'm doing my own thinking, acting, talking, or living. Somebody else is. As though I were picking up signals transmitted from an outside source, many signals, weak and strong, telling me what to do . . . how to act and feel . . . what to wear and how to think . . . Where are the signals coming from? Who's behind them? I want to find out.

It feels like I'm talking in my sleep. Half the time I don't know if I'm awake or asleep.

So: three people this week. One person with my secretary, another with the few friends I have, still another with my kids. The first person lives on the phone and in meetings; he's designed to manipulate and get results. (That's why we're in business.) The second person likes to play tennis and socialize. The third tries to be fatherly, but without success. (The more time I spend with my kids, the less they like me.) Sometimes it's confusing, being all these different people. I go home at night but can't make the transition from one to the other. I insult those few friends, thinking they are businessmen. I try to be overly protective and paternal with my women. I try to be "friends" with my kids. And some weeks, when the seasons in fantasyland change, all the different people I'm supposed to be run together. I'm mean and aggressive one minute, sweetness and light the next. I fight with everybody over petty things (which is one reason my first marriage broke up) and then bring them roses (especially if I've insulted my secretary) to make up.

It's very confusing, as I say. And after a while I go numb. I can't decide on anything. Making even a simple choice as to what to eat for dinner or whom to call or where to go for a good time becomes the hardest thing in the world. Midnight comes and I can't fall asleep. I take Valium and Nembutal and I drink but sometimes nothing seems to help. Even when I do manage to fall asleep, I feel my dreams don't quite belong to me. I don't recognize the people in them, I don't identify with any of them, and I'm often puzzled as to who is actually having the dream. This may be the result of working all these years in the Industry, producing pictures. The pictures *are* your dreams. (I see at least one every night and often as many as four or five over a weekend.)

We do your dreaming for you. We give you ninety-minute fantasies (which is about how long all of us dream, cumulatively, every night) and if the fantasies are *there* and connect, we make money. That's how we've made money in the past. . . . In my dreams, I see cars crash and bombs explode and naked ladies, with dark wiry pubic hair, spread-eagled on beds covered with white satin sheets. I see these things but I don't believe for one moment that they are real . . . or happening to me . . .

Years ago, I fell in love with a girl named Jill McCorkle. She had bushy eyebrows, eyes dark as night, apple cheeks, and a bony figure. She was smashing. I don't remember how old I was, but we went to the same school together back East. Jill McCorkle—"Corky," we used to call her—was slightly boyish in manner and appearance (those apple cheeks were pretty hard). And she liked to spend all her time with the boys. Still, she'd come to school wearing lipstick, white satin blouses, and, around her pretty little neck, chokers made of black velvet, gold hearts dangling from them. I had a terrific crush on her. But we lived in very different neighborhoods—her family was well-to-do, mine wasn't. Her father was a plastic surgeon, mine sold junk. I laugh to myself when I think about it. She had tiny feet. She'd bring her toe-shoes to school because she was taking ballet, and I remember thinking, "How can she dance? Her feet are so tiny!" And she signed her name in a strange way, with large looping letters. (I signed mine with small letters, or often just initials.) When I asked her out for dates, she turned me down flat: "Tony, I can't." *But she never said why.* And I never knew if she turned me down because her father had money and mine didn't, or because she thought I was a *shmuck,* or because I wasn't handsome enough for her. I never knew—it's a mystery. Why am I still hung up on her? Why do I keep thinking about her? I fell in love with Jill McCorkle. Do people fall in love anymore?

All these different people, I'm beginning to realize, are never satisfied. They all want More. The businessman wants More, so does the man with friends and the man with kids. Probably they all want More just for the sake of having More and not for anything specific. Yet having More probably won't make them any happier. In fact, I'm pretty sure it won't. The more *things* I have (most of which are really toys, like my German cars, which are loaded with gadgets and gismos), the less satisfied I get. I think I want a new car, a larger house, more money in the bank, more women to sleep with. And all the people I know, both in and out of the business, want those same things. (Ours is a city of Extreme Want—and a city where you're led to believe that you *can* get everything you want.) The trouble is, nobody can wait anymore. I want all my desires to be satisfied *right now*. (This week I want to get laid by three women I don't know very well.) I can't wait, I want instant gratification. And that goes for *every*thing.

Back East I remember my father and my uncle both telling me to wait, telling me not to demand the world instantaneously. My uncle said, "The longer you wait to *shtup* a girl, the better it is." I grew up waiting. . . . One day I packed all my things in a suitcase and, with sixty dollars in my pocket, I headed out West for a shot at making it. The motion picture business seemed the best shot, one that I'd dreamed of as a kid (Gable and Bogart, Cooper and Cagney, Howard Hughes and Orson Welles were my idols), so that's where I pointed my guns. I figured I'd stay until my money ran out. Which of course it did in exactly one week after my arrival. Then I wired home for a return bus ticket, which my folks immediately sent. But luck was with me, and somehow I managed to get a break. So I kept the money my folks sent me (using it to buy a brand-new suit) and began working here, at this studio, first as a messenger boy, then in the mailroom for twenty-five (no, thirty) dollars a week. In the years since, I've tried not to forget how poor I was—and how lucky to get that break —but I still hate to be reminded of my roots.

I hate to be reminded, I suppose, because I think they're a sign of weakness, and weaknesses (no matter how small) are always exploited in our business. Most of the time I cover up my origins, my family back East. In conversation, I never offer more than a bare minimum.

"Where you from?" people ask.

"The East."

"What part?"

"Different parts. Dad sold things, so we moved around a lot."

End of conversation.

I love to talk about the Industry, about the dream factory where I work and to which I owe all my good fortune as well as my misery, though I'm beginning to think that I owe the latter to myself. (I mean, I create my own misery.) Yet what is wrong with me is probably what's wrong with the Industry. And the other way around. So maybe what's wrong with the Industry is wrong with the country, I don't know. I do know that, contrary to what you might think, we try very hard to reflect what is happening in the country, and what is wrong. . . .

In my mind I thrilled to being naked with her. I wanted to stroke her breasts . . . which were large and soft and nippled just right. I wanted to stroke them as tenderly, lovingly as I rode my bicycle to school. . . . Then my best friend boasted that he'd made it with Jill McCorkle, screwed her under the fire escape.

"Take it back!"

"You kidding?" He laughed.

I got into a fight with him and was sent home from school for the rest of the day. At home I told my parents: "She fucked another kid." (It was the first time I'd ever said the word "fuck"—I didn't know exactly what it meant, what fucking *really* involved.) Mother was furious because I'd said "that word" and she told Dad to punish me, which he did by sending me to my room without dinner. Neither of them cared about my being sent home from school, or why.

The studio where I work is a dream factory, just like all the studios that make up the Industry. (We've been calling ourselves a dream factory for so long that we've grown to believe it.) The dreams we manufacture used to be in black and white, and we made hundreds of them before and shortly after the War. And millions of Americans went to see them week after week, rain or shine, because they shared those dreams and believed in them. (They were hooked, and we couldn't make enough dreams to satisfy the addiction.) Back then, the studio was alive with talent and energy; the opportunities were enormous because there was so much production on the lot. Everybody seemed to have a shot. Unknowns (mostly actors from the Midwest with long faces and equally long bodies) became stars overnight. (They didn't have to wait ten years to be "discovered" overnight, either.) And being a star really *meant* something: You could do whatever you wanted, and nobody could say anything. The old-timers tell me you could be free sexually (morality was never an issue), and you could live any way you wanted, royally, extravagantly, as most stars did. . . . In real life and on the screen,

you acted out (almost mythically) the fantasies of
the people watching you, and you fulfilled a certain
destiny in every picture. And that's why people
came to see you no matter what the vehicle. . . .
But soon television came in, about the time I came
out West with that suitcase and sixty dollars. Television came in and, for a while there, I remember
people being both curious and excited about the
medium. (I also remember people hating the "glass
eye" because it made everybody smaller.) Nobody
saw television as a threat to motion pictures—at
least not until it was too late. But of course it was
a threat, and before too long it took over our business. And then, in no time, advertising took over
television, and that's pretty much where we are
right now. (The medium has no other purpose
except to sell products, and the "actors" who appear
on it become products, too.) Ninety percent of all
the film being shot in the Industry, I'm told, is for
television commercials. The look and sound and cutting of a commercial are the product of the highest
craftsmanship our Industry can achieve. And the
advertisers are not unwilling to pay for that. They
pay astronomical sums, tens of thousands of dollars,
for just thirty seconds of film. (I've made those
thirty-second spots and I can tell you it's the most
boring, stupid work you can imagine, and everybody who does it hates it—or else *loves* it, which
is even more bizarre. Only the money—thousands
of dollars a day—helps deaden the pain: You feel
disconnected from anything important, you think,
"Why am I wasting my life away like this?") Some
say commercials have replaced our dreams. At night
I know I have a tendency to dream in those thirty-
second spots; my dreams are zingy, wild, often
broken up into fragments, quick cuts like Coke

commercials. I know, too, that I'm always hungry and thirsty in my dreams; I can't seem to drink enough. . . . I can't remember when last I had a long dream. . . .

I wish I could forget Jill McCorkle, but I can't.
I look for her in starlets I meet.
"Pretty good piece of nooky," my best friend said.
I like women with soft shoulders and lacquered nails and tiny feet.
I half expect her, I don't know why, to show up at the studio one day looking for a job.

Our studio used to manufacture dreams for mass consumption, but we don't anymore. We stopped doing that a long time ago, when everybody stopped going to the movies on a regular basis and just stayed home and watched the Eye. Our studio now manufactures about ten or eleven pictures each year, and these are called Product. Product means a film that sticks to the old formulas (whether it's comedy, gangster saga, action-adventure story, Western, or science fiction) and doesn't take any chances and repeats what's been done before. (We call these "movie-movies.") Product means that the studio has a better chance of recovering its investment than if it tried something new. Which is perfectly understandable, as far as I'm concerned, because the theory behind it is that what's worked before with an audience will work again. And again. And again. . . . You see, every year there are kids growing up who haven't seen the old formulas and will laugh at the same jokes their parents, and even their grandparents before them, laughed at. Product also means that the film I produce for the studio can be properly sold and marketed and promoted through advertising. (In fact, Jake the studio boss doesn't like to make any films that he can't "see" the advertising for.) And every year the cost of Product goes up, doubling and quadrupling, ten, twenty, thirty million dollars sometimes just for the film negative, even *before* you take into account the additional costs of advertising and distribution. So with that kind of investment to protect, we want to be sure of what we've got, sure it repeats the old formulas and last year's hits, because a couple of bombs and we could be in serious trouble. We talk about being "gamblers" and living by instinct, but in truth Product means (for all of us) playing it safe and hedging our bets. . . . (The studio boss Jake doesn't think of our business as "gambling," though he admits being a "conservative gambler," which to me sounds like a contradiction in terms, yet if he's one I'm one too. It's not "gambling," he says, because we're like the house in Vegas: We always seem to come out a little bit ahead of the man trying to beat the house.) Which is true. Last year, profits were way up—but not because we took any real chances—and this year things look even better.

Ultimately, our Product is disposable. Like everything else these days, it's manufactured for quick consumption. In fact, our Product is consumed several times, first in the movie houses, then on television, then on foreign television, where it's dubbed into a dozen different languages. (Our stars sound very strange indeed, speaking Greek, Italian, and Japanese—but that's something else again.) But unlike a book, say, which is the same in hardcover as paperback, our Product undergoes a horrible change by the time it reaches television. The TV censors chop out all sex scenes and four-letter words

and re-edit it as they please, often without logic
or continuity. (All our talk of "integrity" doesn't
stop it from happening.) Then our Product is ready
to be cannibalized by television commercials. And
before it's all over, it bears no resemblance to what
you saw in your neighborhood theater. For you
don't see movies on television. What you see on
television is television.

The studio lies in the Valley. We are just over
the Hill from town—you drive ten minutes on the
freeway and take the second exit to your right and
wind down the road until . . . (Like our Public
Relations men say, we are located in the "gateway
corridor between the Valley and the Basin.") The
studio is a city unto itself and could be its own
movie set. (The PR men say we are a "complete
business and pleasure environment.") There are
office buildings and sound stages (more than three
dozen) and departments of all kinds (Art, Editorial,
Camera, Sound, Wardrobe, Construction, Grip,
Prop and Set Dressing, Electric, and Transportation,
to name just a few). At the center is a Tower. The
Tower rises many, many stories into the hot Valley
sun and is often capped with clouds. The Tower is
made of steel and glass. In the lobby is a bust of
our founder, Max Schumacher. Studio executives
work in there, the moneymen, the decision makers,
and the higher the floor they work on, the more
power they're supposed to have. (Their power is
also measured by where they park, and whether the
company leases them a car. Parking in the underground lot of the Tower means more power than
parking outside, though if you do park outside, it's
important to have your name on the space.) Men
who work in the Tower must wear black suits, white

shirts, and black ties every day. (I don't know how that got started; the studio boss and the man before him whose bust is in the lobby laid down the rule. They must've had their reasons. . . .) We call these men who work in the Tower "Suits," or at least I do, and I'm glad they wear suits, so you can tell them apart from the rest of us. If the studio were a casino, the Suits would run the house. The rest of us are Players.

My office is in the Producers' Building adjacent to the Tower. I'm on the first floor, in a suite of offices with large glass windows and a patio terrace overlooking our backlot. The office is tastefully furnished by the studio chief's wife, who decorates many of our offices and rents out antiques to us. (Everything we have is rented—for tax purposes.) On the walls I have movie posters of pictures I've made (just as everybody else in the Industry has) and photographs of me with various stars I've worked with as well as plaques and awards from European festivals and competitions my pictures have won. The office is large and comfortable because I had a hit a couple of years back ("a few *too many* years," my secretary Cinnamon says), and to some extent I'm still riding the wave of that success. Technically, I am a producer. I call myself a "dependent" rather than an "independent" producer, because I must rely on the studio for approval and financing of projects that I bring to them. I don't have autonomy (how many producers in the Industry do anymore?). They have final say.

My deal with the studio is to make three pictures here, but they still call the shots because they're the ones putting up the money and taking the risks. Simple as that. Though I'm a producer, I've also done acting and writing (which is where I went after my stint in the mailroom) and directing. But what I am, in essence, is a Player. Just as there are executives in the Tower—and fortunately you can tell them apart from us because of those black suits they wear—there are Players at the studio. We are in this building or the one across the street or on the other side of the lot. Players can be actors, writers, directors, or producers. (In fact, it makes no sense anymore to talk about "actors" or "writers" or "directors" unless by that you mean the technical function they perform.) Either you are a Player, or you're not. Either you're in the game, or you're not. I know Players immediately, and they know me. I know them by the way they talk and walk, think and act. Players can wear cheap clothes or expensive ones. Players can be tall or short, black or white, straight or gay, men or women, actors or directors. For, on the bottom line, all Players are businessmen, and if they're any good at all, businessmen with balls.

The game is fast. (If someone pitches me a script or a story, I say, "Give it to me in three sentences.") Compared to most businesses, it's all-consuming. The excitement—the action—is everything. (To become a Player, all you really need is a property, a book or story or script that you've optioned. Once you've done that, you're in the game.) Sometimes it's so fast that Players burn out young, by the time they're forty, and sometimes before they've truly had a chance to do their best work. I hate to see it happen—Players with holes the size of half dollars burned through their stomachs—Players who've lost the touch and flipped out and driven everybody around them crazy: casualties of the Industry. Often they get used up and discarded after the studio has made the deal and manufactured the Product and recouped its investment. Or they don't know what to do with themselves after they've made it. (Players share very similar goals: a chocolate brown German car, money in the bank, a chance to fuck starlets.) They get confused by success, blunder into bad deals, make too many enemies. . . .

The game is fast because the stakes are so high. One day you're busted on your ass, struggling to pay the rent, and the next day you hit the jackpot. Bingo. Suddenly you have more money than you know what to do with. The highs and lows are higher and lower than in any other business I know. And luck more than talent can make the difference. Which is probably why everybody in town wants into the game, wants to be a Player. Which is probably why Players jump from one studio to another, like chips on the board.

I like the speed, the action, which never ends (like Las Vegas), which is everything. But I know if I'm not careful I'll burn out very soon, too. And I worry about that. (You always bet on the come, but what happens if one day nothing comes?) Directors have a life span of about four years if they make it; four years when they're hot and productive and can do what they want. Studio executives last two, maybe three years at most before they're quietly transferred, or phased out. Actors burn out immediately, or become stars and last forever. Actresses can work for a few years as "unknowns," suddenly become stars, and just as suddenly be forgotten within a year. Writers? Unless they can preserve their uniqueness, their individuality, they burn out faster than anybody; one script and many already start to repeat themselves, failing to get better. Nobody in our business ages very well anymore. And the game is so fast that once you're in, you can't get out. Ever.

I don't exactly fit the image a producer is supposed to fit. I'm not fat, don't wear sharkskin suits, don't have on thick black horn-rims. Don't smoke Havana cigars. Nor speak in malapropisms and use "fuck" in every sentence. (The Public seems to think that all producers are like that.) In truth, however, I've been fat, I've smoked cigars and sprinkled my speech with "fuck." How *should* I sound? How should I look? After all this time in the business, I'm really not sure.

So I've started to look like everybody else.

I'm neither too fat, nor too skinny. Too grubby nor too handsome. Too short, nor too tall. I'm ageless, a sort of perpetual thirty-nine. (In fact, I always lie about my age.) My hair is neither too long nor too short. Sometimes it's sprayed, sometimes it isn't. I wear my shirts open three buttons at the throat. I try to have a good tan—and work on it. My nails are manicured. I part my hair on the same side as the studio boss Jake parts his.

"Why?"

"I don't know—it's easier I guess."

"Doesn't it bother you?" My second wife Sandra laughs.

"No."

"It doesn't bother you?" She looks surprised.

"Not at all."

"I can't believe that, Tony." She looks hurt somehow, though being an actress she may be "acting" hurt.

"Why not?" I'm curious.

"Why would you want to look like everybody else looks?"

"I told you—it's easier."

"Easier than what?" I don't know if she's being genuine or playing a game with me.

"I don't know . . ." I turn away, the words trailing off my lips.

"But nobody knows who you are."

"I don't care."

"Don't you see?"

"See what?"

She pulls me back.

"You borrow."

"Borrow?"

"Yes. You borrow. You take pieces from the people around you."

"So?"

"You do it to get what you want."

"So?"

"You're adapted, Tony."

"So I'm adapted."

I remember as a kid trying very hard to be my own person, trying to think and act and talk for myself. But . . . if Dad told me white, Mother told me black. If Mother said white, Dad said black. Half the time I didn't know whom to believe. If I believed my uncle Saul, who visited us frequently and wanted me to go into show business, I couldn't believe my father. (Uncle Saul is another story: He was a midget, though for a long time I could never remember the difference between a dwarf and a midget. . . . Midgets are normally formed and proportioned, but diminutive. Is that right? Anyhow, he loved show business and was always entertaining us, a real *tummler*. At night he worked as a waiter

—"Uncle Saul never had to stoop for the tip," was the family joke.) Uncle Saul wanted me to agree with him against my father. And Mother wanted me . . . against Father. And Father against Mother . . . One day I began agreeing with everybody.

At the studio I am a totally Adapted Man. I take on the characteristics of the people around me. Like the studio chief, I want to know everything. Like the man who runs Television, I get nervous, twitchy, and run scared whenever I have to make a decision. Like the man who handles Publicity, I can be suave and debonair, a charming rattlesnake. Like the actors who act in the television shows we produce, I can Go Crazy from time to time. And like the man who runs Film and appears to be next in line of succession to our chief, I can manipulate and control thought. Of course, I don't do any of these things nearly as well as the originals, which probably makes me more human and less successful than any of them. It also makes me more vulnerable because part of the time I don't know who I am, if I belong to them or to myself. Basically, I try to do as I'm told and feel as little as possible.

For example, I almost never laugh. It takes something extremely funny to get me to laugh. And when I do laugh, it's never spontaneous. I must be prepared and set up to laugh. If somebody in a group tells a joke, I wait till others laugh first, and then I only laugh as loudly as they do, never any louder. I used to laugh a lot more. Things were funnier, more hilarious in my youth than they are now, or at least they seemed that way. In fact, I used to tell jokes myself, but seldom do anymore. (For one thing, I can't *think* of jokes to tell. Maybe all the jokes have already been told, maybe somebody has put the lid on jokes and stopped their flow through society—I don't know. All the jokes start in prisons, I'm told; so there should be more jokes because there're more prisons now . . .)

At any rate, the studio doesn't mind me being like this—an Adapted Man. They *want* me adapted for obvious reasons: I'm less of a threat, more pliable and controllable. As I told my second wife Sandra: "So I'm adapted." But sometimes it makes me angry as hell. I get angry, but nothing registers on my face, for I've been conditioned over the years to hide what I feel, to internalize all my anger and frustration. . . . You see, the studio has everybody where it wants them and where it thinks they'll fit in—not necessarily where they'll do the best job.

If you are unhappy—and last year, despite our record profits, there were more unhappy people than the year before—the studio cannot admit to it. They can't accept the fact you might be unhappy; to the contrary, they think you're *using* your unhappiness simply as a ploy to Get More Money. So . . . they offer you More Money, and keep offering . . . and keep offering . . . until they reach a point, finally, where you can't turn them down. (We all have our price.) Which makes you even *more* unhappy because you know, as they know, that you can be bought. And once you're bought, you've become a prostitute. One man I know calls this buying of people the "Golden Handcuffs."

I'm always up at five and in my office by six or six-ten. I'm out of bed in a shot, usually in the middle of my last dream of the night. (I'm terrified of oversleeping.) I jump into the shower for precisely three minutes, starting very hot, almost scalding, and finishing with a douse of cold. I shave with a straightedge, always beginning my stroke on the same side of my face, which is delicate, cutting myself at least once under the chin, just above my Adam's apple, blood trickling down my neck. I dry myself very quickly. Put on a fresh shirt every day. (White shirts are preferred at the studio, though colored shirts are okay—ever since the man who hosts that late-night talk show started wearing them a few years back.) Shine my shoes, and clean the polish from under my nails. I sit down at the breakfast table and wait for the coffee to perk. I scan the trades (which arrive before breakfast, thanks to a special delivery service I subscribe to) to see who's making it and who isn't in our Industry, and for gossip. I love gossip. The coffee perks, I pour a cup. I scan the trades for the grosses on our studio Product. The grosses are: smash, tame, sparky, brisk, languid, hefty, soft, dapper, lusty, sweet, zippy, dull, fat, nice, thin. And so on. I eat a couple of slabs of toast with jelly, then reach into my vitamins (B_1, B_6, B_{12}, C, D, E) and pop four of each, often as many as a dozen pills at a time. I read the local morning paper for the main news of the day. Terrorism is threatening the Middle East. Civil War looms in Africa. Our cities are decaying badly. Our politicians are corrupt. Things are getting worse, not better. I read the paper, essentially, to confirm my view of the world. By the time I'm out the door it is five forty-five at the latest, and I'm quickly on the road. Takes me about nine minutes to drive from my house in the Canyon to the studio. The freeway gets me there fast. I like to drive the freeways (I don't believe anyone who says he doesn't) and think I drive them well. I like my German cars, I like the performance, handling, comfort, style. (Sometimes I can't decide which German car to take, even though they're identical.) I like to speed on the freeway, switching from lane to lane. I like the adrenaline rush. My eyes become very focused, alert, I feel suddenly awake. I speed because I like the flirtation with danger, I speed because it *is* dangerous. (Cops here seem to understand this intuitively—so when they stop you, pull you over, even if you've been going ninety-five in a forty-five zone, they don't feel compelled to lecture you. They just write out the ticket—I appreciate that.) The way people drive, I figure, tells me a lot about them, tells me how they react, what their reflexes are, and if they have an instinct for taking chances. Every now and then . . . I drive the opposite way. Instead of speeding at every opportunity, jumping from lane to lane, accelerating, braking, hitting turns at the danger mark, I drive . . . loosely, letting my beast (which is what my mechanic calls this car) float along, almost laughingly. (I feel good in my car and even break into a smile, or try to laugh.) The freeway offers me a piece of time in which to collect my thoughts before work. I think of things. I talk to myself (better myself than a stranger), having very intimate conversations about my private life, my sex life. . . . There is something very *secure* about the freeway, I don't know. You never get lost on the freeway. (My friends back East can't quite understand this—they're terrified of driving them, afraid of losing their way. I tell them, "You get lost on the *side* streets.") I like the freeways because, ultimately, that's where the city lives; we're a city built to be seen and felt and lived through the insides of a machine. . . . At five fifty-five, plus or minus one minute, I'm at the main gate. One of the security guards, Benny, lets me drive through; he knows my car and I always wave to him. "Morning." "Morning, sir." Benny is of indeterminate age—he could be thirty-two or fifty-two—a little guy, with a crackling voice and a face perpetually red, flushed, skin peeling and spotty, as though he has a drinking problem. Benny keeps pretty tight security these days; careful about whom he lets in. (I've seen him turn away agents and writers who don't have appointments.) There is some kind of fear in the air, I don't know what it is. Fear we may be attacked by terrorists, or mad bombers. "It's his paranoia," we say, referring to Jake the studio chief (who recently tightened all security on the lot). In my office I call New York and talk to agents I know there, looking for new material (producers live and die on their material), books, stories, whatever. I call my second wife, Sandra (the actress), to see how my boy is doing in school; she says, "He hates school." I call Arizona, where a TV director I don't trust is shooting on location; I tell him not to fall behind schedule on the picture. I call one of the Suits in the Tower who comes in way before all the other Suits, asking, "When's our starting date? We're ready to shoot." He balks and hesitates and says he'll "get back to me." He's a junior, he talks in rectangles and boxes within boxes. I call the man who does special effects at the studio because I want to know how ours are coming for the picture I'm preparing to shoot when the junior gives us a starting date. The standard joke about the special effects man is: "If you ask him what time it is, he'll build you a clock." I hang up before he has a chance. I call BB, the actress with whom I spent last weekend at the Beach; I tell her to get out of bed. *She* hangs up. I open my first bottle of Coke (I prefer bottles to

cans). Before the day is over I'll drink at least a
dozen bottles. (I have a Coke machine in my office.)
The sun is trying to come up over the Hill.

Six forty-six and the cleaning crew has completed its job, leaving the insides of my building,
this white marble ziggurat next to the Tower,
immaculate. "Boss likes 'em clean," they hum. . . .

Seven-o-three and the Suits are arriving. They
start early and work hard; there are very few late
nights for them—parties that extend beyond midnight or even eleven o'clock.

By seven-sixteen the truckers (Teamsters) are
back from location shooting. They shuttle crews
and supplies back and forth all day long. . . .
"Damned hot out there!" Seven hundred drivers
come and go. . . .

The mail arrives in my office at seven-forty—
the earliest in weeks.

Eight-o-one and there is a long line at the tiny
kiosk in front of the studio commissary. People are
buying smokes, coffee and donuts, and the trades
for their daily fix of gossip.

Eight-o-two and the first studio tour begins, and
will continue every few minutes for the rest of the
day. Thousands of tourists will see our backlot and
hear about the Product we're making and (they
hope) catch a glimpse of the stars. . . .

Eight-o-nine, the secretaries are pulling into the
south parking lot in their compact American cars.
They have to pay to park—and then walk a half
mile to the Tower.

Before eight-thirty our set designers have "dressed"
a dozen different sets on the backlot to look like a
dozen different cities and locales in the world.
Nothing is as it seems. . . .

By eight-thirty in comes Alfred Hitchcock. He has on the same black suit and black tie that he wears every day to the studio. He has three parking spaces in front of his offices, a pink stucco complex of buildings near one of the sound stages. "Anyone who happens to park in one of his spaces is subject to immediate death," is one of our jokes. Though in his seventies, and suffering from a heart condition, Hitch still wants to direct another picture, but he has trouble climbing up and down stairs. "He could phone it in," somebody suggests. Hitch has thought of that. He and the studio chief have lunch together Thursdays at the commissary; they'll talk about it. . . .

Eight-thirty-eight . . . crewmen tool around the backlot in electric carts, stopping here and there, chattering about horses they bet on at the track. . . .

Nine-o-six and agents whose "territory" is our studio arrive for meetings with both Players and Suits. Agents have more fun than anybody else in town, and they run a helluva lot of the business. "Westerns are next," they whisper. Last week it was comedy and the week before that science fiction.

Nine-ten and the head of Publicity is doing yoga in his office, the door closed. . . .

Nine-eleven and our Casting Director is in her squat, low-ceilinged office interviewing actors for potential "term contracts," meaning seven years in which you work exclusively for the studio.

In a dressing room painted black from floor to ceiling, an aging woman star is being made up for her small part in one of our big-budget, all-star-cast pictures. On the dresser by her mirror is an urn containing the ashes of her first husband. "I like to keep him with me," she says. The door swings open and in pours a crowd of reporters and tourists.

She gets up and they applaud her spontaneously. "You'll pardon me, gentlemen, but I must get ready for my scene."

The sun is now staring me right in the eyes.

Before any of this happens, or indeed *can* happen, Jake the studio boss is up. He's up at four in the morning (as legend has it) while it's still dark outside and the rest of us are asleep. He drinks Brim or Sanka. He fixes breakfast for himself while his wife is still asleep. He reads the papers, he reads every magazine he can get his hands on. He calls New York, he calls London. He wants to know everything about everything. He appears in his office at six or six-ten—I say "appears" because I know he sometimes plays a dirty trick on all of us by hooking up his office with his home phone, so you think you're talking to him at the studio when actually he's at home. Nothing is as it . . .

Jake Steinman is admired—and feared—by everybody, though not feared as much as he once was. A man of great height, extremely thin, with light blue eyes, he cuts a sharp profile. His hair is silvery, his face darkly tanned. In fact, his tan is darker than that of any man I know in the business. By turns he can be warm and cold, sweet and savage, mean as hell and your best friend. The trade papers call him "the most powerful man in the Industry," and they've *been* calling him that for so many years that everybody has come to believe it. Jake works harder than anybody here—and longer, despite his age (he looks as though he's been around forever). He wants to know everything and he *knows* everything. He knows what you're thinking and feeling, and has known for years.

I half expect him to call right now and tell me, in

his icy voice, to stop saying what I'm saying. "God-dammit, Schwartz!" I can hear him on the phone. "Stop your *kvetching* and get to work!" And he's right. (He doesn't really care what your grievances are, just so long as you're not wasting the time you're getting paid for.) I half expect him to threaten me —if I go on like this—with a refusal to renew my option, which is what getting fired is called here, or perhaps the ultimate threat: "You'll never work in this town again!" Christ, I'm *still* frightened of the man after all these years; I feel a slight chill running down my spine. . . .

I don't care.

Let him call.

I won't answer the phone.

If he calls, I'll just let it ring.

It's ringing now. Three, four, five . . . nine times before it stops. It's ringing again. Should I answer it? The more I'm left by myself, to my own thoughts and feelings, the more malcontent I grow. . . . I get angry, I want to hit somebody, and get it off that way. I fade in and out of this terrible mood; it comes and goes—I'm not sure why. The studio tends to bring out the best and the worst in me, the most generous and the most selfish. . . . Off and on now for the past couple of years I've been a malcontent. My trouble is, I don't know why, but I am. I'm not supposed to be, but I am. I wasn't told to be, but I am. I don't want to be, but I am. I'm a malcontent. There are malcontents in every division and department of the studio; everybody deals with it differently. Some dry up and crack, like old shoes in a closet. Some go calmly along, until one day they flip out completely. Others get loaded on dope or booze, or both. Their faces look weary, grizzled.

The alcoholics (and there are many among us) tremble uncontrollably in the morning before having that first hard drink of the day. Others keep changing jobs, jumping from one studio to another. Still others drop out of sight for a while and write film scripts. ("Everybody in town is writing a script," people tell me.) The scripts aren't very good, usually, but that doesn't stop everyone from trying to sell the material to the same studios they left in anger and frustration. (The studios reject the scripts, but these malcontents personalize the rejections, thinking they've been turned down because of their "politics" or because "nobody likes them," when in truth they've been turned down purely for "commercial reasons," nothing else. The studio, as we all know, is in business to make a profit and could care less about your "politics," or even if you're a malcontent at all.) But I know and recognize malcontents. Unless they're extremely clever at hiding it, which most aren't, I can spot them a mile away. My theory is that the whole Industry is run by malcontents, by unhappy people. Even those at the top aren't happy. Jake grumbles more than he should: "Some weeks we win, some we lose." His staff is mercurial, and their decisions often defy all logic. (They made a picture in which the stars were imitating the stars of another period in pictures; it made exactly one hundred and forty-four dollars in gross returns, in New York, the second weekend it played from six on Friday to midnight Sunday.) This unhappiness filters down to all levels, especially to the crews and workmen, who say very little (except to the unions: *We want ours. . . .*") and curse under their breaths when you ask them to do something. . . .

*   *   *

Maybe we're not happy because we're spoiled, maybe we're not happy because we haven't grown up. Everybody here is a kid. I'm a kid—I look and act and talk like one most of the time. Producers ten years my senior do the same. Writers who are thirty-three say they are "thirty-three going on ten." Actors are mainly crazy kids. (They get into fights and throw tantrums.) Directors are smart kids, sometimes crazy like actors; they can yell louder and talk faster than most other kids. The Suits are manipulative kids who spend a lot of time figuring out ways of getting what they want. Jake the studio boss, who's in his sixties, is the smartest, craziest, toughest kid of all. He *always* gets what he wants. And we manufacture a Product mainly for kids. If it reflects what the kids out there want, what their fantasies are, or what we *think* they are, we have a hit: All the kids in the world are connected with the same fantasy at the same time. Maybe we're malcontents because we've been kids too long—and kids can't be kids forever.

I picked up the phone. It was Cinnamon, my secretary.

Her car won't start, she'll be late.

For a moment there, I thought Jake was reading my thoughts.

I don't know what to do without Cinnamon—she's been with me for years. . . . Like most of the women who work at the studio, she is quite attractive, with classic features and a beautiful deep olive complexion. (She claims that her mother developed it by starting her tan from age three.) She dresses chicly, in the latest fashion. Her voice is pure Lauren Bacall, at times bitchy as hell—and for some reason I like that in a woman. I've slept with her a number of times, but never allowed anything serious to happen. We both have terrific respect for each other and work well together. I think she wants to be with me when I hit again, when one of my pictures *really* connects with all those kids out there. And suddenly all the phones are ringing with reporters begging for interviews, demanding to see us . . . with stars sending scripts that they want us to produce . . . with the front office making half a dozen stroking calls a day because my picture has 'em lining up five times around the block. . . . (For that brief period when you have a hit, it feels like you're the psychic center of the whole world.) Of course, I don't know if I *will* hit again. I want to, but certain practices in our Industry are so destructive and self-defeating that I wonder if *any* of us will ever hit again. One hit for every five, ten, fifteen, twenty misses—the odds get longer all the time. Cinnamon keeps thinking that we will hit again, which is good, and she encourages all the people who pass through my office to think that, too. I probably spend more time with her than with any woman I know, and more of my life passes through her than all the telephone lines and circuits to which I'm continually hooked up. (This is a business totally conducted on the phone, and in the men's room.)

Other women in my life right now: BB, Sandra (my second wife), Daphne. I like BB because of her boniness: She is tall, skinny, almost fleshless. She is a model trying to make it here as an actress. (Barbara is her first name and her last begins with a B; she's done a lot of commercials on television for beauty products.) "They tell me I got the highest fee ever paid for thirty seconds," she likes to tell me.

Since coming out here, BB's had her face planed, her nose bobbed, ears pinned, and teeth capped. (I don't know why; she showed me her "before" pictures and I liked them better.) And she takes acting lessons. The trouble is, when BB acts she thinks she *must* act. So she looks mannered, modelish. She could develop into an actress of some talent (she already has the looks), but I don't think she's willing to work at it. She's hoping that if she hangs out long enough with the right people, she'll be discovered. It's another version of the they'll-find-me-in-the-drugstore dream.

BB happened to come along at a time when there was a void in my life (Sandra my second wife had just left). I think she'll stay with me until she finds somebody who can advance her career faster than I can. I like her boniness, those rounded shoulders, small breasts, flat stomach, long legs (with knock-knees), soft feet. . . . We make love at her place. We make love on the kitchen floor (the checkerboard tile cold as ice on our backs), standing up in the living room (that hurts), sitting down with her legs above my head (which I like), on the living room sofa (we keep falling off), in her hot tub (though that's more difficult than you might imagine—I go soft, rubbery). I spend the night, then get up early while she's still asleep (usually curled up on her left side, bones in a zigzag) and make breakfast (scrambled eggs and bacon) and run on the Beach near her house (chased by several dogs)—and leave.

"I have to go."

"Don't."

"Why? I can't stay."

"Stay."

"I can't."

"I want you to stay, Tony."

"You know I can't."

"Just this once."

"We talk in clichés."

"So?" She doesn't seem to mind.

"Did you ever think about that?"

"Don't go."

"I have to."

Wherever we are BB makes love very quickly. And with a minimum of passion. She prefers a kind of limited sensation, a shot in the gut. At the moment of climax it's as if we're hooked up to each other by a mesh of wiring and circuitry. She gasps suddenly and lets go, her body quivering in release. I feel like she's at once ice and electricity—nothing very sensuous or caressing, just a series of quick jolts.

We never talk afterward. Nor, really, even before, and in that way and certain other ways I find BB different from most actresses I've slept with. *She doesn't want to be loved.* Most actresses desperately want to be loved, and at the same time they don't want to be loved at all. (They can't make up their minds which it is they want. And it's this quality of indecision that accounts, I think, for their being actresses. If they're very good, if there's a lot of tension—sexual—between being loved and not being loved, they have presence. Presence means that you know an actress is *there;* she takes up space.) If you try to get too close to an actress, she'll slam the door immediately in your face, *but if you don't try,* she'll either think you're a faggot or do everything possible to get you to come. BB doesn't want to be loved nor does she want to be rejected—which makes her more of a *starlet* than an actress. Most starlets are young and pretty and want to advance their careers. For that, they'll do anything—take incredible abuse (and, face it, our Industry can be very cruel), and I feel sorry for them, for these starlets like BB, because everybody knows they're willing to be abused, mistreated just to become stars, or even get a shot at becoming stars. . . . Knowing this, too, starlets will only allow you to fuck them (BB is no exception); they won't give you anything more than a quick lay, a chance to get your rocks off. (Most of them are so young and inexperienced in everything except the Art of Getting What They Want that they really *can't* give you something else, even if they want to. . . .)

After we make love, BB tends to fall asleep right away, her eyes shut tight, her bony body curled up like a child's, soft and naked. But I stay awake, I can't seem to fall asleep no matter how satisfying an orgasm I've had. I'm afraid to sleep because of what I see at night. I plead with BB: "Don't let me see that picture again." But she's sound asleep, nothing can disturb her for the next hour.

So I lie awake, and begin shaking in bed.

Suddenly my breathing stops.

I lie motionless again.

My eyes open wide—fixed on a white screen . . .

I am sitting in a room at the top of the Tower. The chairs are made of hard green leather; they squeak when I touch them. The room is filled with studio people in black suits; I see Jake and his cohorts, their faces like masks of simulated flesh. Mark is whispering in Jake's ear. I catch a glimpse of him: eyes glassy, head made of steel, teeth flashing like fangs, a deadly snake ready to strike. I see a woman dressed in white whose face is obscured, a mystery. In unison, the men say, "We must control."

"No."

"We must control."

"More time," I say, my tongue curled back in my throat.

"Join us."

I look for a way out.

There are no windows in the room, just a white screen on the wall. . . .

I hate it, I don't know what to do about it. I told BB and she doesn't know what to do, either. All I see in those pictures at night is failure, my inability to resist the studio people who want to control. . . . I'm terrified of resisting these people, and at the same time terrified that if I *don't* resist them, sooner or later they'll control everything I do and think and say and feel. (Small wonder the new code word is "integrity.") Yet if I *do* resist, if I fight back, I risk losing my job, being thrown out in the cold —without a contract. And then who pays for my two ex-wives and my kids and my house and . . . They know this, too. I'm sure they know it. Jake Steinman, as I said, knows everything, sees all and makes you feel as if it's impossible to keep a secret from him.

Cinnamon called. She can't start her car.

This is the second day in a row that she can't start her car.

BB called. "What the fuck did you mean by ringing at dawn yesterday?"

Jake knows where we are most vulnerable. He knows perfectly well. He knows we're afraid of failure. I know I am, and in fact, that's one of the reasons I came out West. I came out knowing that either I made it here or not at all. It didn't matter, necessarily, what business I was in—I could've been a real estate developer, aerospace engineer, or a gangster—just as long as I was successful, because being successful was everything; I'd make my parents proud. "Remember—you're the hope of the family, Tony." I know how deep that feeling runs and how the people who came out before me shared it and the ones before them shared it and the ones . . .

I hate seeing any signs of failure around me. I'm not comfortable with people who've failed, I don't want them to touch me for fear that their failure will somehow rub off. So I avoid them at all costs. In my time I've known failure—and I don't want to repeat it. (The men I see at night know this about me too, I think.) My first marriage was a failure, so was my second. (For reasons I don't care to get into right now.) And because I'm terrified of failure, I don't like to see success in others. When a Player has a hit, when he makes a picture that gets good reviews and lines around the block, I send him a note of congratulations (it's a common practice in our Industry), but underneath it all I'm jealous as hell of his success. If he succeeds, then somebody else must fail—and I don't want that somebody to be me. So I don't wish people well, and I know they don't wish me well, either. If I succeed, they'll ask themselves: "What has *he* got that I haven't?" And they'll keep asking: "Why *him* and not *me?*" Naturally I do the same thing.

In this business, it used to be that you were entitled to your failures as well as your successes. Both were equally unpredictable, fickle as love in winter. And probably in the end, all the hits and misses would manage to even themselves out. The main thing was to keep working. As one kid director (at twenty-one he directed Joan Crawford on television) put it: "Build your bridges ahead of you faster than the ones behind you get burned up!" But now our business won't allow you a second chance. If you fail you're out.

Unless you fail lavishly.

At times I'm so afraid of being vulnerable that I don't see things very clearly. Decisions scare me, I go numb. My thinking gets all fuzzy, thick as fog. I talk for hours on the phone, but it's just a way of avoiding what I have to do, and it makes me even fuzzier, more confused. I bullshit to people and don't believe half the things I'm saying. (I'm surprised when somebody actually takes me at my word, actually *believes* what I'm saying.) I tell wild stories and gossip about people I don't even know . . . and pretty soon as the day wears on . . . I get more and more fuzzy. I forget what I've told people, I fuck things up. . . .

Maybe the air has something to do with it, I don't know. We're buried in smog (we call it "morning haze," but it's smog), smog that burns your eyes, throat, lungs, smog that burns your insides. . . . (The smog even comes in colors, depending on where you live: soot black in town and all the way out to the Valley, dark brown to the east, and green to the west, as you go out to the ocean.) Only in winter is everything clear. The winds from the ocean blow the city clean, and you're stunned because all of a sudden you can see for miles and miles in every direction. The view is magnificent, like no other city in the world. The atmosphere is more relaxed, less frantic. Visitors come from the East at that time of year; deals are made, little tours of the town and the studio given, friendships renewed. In the air is a feeling of change. The studio people are back from trips at Christmas to Palm Springs or Acapulco.

Anxiety levels are down. January and February are the clearest times, though if it starts to rain, if the winter rains come (and they haven't for a long, long time), it can really drive you to the Edge. You see, the rains keep everybody inside—and you go crazy inside. For this city has no inside. We are all exterior, façade, surface; our skin is metallic, our eyes like a set of mirrors. We live to see and be seen, we live outside, exposed and vulnerable.

Everybody wants to be in a movie here. BB's in mine, so is Cinnamon. Cinnamon likes BB, but hates my second wife Sandra. Sandra likes Cinnamon, but hates BB. We're in each other's movies. And we know all the plots. I know the struggling producer movie, the starving artist movie, and the plots of both. But we don't exist unless we're seen, and our movies don't exist unless they're seen, too. BB has to be seen, photographed, and named in gossip columns. If she isn't . . . Somebody else (I'm convinced) is watching and recording our movie. Even when BB and I make love and the doors are locked and the shades pulled down and the phone off the hook and I'm deep inside her and she's looking for a way out, I still feel like we're being watched. . . .

Despite the smog, I like it here, I like this city. We have more space than New York, and we're more hooked up to each other mentally than people are there. New York is all paperwork—I don't know what we are but we're not paperwork. New York synthesizes what happens elsewhere, while we try to make things happen. The New York movie is dying, ours is still alive. On the other side, we used to mirror what most Americans thought their world should be. I don't know that we do anymore. And while New York has taste and speed, we have speed but admittedly very little taste. New York is being torn down and rebuilt all the time; we're waiting to be rebuilt. . . .

In essence, ours is the first modern city of addiction. You can get hooked on anything here: sex, violence, drugs, film, voodoo, witchcraft, religion. Everybody is pushing something, so it's not difficult. But once you're hooked you become a pusher, too. Pushers and addicts, that's what we've become. I don't like it—it scares me. Half the time I don't know whom to believe anymore because everybody is always selling something and their pitches are so smooth that it's often impossible to figure what's true and what's not. . . . And they're always trying to sell us things we don't need . . . when what we really need . . . it embarrasses me to say this . . . is each other.

I remember being scared as a kid, I remember Uncle Saul scaring me with his stories about "Dan," this shadowy, mysterious figure. "Dan" was coming, "Dan" would get me if I were bad. . . . I remember being scared of snakes and lizards and Gila monsters, scared of doing badly in school. I remember being scared of being a midget, like Uncle Saul. Scared I didn't smell right, or look right. Scared the girls like Jill McCorkle would think I was a jerk. I remember going to horror movies to *be* scared and wondering why I kept seeing them if all they did was scare me. . . . Now I'm scared and think I know why, but that doesn't stop me from still being scared.

I'm kissing her softly.

It's night.

We're sitting in an old movie house, with creaky wooden chairs.

I'm kissing Jill McCorkle and also feeling her up.

She is trying to stop me, but my hand won't go away.

I have an erection.

My hand has now worked its way inside her blouse and succeeded in unhooking her bra and gently worked its way back to her tits.

Which are smaller than I expected.

The nipples are erect, hard.

I want to bite them.

A Western is flashing on the screen. The Cowboys are shooting the Indians and the Indians shooting the Cowboys; I wonder why.

I stick my head inside her black-and-white checkered blouse and begin sucking and biting.

"You're missing the picture," she says.

I take her hand, cold as dry ice, and have her reach inside and fondle me.

I bolt out of my chair and onto hers.

I'm just about to come when the film breaks down.

The Cowboys stop shooting the Indians.

Lights go on, I'm blinded for a moment.

People are standing around the theater, looking at us with glassy eyes.

Jill McCorkle slaps me across the face and runs out, half-undressed.

I cough nervously.
The people start coming toward me.
I see deep scars running down their cheeks.
"Gimme time," I say. "More time."

I could see Jill McCorkle playing the lead in a
film we're planning to shoot on the backlot. The film
is called *Studio,* and a friend of mine is set to produce it, though he's having problems. . . . *Studio*
is what we call a "concept" film, one of those
projects that develop when some writers and producers have a meeting and sit around in green leather
chairs and ask, "What if . . . ?" In this case, what
if our studio were somehow taken over by a group
of revolutionaries (urban guerrillas) who occupy
the Tower and, in a weird twist, hold Alfred Hitchcock, along with others, for ransom? The men in the
front office like the idea of using our backlot as this
gigantic movie set: It helps keep down costs (we're
going through a period of stringent cost control in
spite of last year's hits) and allows us to maximize
the use of our contract players (actors who are on
salary). Plus, we don't have to shoot on location.
But the real reason that the Suits want to make this
picture (and the reason for all "concept" films) is
advertising. This is a picture that can be *sold*—I can
see the ad campaign for it already—and that means
we have a better chance of reaching our target
audience. (They'll see the ads and know in their
minds exactly what the picture is.) If the advertising helps the audience identify with the Product,
we're there. *Studio* will hit. (In this business, like
most other businesses, audience identification is
everything.) Now all we need is a plot, and this
is where we're having problems. . . . Beyond what
we have already—these revolutionaries taking over

the Tower and holding Hitch hostage—nobody knows what should happen next. There is the young actress whose boyfriend is one of the revolutionaries, and she's sent on a mission to persuade him to release all those held hostage. And other actors who work here stop what they're doing (cop shows for television) and join forces to fight the crazies. In other words, you see actors and actresses stepping out of their fictional roles to combat the menace. And in the end—after we've seen a daring chase sequence and much violence (bodies hurtling out of the Tower)—they persuade the terrorists to surrender. (The part of the actress is perfect for an unknown like Jill McCorkle and would make her a star.)

Personally, I think the plot line of *Studio,* such as it is, stinks. And I've gone so far as to tell Irv Steingart, the producer on the project, just that. He admitted that he thought it did, too, particularly the whole notion of urban guerrillas taking over the studio. *Are* there any more revolutionary groups in America? And if there are, do we *believe* them? In the news and on television don't they appear as actors playing the *parts* of revolutionaries? Aren't they packaged in there with the commercials for dog food and deodorant like everybody else? In short, are they scary? Can we make them scary? And why would they want to take us over? I told Irv that we'd end up making a picture intended to be scary (scare movies have traditionally been good box office) but that everybody in the audience, all the kids, would soon be laughing at. Sure, revolutionaries could be an element in the plot, I told him, but not the premise on which the whole thing was based.

The trouble with "concept" films is that they start out as this terrific idea and then quickly turn into a joke. So we make a picture based on a joke. We hire writers to write a script based on a joke and then get angry because the script isn't any good because it's based on a joke. We hire other writers to rewrite the script and their scripts aren't any good either, because they're based on the joke. The director shoots the picture thinking it's a joke. The actors laugh all the way through shooting. The crew knows it's a joke but doesn't laugh. The Suits get worried because the joke is costing so much. In their reviews, the critics point out all the jokes and we get angry at them because they don't take us seriously. We expect the audience to sit through our jokiness and believe it, take it seriously. Which is a joke on us.

"So what do we do, Tony?"

(Irv the Suit and I talked about the making of *Studio* last week—on the day Cinnamon's car broke down for the second time.)

"I don't know," I said.

"What do we do for Bad Guys?"

"It's a problem, all right."

"I know it is."

"Used to be a lot simpler," I said.

"I know."

"There were Cowboys and Indians."

"Sure." He laughed, though I didn't think it was so funny.

"How can you have Bad Guys when everybody gets away with everything . . ."

"Damn."

". . . when *every*body's a Bad Guy?"

"Dammit—think of something, Tony!" he commanded.

"I'll try."

I promised him that I'd make an effort (as a personal favor) to dream up a better plot line for *Studio* and solve the Bad Guys problem, if in fact it could be solved. I didn't want to tell him during our meeting that there was, indeed, a picture to be made about a studio—*this* studio, with its tyrants and courtiers, fools and pretenders, its glamour and debauchery, waste and extravagance, struggles for power—especially as to who should succeed Jake —and petty squabbles.

"I'll think on it," I told Irv.

He seemed relieved.

Irv is one of the vice-presidents in the company that runs the studio. Though in his mid-fifties with a shock of white hair, he looks younger because of his recent face-lift. (He described the operation to me in great detail one night at a party when he was more than slightly drunk.) He always wears a suit with padded shoulders and addresses Jake as "Mr. Steinman." He's also a crude man, and yet for some reason loved by all. (Cinnamon thinks he's a "doll.") Irv is terrific at thinking up ideas for movies and is credited (rightly) with inventing the whole concept of "concept" films and selling it to Jake and the other men who sit on our board of directors. Irv's ideas are the result of long meetings on the top floor of the Tower (his office is down the hall from Jake's); they rarely come out of anybody's experience or bear much resemblance, in my view, to what is truly happening Out There. Still, Irv is good at what he does, gets paid well into six figures, and is respected. (I like him but I don't know why.)

On this project Irv wants his assistant, Frank Shelby, to co-produce and direct. Frank is also in his mid-fifties but tries very hard to look young; he wears his hair long and rides a motorcycle and comes to work in suede. Suede jacket, suede shirt, suede pants, suede shoes. Well, a number of years back Frank directed a hit comedy that won some awards and scored at the box office, though he hasn't done much of anything since—mainly because he's a terrible director. Irv, in any case, is backing Frank for *Studio*. He says he wants Frank to make a comeback, meaning that Frank needs the money to support his third wife, an English actress with a taste for expensive cars. So Irv (whose power is considerable) is giving Frank a shot at it, even though he knows it's risky and the other boys in the Tower keep asking, "Hey, what's Shelby done lately?" It's the kind of project that sounds all wrong. The concept is wrong. Frank is the wrong man to direct. Irv is wrong in backing Frank. The plot is wrong. It's the wrong time for such a picture. And everybody knows it's wrong. So the picture is sure to get made.

Irv wants me to write a treatment, and I hate writing treatments. I hate writing these little five-page jobs that are supposed to give you a compressed, often truncated version of the plot. (But I'll do it—do it my way.) The characters end up cartoons, the plots mechanical. The important thing is, you have something *on paper,* and with that you can generate some excitement, some "heat." Nobody in the Tower believes you have a story unless that story is committed to paper; of course, that doesn't mean they will actually *read* what you've written. (The higher up in the power structure you go, the less reading anybody seems to do—except for the men and women at the top, who read *everything*, including your thoughts.) These treatments are primarily designed to sell the idea for the picture, but since Irv has already sold the idea for *Studio*, I think what he really wants from me is a believable story. And believable stories no longer exist. If they do, I want to find one, just one, and make it into a feature, which everybody will see because it's believable and the critics will love because it's believable—then I'll retire forever. Yet there probably is a *very* believable story about this studio; I do know that the studio brass wants Irv's concept made, I can sense as much in the air. They don't know *what* they want, and if you ask them, about the best reply you'll get is, "We'll know what we want when we see it!" I'm sure at some level, a gut level, the boys want a roller coaster ride—a picture with lots of chills 'n' thrills, climbs 'n' plunges, stars in danger. Just like that very first roller coaster ride you saw years ago in Cinerama. . . . If Irv can do that with Frank directing, they'll buy it. (Most of our products now are just roller coaster rides, anyway—rides designed to make you sweat, jack up your pulse rate, work on your nerves, scare you jittery or hysterical. If that happens, you got your money's worth, say the cynics in our business. People pay for physiological changes. That's the only "content" to a roller coaster ride.) But in *Studio* what I think the boys want, in addition to the ride, is to show everybody here, all the Suits and Players, crews and workers, putting aside their inflated egos and debasing cynicism just long enough to fight the enemy . . . everybody working together courageously for the common good. And so *Studio*, in their thinking, will create another myth, another fantasy about the system—that the men and women at the studio can, under difficult and dangerous circumstances, serve their dream factory proudly, as one big happy family.

In fact, Jake Steinman likes to think of us here as all one big happy family. And goes out of his way to keep us happy. (He pays us well and allows a certain group of us a share in the studio's profits.) I'm sure he'll do whatever is necessary to keep Irv happy and Frank happy and . . . Jake is very paternal, though he's paternal without being bossy. He believes that the way to run the company is acquire the most capable, efficient executives and let *them* run it. "We're in a people business," he's fond of saying. "We're dealing by and large with the judgment of what the public taste may be anywheres from three months to three years into the future. If our management expertise is right more often than they're wrong, we do very well." Simple as that. Jake's been in this business fifty years. "I sold candy in a burlesque theater in Chicago when I was twelve, thirteen years old," he once told me. He loves film and has seen every major motion picture since Sound came in. "I'm the best film buff you'll ever meet," he says. (He once ushered in a Chicago movie theater from six to midnight.) "I'd rather talk to you about film than about money." However, he makes the best deals in the business. If you want something, he'll take half of it away from you and you won't know *how* it happened or *when*. And there's no bullshit with Jake —you tell him exactly what something costs, how much we made, how much we lost. Jake Steinman has been around for so many years and seen everything and survived so many regimes and power struggles that I guess he's earned his reputation as the most powerful man in our Industry. Survival is the name of the game, and Jake and his studio family have most certainly survived. . . .

He took over the business in the Sound era (when we were making over a hundred features a year) from the original founding father, Max Schumacher. Max was an Austrian immigrant who came as a young man to this country around the turn of the century. (A little guy with a big sense of humor, Max was the first son of parents who were, needless to say, shoemakers in the old country; he had a brother called Moritz—his parents naming their two boys after a pair of German comic characters very popular late in the last century.) Max heard from a friend how great the climate was out here: "always sunny," which is why he came here rather than San Francisco. Anyhow, he managed through various means (he'd been in the clothing business before) to buy up some land, sell it, buy some more, sell that, buy still more . . . Before he knew it, he had all this land in the Valley but nothing to do with it. One day, as legend has it, a friend of his brother Moritz invited him to see something in a penny arcade. "They got the darndest thing in there," the man said. "They call it a motion picture." Max saw it—a peepshow with naked ladies—and was thrilled. He decided to build a film manufacturing company on his land in the Valley, around the same time (before the First War) that Carl Laemmle founded Universal Pictures, also in the Valley, and Thomas Ince started a company in Malibu Canyon. Back then the studios were called "camps" and everybody had a lot of fun. One day Mack Sennett came trouping into town with Fred Mace and Mabel Normand and started making terrific little comedies. One day, the story goes, when Sennett was sitting in his office, he saw three little extra girls come up the walk, arm in arm. All of a sudden he ran out the door and stopped the girl in the middle and said, "You're going to be a very famous star!" She was stunned. "What's your name?" he asked. "Gloria Swanson," stammered the extra girl. Well, Uncle Max (as Schumacher came to be known) did a similar thing by hiring Gladys Smith, "the little girl with the curls," as she was known, for the then-outrageous sum of one hundred and twenty-five dollars a week—and made *her* into a star under the name of Mary Pickford. Uncle Max was indeed a showman. He produced over three hundred shorts and two-reel comedies his first year. He hired good people and made everything from Shakespeare to Westerns. He opened up the "camps" to the public, charging visitors two bits apiece admission for a chance to watch silent pictures being made. He had a Rolls-Royce and drove around with a raccoon coat on even the hottest of days. He cultivated a deep tan. He lived in the most fashionable hotel of the period, the Lorraine. He could always be seen wearing a little brown derby and walking with a cane. He was quite a ladies' man. He fell in love with Clara Bow, that crazy flapper. He used to go to Valentino's home up in the Canyon (Falcon's Lair—which was painted solid black on the inside) and snort coke with the star. Uncle Max prided himself on knowing what the public wanted because he thought of his own taste as simply an extension of theirs.

He's still alive today, I'm told, easily over a hundred years old, living quietly in a private rest home. He says that the secret to his longevity is the fact that, in his entire life, he has never exercised. Uncle Max doesn't hear very well anymore and the word is that he hates to see movies now. I saw him not too long ago, when they wheeled him out in a mechanical chair—wearing a tuxedo, his right eye covered with a black patch, his face shriveled up, though still very handsomely tanned—for a banquet honoring his contribution to the "art of motion pictures." He cracked right away, "Never said it was an art." The audience loved it, broke up laughing. "Art can't make money!" he roared, getting more laughs, before they wheeled him off.

Surgery takes about ninety minutes—Irv was telling me—sixty for the face and about fifteen for each eye.

They start by giving you anesthetic, but only a local—so you're completely awake.

The nurse is cute and wiggles her behind.

The doctor comes at you with a knife.

The blade is sharp.

He makes an incision beneath your lower eyelashes about one inch long. You can feel it.

You bleed.

He loosens up the skin of your lower eyelid and shapes it gently, softly, like a sculptor in white.

He clips away the excess tissue, your dark bags and wrinkles. Sews up the incision with plastic thread, making very tiny stitches.

Repeats the operation for your upper eyelids. Takes out the puffiness and wrinkles. (The operation is very exacting because eye tissue is the thinnest and most delicate on the face.) Applies no bandages.

For the face, he makes the incision around the

ears and in your hairline at the nape of your neck. You can feel that too.

Pulls the skin taut to see how much should be clipped away.

You hear him clipping away.

He sews you up, leaving a long scar hidden in your hairline. Applies pressure bandages to reduce swelling.

You wear sunglasses for several days until the swelling goes down and the stitches are removed above and below your eyes.

"Ah, now I can see what the public wants," says Irv, peeling away his old face, looking at himself in a mirror for the first time.

Uncle Max's philosophy: Find somebody who can do your job better than you can and let him do it. From the day that Jake Steinman stepped into Max's office, where he started as a low-level promoter and booking agent, it was apparent that he would one day become . . . president of the company, head of the studio. (Or so the old-timers here tell me.) Jake didn't have to utter one word that first day of arrival—everybody knew. Max must've known, too, for no sooner had he hired Jake than he began teaching him everything that he, Max Schumacher, knew about the business. (Jake started at sixty dollars a week and moved up fast from there.) Jake learned quickly, and sure enough, ten years from the day he arrived he became studio head, taking over from Max. Max didn't exactly retire; he still came into his office every day, made calls, sat in on meetings, ate lunch with Jake and others at the studio commissary (always in the back corner table). He and his third wife began collecting antiques (which once filled their sprawling Tudor mansion) and giving lavish parties for all the "A" people in the business. Through a series of investments in the stock market, Max had become very rich (he had something he called the "Tao" system) and was content to enjoy himself in his later years. Jake was in full command.

His rise to power was a remarkable feat in itself. For Jake started with nothing. He came from a poor family in Chicago's East Side—never had time to finish high school because he had to support his brothers and sisters after his father was killed in a railroad accident. Worked in a burlesque theater selling candy for a man named George Young. Young got him other jobs as well—some of them connected with organized crime. Jake had grown up on the street, knew its language and rhythms, and could've become a successful criminal, like most of the other kids who had nothing in his neighborhood. Yet he found he had a certain gift. While most criminals use violence or force to get what they want, Jake used talk. He would talk and talk and talk until he got what he wanted. And this made him into the Consummate Pitchman. "He could sell you *anything*," old-timers tell me. Convince you to buy what you didn't need. Convince you that he was really doing something *for you,* and that by buying whatever he was hawking, you were doing something for him, too. Which is central to the con man's art. So Jake survived and kept his family from going hungry—but he never forgot the experience, never forgot that he started with nothing. . . .

When Jake took over from Max, it became clear to everybody that he wanted this studio to be the best in the Industry. He wanted us to have an identifiable name with the public, just as Disney had (Uncle Walt was also a Midwest boy and he and Jake were good friends for years), so that the moment you saw the studio emblem on our Product, you knew what to expect: entertainment of a high order, entertainment for the great mass audience. He wanted our distinct studio style (our Product wouldn't be interchangeable with the Product of every other studio in town)—and went after the talent to produce it, no matter what the price. (On reflection I'm not sure he was as keen for *quality* Product, knowing that quality always took more time and therefore more money, and the results could often be mixed.) Jake made some incredible deals for stars, offering them a million dollars a picture or a chance to participate in the profits— just to keep them happy. ("Participation," as it was called, started a whole new pattern for the Industry in that the stars owned half the profits from a picture.) Jake had everybody under contract to us: Bette Davis, Joan Crawford, Ann Sheridan, Dennis Morgan, Jimmy Stewart, Barbara Stanwyck, Johnny Garfield, and, if you'll pardon the expression, Ronald Reagan. He worked hard and pushed his people to the limit. (And while other studio bosses seemed to cultivate public images and indulge in the wildest night life in America at the time, Jake maintained a low profile. Rarely went out to parties. Didn't seem to have much outside life at all. Guarded his privacy with extreme care, refusing to divulge much of anything about how he lived. Did he drink? Have any vices? Throw extravagant parties at his palatial house on the other side of the Hill? The gossip columnists wanted to know but never knew.) Shortly after the War, Jake Steinman almost realized his dream: Our studio was well on its way to becoming the best in the Industry.

But then television came in and changed everything around (as television commercials changed television around later on). And the dream began to fade. . . . What was once larger than life was now diminished to merely a series of dots on a glass eye encased in a box. Actors thirty feet tall shrank to the size of comic strip characters. The fourth largest industry in America soon became . . . Needless to say, we tried everything to compete —from biblical spectacles and 3-D to Technicolor and Cinerama—but we failed. And seeing that our dream of building a truly great mass medium—one capable of turning out fantasies at better than one a week and in effect controlling the dream life of the Republic—seeing that this was fading and that *film* was becoming a medium (in the form of television) for selling products and nothing else, we grew disillusioned. I think Jake grew disillusioned as well, though he kept it pretty much to himself. Publicly, he said: "I don't think television is going to go away," as some wistfully imagined. "It's creating a whole new audience for us, because anyone watching television is a customer for motion pictures." Nobody believed him.

He dealt with the threat of the new medium that wouldn't go away not unlike he dealt with most threats in his life—by confronting it. One day he went out and bought as many TV sets as rooms in his house and, in fact, put one in each room and watched the Eye compulsively, obsessively . . . for days at a time . . . until he knew . . . everything there was to know about it.

The television business is one of the most highly complex, interrelated businesses you can imagine. Very few people really understand what makes it work. The risk factor in producing a television program is less than in features: You know who's paying you and how much you'll get paid for a show. But it differs from the feature business in one major area—you can't have a big hit. No matter what the numbers (ratings) are on a particular show, you're still paid a fixed fee. And the fact that a TV show is a smash doesn't mean that you can maximize your revenues (through advertising and promotion) the way you can with a hit picture. Nevertheless, with preselling and the creation of the late-night market (for reruns of our cop shows), and maximizing foreign syndication, television can be a very good business. What makes it work here is the fact that it's an integral part of our studio operation. We use actors who are contract players; we have streamlined production facilities (an intensive, six-day work week for all those involved —programmed for efficiency by computer). We originated the idea of "Movies for TV" and consequently were the first to manufacture films for that market (which was very profitable). We devised the "best-seller concept," whereby novels could be adapted to television and serialized. Our library of feature films and TV films provides substantial cash flow. And we use the studio tour to reinforce audience identification with our TV Product. (The tour *lives* because there's so much TV production on the lot. Tourists look for their favorite TV stars at work—most of our features being shot away on location—see the sets and sound stages where the cop and doctor shows are produced—eat at the commissary where the TV stars eat. And continuously, throughout their visit, see posters and placards and illuminated blowups of those TV stars. . . .) In our studio family, television is the favorite child.

The man everybody is saying Jake will pick as his successor comes out of television. In fact, he used to head that division of the company until Jake promoted him to head Film. So he knows as much, if not more, than Jake knows about the medium. Mark Fowler is in his late thirties, cool yet extremely aggressive (he sold nineteen hours of our programming—cop and doctor shows—to the networks one year). He's an imposing figure: tall, steely in build, with dark, penetrating eyes. He speaks in a deep booming voice. And has the smile of a cobra. He can be a real *putz* at times, or a charmer. He's part of a new breed in the business: the snakes. He started in the legal department (after law school in the East and clerking for a judge) and quickly worked his way up the ladder—something Uncle Max always liked: executives starting in the mailroom or the lower rungs and vaulting to the top. Like Jake, Mark is a shrewd, tough negotiator. Making a deal, he'll take your scalp, your tongue, your teeth, even your heart, and he'll tell you at every step along the way what he's taking and you'll watch him taking it and you'll feel the pain, but there won't be a goddamn thing you can do about it. . . . Mark's mind is analytical, like Jake's. I've seen him thinking twenty-five moves in advance, like a world-class chess player, calculating ways of selling our Product to the networks, plotting production schedules, assessing talent, making decisions on which film projects to go ahead with and which not. . . . He and Jake have started to meet and confer more frequently these days (which has led to all this speculation that Jake will name Mark to take over as studio head). They confer over lunch at the commissary, they confer in Jake's office when the computer grosses come in hourly, telling us how our Product is doing in various "situations" around the country. They plot marketing strategies and try to find the right "media mix" (radio and print, print and TV advertising) for each picture, and Mark is a wizard at that sort of thing. (And he sells every picture to the exhibitors by saying, "It's a microcosm of American life.")

Yet in his day-to-day running of the Film division (which of course involves me), I think Mark has fucked up. (Incidentally, I'm not afraid of him, though just about every Player and Suit I know is.) He watches every penny like a hawk, probably as a result of working all those years in television, where everything is so heartlessly programmed, so impossibly tight in terms of budget and shooting schedules. He watches every penny and makes everybody who works for him paranoid because they feel as though all he's doing is watching *them*. If you're shooting a picture and it goes *one* day over schedule, you can expect a long phone call, often threatening, from one of Mark's boys in the Tower. The boy won't say he is calling because Mark is concerned, though you know Mark Fowler is behind it and that he watches your rushes as they come in and keeps close surveillance on the shoot. *Two* days over and a Suit appears on the set with orders (he won't say under whose authority) to "look into the situation"; you could be in Taiwan or Timbuktu, but that is no deterrent. *Three* days over and somebody is sure to get fired, and then three hours later, mysteriously, rehired again. *Four* days over and they can close down the production altogether, fire the director, and issue a stiff warning to the pro-

ducer: "Your option won't be picked up." If you're
an independent producer, you have to sign the
Studio Standard Distribution Agreement, and that
means they have approval of script, cast, crew,
locations, starting date, labwork, the musical score,
screen credits, and all advertising for the picture.
They have a right to see the rushes, to recut or re-
shoot the final film. They have control over everything, except, according to the Agreement, "for the
epidemic outbreak of plague" and "acts of God"
(seriously). Before you get paid as a producer, you
have to wait till the studio deducts from its expenses
the cost of prints, distribution, advertising, screen
titles, residuals, insurance, copywriting, etc., etc.
And that covers all "territory." Territory, according
to the Agreement, means "the entire universe." So
Mark Fowler knows that the Agreement we sign
means he has everybody by the balls, and yet he
still persists in watching over us like a glass-eyed
demon, buggering us—I mean bugging us—whenever he has a chance.

Mark has also fucked up with creative people,
alienating some very promising kid directors and
writers. I think he tries to motivate them by fear
—which is the way he motivates the Suits on his
staff—but the trouble is, fear doesn't always work
with creative people. They're sensitive and emotional and want to *believe* in what they're doing, unlike
the rest of the Suits, who haven't believed in anything for years. . . . Come to think of it, I wonder
what Mark's true power base is. . . . I know that
Irv doesn't like him, is jealous of him (because Irv
wants to succeed Jake as studio head himself). I
know the "dependent" producers on the lot like
myself aren't pleased in our dealings with Mark. He
insists on deciding which pictures to make and

never lets us forget that he has the power to do that. I suspect that, privately, Jake wants Irv to succeed him but feels Mark, with his computer mind and television track record, is a smarter choice. . . .

But the one thing that mind seems to lack is the one thing that's crucial to this business: intuition. Either you have it, or you don't. Jake had it—as did Uncle Max before him. Intuition comes down to this: knowing what to make. (I remember Uncle Max saying over and over again, "The most important thing in this business is to know what to make!") And as more and more of the Industry is being taken over by lawyers and accountants and men with computer minds, I see less and less intuition in practice. I see Mark's staff using market research in the decision-making process. I hear them talking about audience testing and demographics and something called "psychographics," which is supposed to tell you what the movie audience is feeling and which kinds of films they're most likely to identify with. . . . And if it keeps up like this, all the intuition will be taken out of the game —and also *all the fun*, which is what keeps everybody awake and alive. If Mark's boys use market research before placing their bets, I wonder if we'll be able to produce anything more than pictures that indulge the audiences, products that are consumed, digested, and excreted right there in the theater. . . . I also wonder, with the computer boys running the show, if we'll be able to make anything more than Product that reflects the minds and private fantasies of lawyers and accountants and office managers. . . .

Our Product is already pretty clunky. By that I mean it's like those television commercials you see that look trashy, look as though they were just sort of thrown together, when in point of fact they were not, when every tenth of a second was carefully planned and engineered, shot and reshot, to make it work on you—penetrate your defenses so your resistance breaks down and, presto! you buy the product. The commercials look terrible, but they do the job, right? So we're making Product that is chunky, often with elaborate special effects: cars wrecked, skyscrapers disintegrating, ships exploding . . . Our Product works on your nerves, makes you frightened and uncomfortable, squirming in your seat, or else it shocks the hell out of you. (Those are the kind of pictures Mark Fowler wants to make.) Like TV commercials, our Product manipulates. . . . And the boys in the Tower think we have to keep making "shock" pictures, with expensive special effects that manipulate the audience. And yet, "shock" pictures haven't all done well at the box office—the audience can't be fooled all the time, contrary to Mark's thinking. Some came at the end of a particular cycle, like the picture, the tenth picture about demonic possession—which didn't scare *any*body. (The audience I saw it with just laughed themselves silly; I felt really embarrassed for the producer and walked out after the second reel.)

I think Mark's boys are scared. They keep wanting to make pictures that are surefire box office and spend all their time looking at the data from market research and calculating which formula is supposed to work with which audience. Yet none of the formulas works every time. They're scared because films are a big investment and they want to do everything possible to minimize the risk. If they don't, if they make the wrong choices . . . they're afraid they'll lose their jobs, which is all they really care about, anyway. . . . So they look for "guarantees." Violence is a guarantee at the box office, though the violence in your picture must surpass the violence in the pictures before you. (If twenty cars were blown up last season, you must blow up twenty-one.) Sex is a guarantee (frontal nudity above the waist, full nudity from behind—but no pubic hair). Laughter is a guarantee, though only a few "geniuses" are allowed to make comedies anymore and their names are familiar to all of us. (Indeed, comedy is the last place in our Industry where "genius" is truly acknowledged, even allowed, because we all know how impossible it is to make people laugh.) It's equally impossible to make them cry, though if you can, if you have a "love story," which is something that Jake has been dying to make for a long time, you can strike it rich. But I understand how Mark's boys think and feel probably better than they do. I know we're in business to make a profit, and if by chance a picture comes along that's art and makes a profit, too—well, that's terrific. I know that we have a responsibility to the stockholders of this company, and that if we keep making losers, we're being corporately remiss. But I can't really believe that deep down Jake is very happy with the way things are going. I'm sure he remembers when there was real excitement and glamour to the picture business, when the stories we made really *moved* the audience, when the dreams depicted were shared by a nation. . . . I wonder if, privately, he's actually pleased with our recent spate of films calculated to shock people, offend them with gratuitous sex, gratuitous violence . . .

Or the films that star nothing but machines. Our

films star airplanes and blimps and mechanical sharks, mechanical monkeys and buffalo . . . star trains and cars and roller coasters. . . . Humans (actors) just move inexorably through machines, or fall in love with them, or get eaten by them, or zapped by them in the end. I know that in some of those films I work up more sympathy for the machines—the mechanical sharks and monkeys and trains—than for the humans. When the machines are trashed or blown to pieces, I feel more sorry for them than for the actors involved with them (because, I suppose, the actors aren't really hurt—they're indestructible and survive all the explosions and always return to do battle with still other machines, in other studio films). The machines are often made to seem human, endearing, thanks to the magic of our special effects men, though human and endearing in a very primitive way. The machines are made to seem *innocent*. It's as though they had feelings, sensitivities—and you could identify with them. . . . I know that a helluva lot of time and money is spent building those machines that go berserk, out of control, killing and maiming people. I know I'd like to have points, a percentage of the take on one of those machine pictures that really *hits*, becomes a blockbuster with millions of people lining up three times around the block, in Singapore and Toledo, to see your picture. . . . Yet I can't believe that Jake truly wants our studio to make Product starring nothing but machines; I refuse to believe that.

One by one all the people I know are falling asleep. The people who wanted to do something before, who were out to change things, are half-asleep. They don't say anything, or feel anything. They're just numb at the end of the day. Short-circuited from all the demands and pressures. I'm numb too, as I say. I'm half-asleep, only during the day, because at night I'm *afraid* to fall asleep. I'm terrified of what I'll see. . . . In meetings at the top of the Tower, some executives automatically fall asleep in their green leather chairs no matter what you say. You can be in the middle of what you think is a terrific pitch for a feature project, stop to catch your breath . . . and see grown men at the far end of the conference table conked out, stone cold. I see it happening all the time. One man whose office is next to Irv's does it, and he's a vice-president in our company. His name is Al Lucky, Jr. And his sleeping has become something of a joke about town. Why do they keep him around? He has no taste, no sensibility. No wit, no intelligence. He says, "We want to make the kind of movies that make money." The man is nothing, if not profoundly superficial. But still he keeps getting promoted, and I think it's because he's always *the least objectionable* choice. (Just like the actors who are chosen to do television commercials because they're perfectly bland, inoffensive.) Lucky never offends anybody, either. He's a Face Man —good-looking, with a great tan, well-groomed (conservative clothes: jackets with natural shoulders, cuffed pants, wing-tipped shoes). He has two kids who look exactly like he looks—bland—and a wife who is friendly but bland—and a house that could win awards for ordinariness. But in contrast to everybody else he is "solvent" (we're either in debt or getting there fast). I don't know what Lucky does, except sleep. . . .

I keep telling these sleepers like him that we're

in the middle of a crisis. They look at me with long faces, eyes glassy and half-open, and politely ask, "What are you talking about?" I tell them that the dreams we're manufacturing are becoming more and more tasteless, mechanized. We're not getting people back into the movie houses; we're making these "event" pictures, these terrific roller coaster rides that are consumed right there. Yes, huge numbers of people come out of the woodwork to our "event" pictures, like the one about the mechanical shark and the car possessed by the devil, but at the same time nobody is coming out to see anything else. It's either an "event" picture, or nothing. Like Broadway, either you've got a hit or a turkey. Either you excite that audience in huge numbers, or you've had it. At this rate, I tell them, there won't be a business in five years, and we'll be out on our asses. They still don't understand what I'm talking about and fall right back to sleep. I continue: The seven major studios (the majors) will end up producing just one "event" picture apiece each year—taking all the fun out of the game—and that six of those seven will be "pieces of shit," which is what we call a movie that is just that, and will never make a cent. By this time the people I'm talking to are sound asleep, snoring, farting. . . . So I simply get up and walk out, leaving a few memos scattered on the conference tables that, I hope, they'll read when they wake up. The memos say YOU ASSHOLE! in large letters.

Maybe one by one all the people I know have just Given Up. Maybe they don't want to do anything for the Industry because doing something means taking responsibility. The people who've Given Up now just seem to care about getting by and cultivating their own private interests, such as a better tennis game, a mistress or two, more expensive dope, another room for the house at the Beach, another German car, more antique furniture, exotic clothes. . . . They've gone inward. They don't see anything changing or want anything to change. (Things will always be the same, they reason, no matter who's in power—so why bother? Just work on your house, keep remodeling and adding and building until it's like a fortress.) The men my age, and even those younger, have grown cynical and embittered, and so they take refuge, I suppose, in simply falling asleep.

My competition at the studio, however, is very far from asleep. I know that while I'm trying to figure things out, they're already calling New York and London, Paris and Rome, setting up deals with stars and directors. My competition comes from a team of producers, one being a former agent, Roger Dalton, the other Jake's nephew, Michael Steinman. Both are young. Roger is only in his late thirties, Michael late twenties. I like them both personally (Michael has a terrific sense of humor), but I can't stand how they do business. What they are, essentially, is dealmakers and packagers. They scan the best-seller lists for books that can be turned into movies, or more often, catch those books still in manuscript. They buy what they like and what they think will make for a commercial project, especially a picture with *worldwide* appeal because half our market for American pictures is abroad. From there (once they've acquired the rights to the property), they hire a writer (usually a hack) to adapt the material into a script. With the script they approach a hot young kid director (or, as is more likely, an aging hack director who needs the work and can be kept in line). And with the script and a commitment from the director, they approach one or two of our major "bankable" stars. If the star commits, you have a package. Of course, this process can be accelerated drastically: You can put together a package just on the basis of *commitments* from a writer, director, and star with nothing on paper. The studio may buy it if they like the elements (the "chemistry" of script-director-stars), or the basic material—and decide to make the picture. The former agent and the nephew then take a percentage (maybe five, six, seven, whatever points they can get—and the battles for those points can be incredibly hard-fought, Napoleonic, sometimes even more exciting than the picture itself); they take a percentage of the anticipated profits. If it's a hit—an "event" picture—these guys, who've set up the deal and gotten the commitments from the director and stars, can make millions.

I do pretty much the same thing as my competition, except that I also *work* on a film project. I see it through from the script to the final cut, from the deal to the advertising. Which is precisely what they *don't* do. I try to go for a quality Product, a film with texture, nuance, style. Face it, pictures like that take more time (and you spend just as long on a bomb as you do on a hit), but that's the way I am. I don't like their approach to filmmaking because it focuses too much energy into the deal, into finding the right elements and packaging them in a way that the studio will buy. A lot of times all the energy gets absorbed into the excitement of putting together the package—so there's nothing left over for the actual making of the picture. There's this Trajectory of Enthusiasm after you make the deal: You start high on a project and as more time passes, things cool off, interest wanes, and you go into a tailspin. . . .

I know that the former agent, Roger Dalton, is very shrewd. He can spot writing anywhere and immediately see its potential as film. He plays hunches (as most of us do) and he's *fast*. I mean, he and Michael make decisions on material submitted within *hours*, so naturally all the agents in town love them and keep them on their front list. Roger is British, wears three-piece suits from Bond Street and smokes custom-made cigars (very long and thin). Every time I see him he has on a new pair of glasses: black horn-rims, aviator shades, wire-rimmed specs. He is forever putting on and taking off glasses—as if he doesn't like what he's seeing. Michael Steinman is a freer spirit than Roger; in meetings he cracks jokes, most of them obscene, and he likes to gossip. (In this business, the men gossip more than the women.) He always has a great tan (which he works on mornings, sitting outside his patio office in the Producers' Building) and is a health food nut (he must have honey in everything—coffee, tea, milk, on toast, cereal, eggs). He lives out on the Beach in a spectacular (but very theatrical) wood-and-glass house with thirty-foot ceilings. Every time I see *him* he has another car. In a matter of weeks I've seen him with a Japanese compact, an American luxury car, an American clunker with huge "cancers," as the mechanics call the rust spots, an Italian sports car, a British taxi (authentic—which Roger got the biggest kick out of), and a German insect. He calls these cars his "instruments" and loves to talk about them even more than he loves to talk deals and packages.

Michael Steinman and Roger Dalton—S/D, as

they're sometimes called—work fast, as I say, and have one advantage over me: direct access to both Jake and Mark. (They don't have to deal with all the juniors and sleepers—Al Lucky—like I do. They can accelerate the decision-making process and get quick answers.) I get angry about that— goddammit, I get *very* angry . . . but mostly try to keep it to myself. I like competition—as long as it's reasonably fair, which it isn't in this case. Anyway, I don't want to alienate S/D, especially Michael, because my bet is that Jake picks Michael his nephew to succeed him as studio chief. It's a hunch and I know the odds are long, but if it happens I want to be on Michael's good side, so that I'm not a victim of a purge, so that I càn still keep working. . . .

I remember when creative producers were the dominant force in the producer-writer-director triangle. We developed the script with the writers, we picked the director and worked with him on the shoot. When the principal photography was completed, we supervised postproduction (the score, the cutting, the dubbing). I did that on at least ninety different features. I wrote, I directed occasionally. . . . I made good pictures and bad. But now I have to fight for *any* creative control on a picture. Now some of us are called "line producers," men who look for props and locations, men who watch the budget and try to keep everybody happy with phony small talk and PR. Now producers are synonymous with packagers. . . . I think Jake likes it that way for some reason. (He refused to negotiate any kind of workable agreement with our Guild, further diminishing our power.) I don't know why he wants to see us stripped like this, reduced to the role of line producers and packagers. I don't know but I'm getting angry about it and, I swear, I'll fight him on that.

BB called, she wants to see me.

"I never see you, Tony," she said.

"Look, I got to be three people this week," I said. She wants me to "eat over, sleep over."

I told her I couldn't right now because I was working on the treatment of *Studio* and I'd be up all night, awake longer than ever before.

"Don't drink so much Coke," she said.

She's right—my Coke machine *is* empty.

Only the actors are awake. They're more awake than anybody else in the business—more awake because they're frightened. You look at an actor on the screen and think he's the most confident person you've ever seen, someone who can really get it up. (And that's essentially what actors are paid for— getting it up twenty, maybe thirty times a day.) But in real life, actors are frightened beyond belief. They live on the edge of rejection all the time, and living like that scares the shit out of them, as it would anybody. I've seen actors sit in front of a telephone, staring at the numbers on the dial, and wait hours, days, even weeks for it to ring, for that *one call* from a director or a casting office. As if they were wallflowers at the high school prom. Nine times out of ten that call tells them they've been rejected. And if they're Method actors (and the best ones are), they've auditioned for a part by taking the memory of their father dying, for example, and finding an emotion associated with that grief and using it for their performance. So if you reject them, it's as though you're rejecting their entire emotional life. Living like that keeps you very awake. But it's like waiting to have your fingers chopped off. . . . You smoke, you drink, you take drugs. You fuck out of boredom, you talk endlessly. You live totally in the present. . . . Actors are by nature malcontents: They see so much and feel so much and know how the system works. It's a system mainly designed to defeat them, and so they talk about change (when they're not talking about themselves), but I don't see change coming from actors. If they're any good at all and suddenly get a break, they can become "overnight" stars (which is all they really want, anyway), with more money than they know what to do with. And once you've made it, you get scared of saying anything and pushing for change because you can be so quickly shut up by others who are less fortunate: "Hey," they tell you coolly, "you got yours." Nevertheless, actors have one thing going for them—they're allowed to be crazy. Indeed, they're *expected* to be crazy, though not *too* crazy. The better the actor, the crazier he's expected to be. Up to a point.

Though this can sometimes produce strange results. There is an actor at the studio who is the star of a cop show; the people connected with the show call him Bobby Crazy. He *tries* harder than any actor I know to be crazy. He drives onto the lot in an old Cadillac of his that's covered with pigeon shit and parks it defiantly in the space reserved (forever) for Max Schumacher. Well—one of the security guards, Benny, comes running out after him, screaming: "Put it somewhere else!" Bobby gives him the finger and yells back, "Hey, whaddaya gonna do about it?" The guard can't do anything and Bobby knows it. Bobby's show is a big hit on television and the boys in the Tower want to keep him happy. When Bobby later appears to shoot interiors for his cop show, he flips out, goes wiggy. Demands script changes petulantly. Wants the director replaced. Knocks his fist through his dressing room door. Pretty soon shooting stops. And since this means time wasted and time means money, one of the Suits will come down from the Tower and "see what all the commotion is about" and ask "if we can't find a reasonable solution to our problems." Bobby Crazy tells the Suit to fuck off and leave, or else he's walking out on the show and "fuck everybody." The Suit tries again to calm Bobby down, but he won't listen. Finally they call it a wrap and quit for the day. The next day, Bobby appears on the set and apologizes to everybody: "Sorry, guys. I freaked." And works hard and does a terrific job. Of course, he can do numbers like that and get away with them because he's the star of his own show. But what's the point? He burns up a lot of people's nerves, wastes their energies. . . . Unfortunately, the truth about Bobby Crazy is that his life is solidly booked up for the next seven years (the length of his "term contract" at the studio). And that means there isn't one day out of the next seven years where he doesn't know exactly what he's going to do. . . . And Bobby Crazy knows it and hates everybody, especially the Suits in the Tower, for it. (A lot of people hate him too.) But there isn't a goddamn thing he can do about it. Except maybe appear every now and then on Johnny's Talkshow and complain about the Tower as "this big black box that runs the whole world."

Most of the actors I know, even those who are very awake, have simply become extensions of studio Product. They drive the machines or are destroyed by the machines (eaten, run over, mauled, devoured, mutilated) that star in our films. When the films are completed, they appear on Johnny's show, or Merv's or Mike's or Dick's show in order to promote studio Product. But they're not very good at hype. (They end up making apologies for the Product, or else trying to hype it with fake enthusiasm.) Besides, they tend to look ridiculous spliced in between commercials for dog food, aspirin, and deodorant, and whatever glamour they were supposed to have is quickly diminished. To a large extent, these actors have lost the very thing they need most—their uniqueness, their individuality—and become what I call Interchangeables. They look and act and talk alike, they wear suits and ties and even maintain offices in the Tower, coming in punctually every day, always being polite to everyone, calm and well mannered, smiling blandly at you, almost on command, like Pavlovian dogs. They've become corporate men, which is very weird, which is even weirder because these actors look like they're *acting* the parts of corporate men. . . .

Most actors start out by being crazy. I remember hanging around a couple of them when they were young men in the business. They radiated unpredictability; they could be explosive, often violent. It was a thrill just being in their presence—you never knew what to expect. I remember James Dean being like that, and the young Brando, and, to some degree, Montgomery Clift. They were all so many different people and could change at will. . . . One minute kind and gentle, the next monstrous and terrifying. But now most actors have toned down their craziness. (I suppose they're afraid of not working if they get a bad reputation, and know the insurance companies won't take the risk of backing them in a picture, and no insurance, no picture.) Actors want to be bankable—it means everything. (Your name on the marquee guarantees the success of the picture and you have enormous leverage because of that.) When they're bankable it also means they're dangerous to the studio because they don't need us, we need them. So they can call the shots and have control of a picture, including the cut. We hate them for that and never let them forget it—if, for some reason, they should happen to lose their bankability one day. . . . If they are stars but not necessarily bankable, the studio has them make one picture for themselves, the next one for us. "One for you, one for us" it's called. That means making one picture they can control without our interference, then making one that's strictly commercial, where we can exploit their star value as fully as possible. If an actor isn't quite a star, let alone a bankable star, then he or she has the choice of becoming one of these studio players, under contract for seven years like Bobby Crazy. Which means not only wearing business suits like the boys in the Tower but also thinking and acting and speaking for the company during press interviews. Which means looking clean most of the time, as though your body were sprayed each morning from head to toe. You look and act respectable, and you reflect the studio's point of view and corporate values. If you're an actor who does that, you're rewarded by being made a regular in studio Product.

I think I know about actors, know what makes them the way they are. I've seen several generations

of actors come and go (about seven years consti-
tutes a generation in this Industry). I've known them
when they're up, and when they're down. (I tried
acting myself early on and got a couple of bit parts
and wanted to go further but didn't feel I had the
"instrument," as actors say, for it. I felt I wasn't tall
enough, large enough, strong enough.) And all my
years in the business have given me tremendous
respect for actors, especially those who aren't afraid
to take chances. You know, one actor can change
the way an entire generation thinks and feels and
talks, like Brando or Dean. Most actors, in fact,
don't know how important they can be, what powers
they really have. Sometimes I think they throw away
their powers carelessly, or give up struggling too
soon and become studio players under contract.

He called.

We spoke for thirty seconds.

He speaks to everybody on the phone for thirty
seconds.

He didn't say, "Goddammit, Schwartz! Stop your
kvetching."

He was friendly, yet I'm still afraid of him.

"You're writing it, aren't you?" he asked, knowing I was because he knows everything.

"Yes."

"The story about the studio?"

"Yes."

A long pause.

"Any luck?"

"Well, I'm still working on it."

"When do you suppose you'll have something?"

"Tomorrow."

"I want to see it when you got it. Bring it into
my office."

"Yes, sir."
"I like the title, Tony."
"I do too."
"Studio."

My second wife was an actress—not a very good
one (Sandra was limited in certain ways, her voice
was grating, metallic), though I had dreams of her
becoming a star one day. As a matter of fact, I
wanted to make her into a star, build her career. I
went looking for properties especially suited to her.
I worked on her acting technique. (I got her to study
with an old Method actor who was originally part
of the Actors Studio with Lee Strasberg in New
York. He was a wonderful, though demanding
teacher, who taught her about "private moments,"
being able to stand naked, both physically and
mentally, before a crowd of people and overcome
her fear.) She didn't want to learn about "private
moments," she fought me on that. Our marriage
got screwed up; I didn't know where she was coming from.
    Like most actresses, she was a different person
each day. One day morose, another happy. And she
never seemed to remember what she told me from
one day to the next. I didn't know if she really
wanted to become a star or not. Her presence was
definitely that of a star: Though physically tiny,
with small hands and feet, she nonetheless took up
a helluva lot of space—in fact, every room in our
house. Men used to stare at her from a distance and
she'd stare right back. "Well," she'd confront them,
"did I pass?" She had a weird set of habits—her
shoes, for example. Instead of throwing out the old
ones, she *saved* them. One time I counted the number in her closet: eighty-six. She had another strange

routine. Whenever we went on a trip (to New York, Boston, Chicago, Atlanta, New Orleans, Houston, Dallas, Denver, San Francisco), she always looked for some article of clothing from the place. (If we stayed with friends, she'd ask them for a shirt or blouse or undergarment.) At home she had a drawer filled with other people's clothing, and catching a whiff from one, she said, evoked a whole flood of memories for her.

She wanted to have a kid, then didn't want to have one. But ended up having one anyway, and now Jason is six. (He's a great kid and I love him.) Sandra tried to be crazy, as all actresses (and actors) do, but it wasn't real for her—I don't know why—and something happened to her career as an actress. She left me (we were by this time, late one January, in the middle of the rains, fighting each other almost constantly), and her career went nowhere. She said, "I want my freedom." I said, "Take it." And she left me on a dark January morning for another man. (That night I got horribly drunk, I remember, and smashed up my favorite German car.) I didn't know that she'd been involved with this man—a television actor, for whom I have nothing but contempt (he's grassed out of his skull, like the star of that mechanical-man series)—but she was, and when she told me I felt like a fool. I can't stand the guy, he's a creep, and I keep saying that if I ever see him on our studio lot, I swear I'll beat the shit out of him. So she tried to be crazy, her career dissolved and she's living with a *shmuck*. (The guy doesn't sleep with her every night, I'm told; he likes to play around and get it on with teenage girls who are hung up on his ridiculous TV show. In other words, he likes to be starfucked.)

It's not good for Jason, and I worry about that. Worry about the kind of people he's exposed to. (I've tried to win back custody of him but so far no luck, though my lawyer is working on it). I don't know about Sandra—I see her going from one pill to another, up, down, every whichway. I know she's hooked on sleeping pills and I can understand why after her years as an actress of being awake. It's cruel, but I can't say I mind seeing her deteriorate . . . a jumble of nerves, loaded on pills, often hysterical, panicked about losing her actor-lover-whatever he is. . . . If she collapses completely —and I'm afraid she's long overdue for a breakdown—I should get custody of Jason. Yes, I should get custody of Jason. . . .

So I think I know something about actors, know what it's like to live with them day in and day out and share their terrific insecurities. Know how awake they can be—and how fucked up. Basically, they're a lot of different people. Voices pass through their "instruments," voices from other periods in history, voices from the present, from the street and the Tower. . . . You inhabit so many people and they inhabit you that you feel almost possessed, a devil and a Good Guy. . . . You're fragile and therefore vulnerable. . . . Even the best actors we have, however, tend to be putty in the hands of a certain director or producer. For actors have no idea how well or, often, how badly they're performing (unlike most other arts, where you pretty much know how you're doing), and they want to please so desperately that they can ask the most stupid questions, throw tantrums like spoiled children, be good to you one moment, impossible the next—all of this just to mask the insecurity of not knowing who you are.

Stanislavski said that an actor who identifies with the part he's playing—who really *thinks* he's Napoleon or Churchill—is insane.

Which is true, though every actor knows in his heart of hearts that to be any good at all, he's got to go nuts! He's got to be more people than he's ever been before. . . .

Jake says, "There are seven basic plots. You know that, Tony."

Hitchcock tells me, "IIIIIIII tend . . . to *go* for the in-no-cent *man* in bizzzzz—arrrrre sit-u-*ations!* Like Cary Grant finding him*self* on Mount Russssssssshmorrrrrre."

I'm afraid BB will run away with Mark Fowler, though she hasn't given the slightest hint of doing so. Mark can do more for her than I can, but I'm still not going to let it happen.

Cinnamon's car is called Thumper. I wish I could . . . I can see Michael Steinman at the wheel, driving . . . She's just one of many cars for him.

Tonight, I'm seeing a Clint Eastwood picture. To be honest, I'm seeing it for the violence—I like Eastwood—he speaks with his gun. He shoots people better than any other actor I know. He punishes those elements of society that go unpunished.

Sandra called, Sandra called, Sandra called. She told me Jason said "that word" for the first time. "What word?" "That word." "What word?" "Fuck." Of course, he had no idea what it meant. She slapped him across the face and bloodied his nose. I'm mad . . .

I wonder: How can you make any choices when you're asleep? Isn't somebody else making the choices for you when you're asleep?

Before they hired me at the studio, they took me out to lunch. A man whose only job is to take people out to lunch took me out. Over drinks he asked, "By the way, are you a Red?"
"No."
"Do you have any convictions?"
"No."
"Oh, just joking." He flicked his hand. "Forget it."

There are some former Weather people working at the studio. They wanted to change things at one time . . . but now wear Golden Handcuffs like everybody else. They must like the fit. . . .

Mark Fowler is head of Film, okay? He, along with Jake, decides on every picture we make. Mark was offered a twelve-page treatment by a hot young kid director one year. He turned it down. The kid sold it to another studio and made it in three years. The picture was a fantasy about intergalactic space warfare. The picture hit with the other kids and they saw it again and again and took their parents to see it. The studio's coffers swelled, ours didn't. Mark didn't see it.

Cinnamon keeps my cologne in the icebox. "It's cooler that way," she says. I smell better.

*   *   *

"If you can't do the treatment we want," Mark tells me, "we'll get somebody else."

"Thanks. I'll be thinking about that while I'm writing."

Mark is a son of a bitch, all right. He thinks that's the way you "motivate" people.

A joke, my first in ages: TV producer to TV writer during a story conference: "Listen, I want you to elevate the main character in your script."

"Elevate the main character!"

"Yeah."

"Okay," says the writer. "I'll give him a sloping forehead."

Every day this week, this year, the Suits in our Tower talk to executives in other dream factories. They bid on the same properties, decide to make the same kinds of pictures, even combine their efforts sometimes to produce one gigantic block-buster. Our people are interchangeable with the people in other studios. I know there are counter-parts to me at Metro and Columbia, I know I'm *there*. . . . My counterparts look and act and talk and think just as I do—my doubles, triples, qua-druples, clones of me, the other Tony Schwartzes in the business. I've even met them and had lunch with them and sat in on meetings with them and it's like seeing yourself in a hall of mirrors. There are so many of you . . . row after row of Tony Schwartzes, reflecting the same images, the same Tony Schwartz dreams, same frustrations, ambi-tions, same Tony Schwartz hopes, aspirations, suc-cesses and failures. . . .

*　　*　　*

I wrote the treatment. The plot was easy, it always is. The most difficult thing was creating the main character.

Call him the Actor. He's in his mid-twenties. He lives in the city. He's quiet, lonely. He carries a gun all the time. He dreams about using it one day. He dreams about going into a tall building and killing, at random, any number of famous people. He has a peculiar habit of winking at you one moment, then sneering the next. He wears a blue flight jacket. Chain-smokes. Shaves whenever he feels like it. He likes machines, especially old cars. "Originals," he calls them. He's more comfortable inside a machine than anywhere else. He drives with extreme alertness; quick with his hands. Underneath his jacket is a T-shirt with the lettering HE CAN DRIVE. The T-shirt was given to him by his girl friend. She's an actress, her name is Greta. She wants to be a star. She encourages his assassination fantasy, for some reason. He isn't committed to any particular cause, he's just looking for a stage. He wants to perform. He wants to get paid for his performance. If he holds enough people hostage, he figures he'll be well paid. Meanwhile, he hangs out at Jimmy Ray's bar and listens to the jukebox. He plays the same song over and over again. The song is "Solitary Man" by Neil Diamond. He drinks Coke and listens to the song. He grew up in a dozen different cities, he knows the peculiar rhythms of the street. His father was killed in an accident when he was nine. He can talk his head off and persuade you of anything, but he doesn't want to. He loves Mexican food and is always eating it in his car. He hates movies and never sees them. He's terrified of growing old. He feels he doesn't exist unless he's seen. He belongs to a street gang called the Envies. The

Envies attack people who are well-dressed, attractive just because they're well-dressed, attractive. Greta wants him to hang out at the studio and make enough of a nuisance of himself so that people stand up and take notice. He says, "Nothing means anything anymore." She says, "That's not true." He looks at the Tower and says, "There's anarchy above the tenth floor." He drives the freeway in his "original" clunker. He pictures the city as a city of addiction. Sees everybody hooked on something. Sees everybody pushing . . . Pushers and addicts, he reasons, have taken over. He turns to violence. For a while, he pretends to be a terrorist. He lives mysteriously, always on the run. He assumes multiple identities, several disguises. One day the gun goes off.

I want Daphne to read it. I don't know why but I do. She's the third or fourth or fifth woman in my life. (I'm trying to see more of her these days, though BB doesn't want me to. She knows I'm seeing Daphne—women always know if you're involved with another woman, even casually—and is getting very upset, jealous. Anyhow, I'm going to call her and read it to her *right now*.

"Darling, do you know what time it is?" Her voice sounds scratchy.

"Of course."

"Well?"

"Too late for dinner, too early for breakfast."

"Very funny, Tony. Very funny, indeed." She's being sarcastic. "Can't this wait till morning?"

"No."

"Sweetheart, I'm *very* tired."

"That's good."

"Good?"

"You're a better audience when you're tired."

"I give up."

"Just listen, okay?"

I can picture her rolling over in bed, cradling the phone with one arm (most of the time she uses the phone like a weapon). I wonder if she's wearing jeans. . . . Daphne Jones always wears jeans, she loves them. In fact, she knows everything there is to know about jeans. How tightly they must fit. How to try them on in the shop flat on your back, holding your breath while two or three salespeople zip you up. How jeans have to be broken in properly. How they have to be faded just right. Daphne likes to wear them with the cuffs turned up and with black spiked heels, like they do in London. She looks sexy in jeans, I must admit. Cuts a sharp figure with her carrot-red hair.

"Darling, are they *paying* you for this treatment?"

"No. I'm doing it as a personal favor."

"Personal favor! My God, you're *mad!*"

Daphne is an agent. She works at this terrifically competitive agency in town; it's the kind of agency where the boss is predatory, where the juniors are predatory, where the secretaries are predatory, where even the *janitors* are predatory. Our studio is her "territory," so she comes here three times a week in the afternoons.

I don't feel so bad about calling her in the middle of the night—she often does the same thing to me. One time I remember on the phone: ". . . Redford will agree to Pollack, if Hackman plays the other part. But I'm not going to push it. If Hackman drops out, which I expect, then we can get Nicholson. Has Nicholson ever worked with Pollack before? Do you know? Darling, I'm *worried*. . . . Are you there? Honey, are you there?"

I tell her now that I wanted to give Jake a believable story. I wanted to create a character—a terrorist of another order—whose function in the plot would be as an opposing force. I wrote it my way, partly to show off, partly as a gamble. . . . I doubted that they'd buy it; in fact, I was pretty sure they'd hate it and Mark would get on my ass.

"I want to see you," I tell Daphne.

"It's so late, dear."

Daphne has one singular distinction: She's *shtupped* everybody of any importance in the Industry. She's made it with Frank Shelby, the Suede Man. She's made it with Irv. ("He's so sexy after his lift," she says.) She's banged Al Lucky, Bobby Crazy, a former Weatherman in the Story Department, any number of writers ("They're the easiest," she notes, "but they all feel so guilty about it."), Benny the security guard (I don't believe that). She's even *shtupped* my counterparts, my clones, the doubles and triples of me—the Tony Schwartz who works at Metro and the one who works at Columbia. I got mad at her when she told me, but she just laughed in my face. I don't know how she does it—she's not very attractive in the conventional sense. She has a lot of *chutzpah,* that's all. Now she wants to *shtup* Mark Fowler, though he's been putting her off. . . . One day I have no doubt that she'll become the most powerful agent in the business. How can she miss?

"Okay," I tell her. "Another time."

"Okay, Tony."

"Thanks for listening."

BB is jealous of Daphne, as I say. And Daphne doesn't like BB. (Sometimes she does, sometimes she doesn't.) In many ways, BB simply offers the attraction of immediate physical gratification, whereas making love with Daphne is a form of social climbing. If she *shtups* you (and she can be very aggressive), it's as if you've joined a select club—she's rewarding you for your success. I don't know, it gets complicated. I know with BB there's this feeling we share (even though we say nothing before and nothing afterward). It's this feeling that we've both been used for so long by everybody else (indeed, BB, being both a model and a starlet, has known little else), we've been at the mercy of everybody's demands, we've always tried to please and compromise and do as we were told that we've forgotten what it means to get our own way. She knows this and I do too, and that's why we have this understanding, this feeling. . . . In a sense, we've both been exposed to the public for so long, exposed to the forces of control . . . that we have nothing that's truly private *except* making love. It's the one thing the men I see at night, the men who must control, can't take away from us—the one thing that *absolutely* belongs to us.

So we make love without passion, yet also with great passion. For us, making love is the last thing that's not decided by somebody else, by the people we work for, by the people who own our property, who tell us what to wear and how to speak and what to think. They try to tell us how to make love, too, with their books on technique and tips on what positions are trendy and how often we should do it. But . . . what do they know? . . . Besides, once you realize there *is* no technique for making love (everybody does it differently, thank God, men to women, women to men, men to men, women to women) and it can't be standardized, mechanized, computerized . . . well, you've come pretty far, a lot farther than they want you to come. . . .

It wasn't too late for BB. I drove out to her house at the Beach, and when I got there she was sitting in the living room, barefoot, legs crossed, a Japanese kimono wrapped around her, smoking. . . . She looked angular, for some reason, her long arms and legs intersected. . . . I don't remember what time it was but the sun hadn't come up yet. I told BB about the treatment; she was at best indifferent.

"I missed you," is all she said.

"I missed you too."

In the background I could hear the ocean roaring and the waves crashing and the gulls squawking, though I couldn't make out what they were saying. . . . Stubbing out her cigarette, BB burnt her fingertips. She winced. I thought of the brush fire now raging out of control in the Valley, thought "Scarface," as it was called, might suddenly swoop down here.

We went into the bedroom. I unwrapped the kimono and she stood naked before me. I touched her shoulders, I hugged her gently. I ran my fingers down her back, I stopped at the sweet curve of her bottom and squeezed. I touched her lips and kissed them. I ran both hands through her hair. I picked her up and carried her to bed. I kissed both her breasts softly, I blew delicately on her nipples. I ran my fingers, barely touching, from her nipples all the way down to her toes. I grabbed the arch of her foot, I pinched her ankles. I nibbled on her fingers. With both hands, I squeezed her thighs as hard as I could. I stroked her pubic hair, running my fingers through, back and forth several times. I felt for an opening, I probed with the tips of my fingers. I found the opening and stayed there for a while. My other hand ran up and down her back, while I kissed her, our tongues connecting. I felt for the mole on the lower part of her back and found it. With my fingernails I signed my name on her back. She liked the sensation. She played with my ear, she ran her bony fingers down my back. She hugged me. She scratched the short hairs on my chest. She bit my nose, she blew hard into my ear. She kissed both eyes. She squeezed my behind, she tickled my balls. She touched me where I live, she brought me to attention. I squeezed her breasts, I probed further the opening in her pubic hair. I climbed inside. She yanked her head back, I went deeper. She tossed from side to side, I went deeper. She wrapped her legs around my back, I held steady. She didn't want me to go anywhere. I stayed where I was. She didn't want it to end, I kept it there. She was in no hurry. I was thinking about anything. I wasn't thinking about the past, about tomorrow and what I had to do this week. I began to melt, my body went soft. She wrapped her legs more tightly around the small of my back, I continued to melt. She lifted her legs above my shoulders, I pulled away. She pulled me back. She quivered, I quivered. She held tight, I held tight. She trembled, I trembled. She smiled, I smiled. She laughed, I laughed, she cried, I cried, she nibbled, I nibbled, she climbed, I climbed, I went higher, she went higher, I went, she went, I, she, she, I . . .

Until we both let go.

I'm in that room at the top of the Tower, sitting on green leather.

It squeaks.

The black-suited men, along with the woman in white whose face I can't make out, speak to me.

"We must control," they say.

"No."

They tell me, in smooth voices, why they must control. They are very reasonable. They explain how destructive Man is, what a killer.

"More time," I plead with them, my tongue trying to uncurl.

I plead for more time.

"So we can change him."

They don't like "that word."

What word?

"Change."

I look out the window in the room, I see everything, see it all going by so fast. I see them controlling more and more because we're allowing them to control (they are us and we are them), allowing them to strip away all our privacy.

There's no resistance.

The next morning Daphne called; we talked for a long time about *Studio*. She told me she hates the whole idea of concept films. A plane in danger. A roller coaster gone amok. A runaway train. A gigantic skyscraper burning. A ship turned turtle. A major studio held hostage by a young group of terrorists. (The plots are pretty much interchangeable, just the locations and the machines vary.) She thinks the audience for them isn't there anymore. She says they're a bad investment. Says there's no individuality in concept films. That is, you never have the feeling you're in the presence of anybody, any star or director or writing talent—only a machine in danger. Says there's "nothing to talk about" afterward except one's physiological reactions, if you shivered in fear, coughed nervously, got jerked around, or threw up. Concept films, she told me, aren't dreams—they're nightmares, and you try like hell *to forget them*.

I told her I couldn't agree more, but that I thought *Studio* might be different.

"Bullshit," she said and hung up.

I called up two writers I know and asked them to read my treatment. (My strategy was to get them interested in the project and then talk them up in front of Irv and suggest we go with them to write the first-draft screenplay of *Studio*.) The writers are a team that I discovered and gave their first break. (I figured they'd be loyal to me, and therefore I could control how my treatment was transferred into a script.) The writers are Billy De Witt and Elroy (Roy) Hotchkiss, both in their early thirties. Billy is short, with a bushy moustache and dark hair combed straight back. Roy is tall, lanky—and Yale. Though in his early thirties, he's never left Yale. He looks and acts and talks Yale. While Billy is short and Roy tall, I often confuse one with the other. Like most writing teams—and married couples—they complete each other's sentences, work and think as one person. Both are speedsters (the kind of guys who burn out by the time they're forty)—functioning at a higher rate of metabolism than most people I know. Right now they have a development deal with S/D (Steinman and Dalton) to write a war picture. (War pictures are sure winners at the box office these days because they do great business abroad, where half our market is. War is a terrific commodity to export on film, the Suits tell me, because it can be clearly understood in Third World countries—it has universal appeal.) If I can convince Irv that Billy and Roy are the guys most

capable of writing *Studio,* maybe he'll pull them
off the S/D war project. (That way I'd score points
in *my* war against the competition.)

"We'd love to read the treatment," Roy said.

"Sounds terrific," Billy said. "Send it over."

And if I can get the Kid Writers, as I call them,
to work with me and Irv on the project, I might
save them the humiliation of working with Mark.
(That's no small victory, either.) For Mark Fowler
is sure to fuck them over. (Kid Writers are the most
vulnerable elements in this business; their words
always get changed around, often by people who
have tremendous contempt for the artist and will
do it just out of spite.) Mark doesn't seem to
realize that creative people wear their emotions on
their sleeve; you have to deal with them tactfully.
You can't bully them into submission; they'll hate
you for it and you'll kill their work.

I like the Kid Writers, come to think of it. I like
Billy and Roy, I don't want to see them get hurt or
burn out too quickly. I know how vulnerable they
are now. . . . For a while there *before,* I thought the
Kids might take over, which is to say all the guys
like Roy and Billy who were on the other side of
thirty just a few years back. (Now, of course, they're
on this side of thirty and have wives and children
and lots of worries.) Thinking back, it looked as
though the Kids *would* take over—they had us out-
numbered and running scared when they made
those movies that connected with other kids, some
of which made big money. I know I was scared of
them—with their outrageousness, their powers to
shock us, to defy authority. But at the same time I
was secretly cheering them on, hoping they'd take
over the business and change things around. (Many

of us, in fact, were ready to turn it over to them; I
know I was.) The Kids didn't realize how close they
really came, how much they scared us. (Billy and
Roy have no idea, even now, that everything
could've been *theirs* if they'd just hung in there a
little bit longer.) But the Kids blew it. By their
own admission they blew it. Nobody knows why, I
know I don't. There were "reasons" given: The
Kids fucked up on certain movies and wasted a lot
of time and money. They were "irresponsible" and
couldn't handle the incredible opportunities given
them at such early ages—opportunities only a
select few of us ever dreamed of having. These Kids
were allowed to play with a medium, with toys that
cost sixty, seventy thousand dollars a day to operate
(even more in most cases); they had full command
of armies of people. They were instant stars, culture
heroes fawned over by the Press.

I don't know what happened to them. Did they
think they were "owed" the right to work in the
medium and never realize it was a privilege? Did
they think it wasn't a business like other businesses
and therefore one that by definition had to pay its
way in order to survive? I just don't know. . . . Billy
and Roy don't talk much about that period only a
few years ago when they were shaking up the town
with their low-budget features and threatening to
take things over. Billy and Roy seem to've forgotten, if not repudiated, that period altogether. I still
remember it vividly, though I don't talk much about
it to anybody. I recall those "crazy kids" (crazy in
a good way) who stormed into my office and hustled
projects and tried to intimidate the Suits in the
Tower into doing those projects because they, the
Kids, had the answers. They were part of something
called "the film generation." I remember Francis

Coppola driving onto the lot, on a motorcycle, hair trailing in the breeze, with a black briefcase full of projects he wanted us to underwrite. I remember his sheer *chutzpah* in dealing with us. . . . Some of those crazy kids were terrific—I miss the excitement they once generated. I liked their picture (which stunned the Industry) about the two hippies on motorcycles who were going to fulfill the American Dream: Make a lot of money and retire in Florida. I liked everything they were saying. I wonder what happened. . . .

Some of them turned from crazy kids into freaks, and I know a lot of the freaks were too fucked up to get anything done. (There are still freaks in this business, though usually just in technical jobs, such as cutting, sound, lighting, special effects, camera work; most of them have gone quietly inward—they don't say much, except when you ask them something that pertains to the functioning of a machine. They speak a very private language—almost strangers in their own country.) I miss the crazy kids, as I say. They made us open our doors just a crack and let in a few newcomers. We had to, we had no choice, because all of our big-budget productions were losing money (our musicals failed pathetically). So we let them in, kids fresh out of film school, kids who told us they had something to say, kids who seemed to know how to make pictures that hooked into the fantasies of other kids. While this may seem obvious to other people (letting in the Kids), something that other businesses would've done on a moment's notice, you must understand that our Industry doesn't take very readily to outsiders. Ours is an industry that is largely handpicked, passed on from one generation to the next. (That's why there are so many "Juniors" in the business—

sons of producers, daughters of actresses.) Besides, a lot of these kids were so brash, so cocksure, that they offended many of us; they didn't have any respect for the men and women who created the picture business before they were born. (Ultimately, I don't think the Kids even had respect for themselves, and that was surely the beginning of their collective downfall.)

We don't accept new blood easily, as I say. We believe there is such a thing as paying one's dues, serving an apprenticeship. Nevertheless, every season there are still kids who come out from New York, Chicago, Boston, Denver, San Francisco, wherever. They're not the crazy kids of before but rather self-proclaimed film buffs. They're kids who've watched thousands of movies by the age of eighteen, kids who've sat in movie houses (usually in the same seat, ten or fifteen rows up from the front, always in the center, slouched in their chairs) and *seen everything*. Many have gone to film school and spent several years seeing *more* of everything. I like this generation of film buffs: They're enthusiastic, well-informed, and know film history. (Unfortunately, they don't know a lot outside of film.) Most buffs like to experience film viscerally, purely at a gut level—the way a film can work on them, wipe them out. Mainly they're *fans,* and I know at one level I'm a fan, too. So are Jake and his boys. The film buffs who want to work in the Industry are pliant and easy to manipulate. For one thing, they'll do anything just to *get* a job. They don't know much about the business side of the business.

I have a couple of them working for me—one young writer named Nick Benvenue. He has a thick black beard, unkempt, like Francis Coppola's, which is standard for most film-buff writers in the Industry.

In other words, Nick looks like your film-buff writer is supposed to look, and I'm comfortable with that. Most of his scripts so far (he's written six, sold three, though all are unproduced) are essentially reworkings of old movies. (The one I liked best was a marvelous reworking of that classic Billy Wilder picture with Bill Holden and Gloria Swanson.) Nick grew up in the Valley here not far from the studio, and he has lots of stories to tell about cruising on the Strip, at night, in his hot rod, looking for action, showing off his machine—stories about his parents who went out cruising with him because they'd grown up cruising, too, and wanted to pass on what they knew to the next generation. I've heard them and they're wonderful. "Write about what you know," I told him, as the cliché goes. But he's afraid scripts like that won't sell. And selling for a young writer is everything. (You spend twenty-five percent of your time writing and the rest hustling.) It's tough as hell to sell a script. Our studio, for example, has twenty or so readers and they each read about thirty scripts a month and *recommend* only one. They spend most of their time turning down scripts. That's where a development deal can help.

Nick has one with me. The deal is, we get together on an idea of my choosing. Turn it into a treatment, or a first draft screenplay. I pay him, and if I like it, I pay him for another draft or a rewrite. We keep going on like that, and I'm free to cut him off at any point, so it's advantageous for me because I don't have a lot of money tied up in a property, and I can follow its progress and control the result. Nick doesn't mind because he can pay the rent and keep working.

Actually this isn't such a bad time for writers in

the Industry. (They're no longer considered just *"shmucks* with Underwoods," as we used to call them.) While it's still hard to sell scripts, writers are enjoying a new status, one that I think ranks them above directors. (Without the script, the blueprint for the picture, what have you got?) Most of the Suits at the studio now see the director as the guy who has to get up at four in the morning and put up with all the hassle of shooting the goddam picture—in other words, the director as hack. (Some are even less kind toward them: "Directors are nothing," say the Suits. I think they say it because they're afraid of directors getting too large, too powerful, thanks to the Press and all the publicity they get as "artists," and challenging the authority of the studio, as Coppola and a few others have done.) Here we joke: "A director of genius is somebody who comes in on time." Meaning that he or she doesn't go over schedule and therefore over budget.

Writers, if they're any good at all, can make a lot of money faster than directors. And they're treated with more respect, their contributions held in higher esteem. It's the best way to start out in the business (it's the way I started out years ago). From writing you can cross over and become a director or producer or a "hyphenate": writer-director, writer-producer. And that's how most writers, if they're smart, look at what they do: as a means toward an end. The end may be directing, producing, whatever.

It's strange, but most of the writers who come out here immediately want to write about the Industry. That's their first impulse. (Novelists may save us for their last novels, as Fitzgerald did, but at least they save us. Journalists write about us first, then, if they're lucky, become screenwriters *for* us. Writers are fascinated with the glamour and excitement of the Industry. They love the thrill of being around people who are constantly manufacturing stories, dozens and dozens of stories for mass consumption. They're in awe of all the machinery that goes into operation (whole battalions of people) just to find and develop and produce stories. Most writers can't quite believe all this is really happening—an entire industry dedicated to feeding stories, dreams, and fantasies to the ever-hungry beast known as the American Public. It doesn't seem possible, writers think, for a culture to be so addicted to illusions—synthetic, counterfeit versions of the reality you see and feel and know with your own senses. But the Public *is* addicted, we got them hooked years ago . . . and that's why we're in business . . . to keep feeding that appetite for illusion. . . .

Somewhere in all of us is a little kid who wants to peep through the keyhole to see what the Big People are doing.

Most writers tend to repeat last year's hits. And as I see it, there is nothing wrong with that. What worked before will obviously work again. Most producers *want* last year's hits (I know I do), but it's a lot harder to get them than you might think. For one thing, it involves a very clever kind of stealing —of which most writers are not incapable. (They steal shamelessly from each other, don't they?) Listen . . . if last year's biggest hit was about a shark (mechanical) who eats up the people living in a small coastal town in New England, you take the dominant psychological element from that picture. The element is menace. And if the year before that the biggest hit was a story about demonic possession, you take another element that the audience most strongly responded to—the devil. Combining those elements you get a mechanical devil menacing a small town, which doesn't quite work but is suggestive. . . . Let's say the mechanical object is a car, let's say the car is possessed by the devil . . . and it menaces a small town! Which will sell as a script—in fact, one such script was bought by our studio. (I don't think the script was written as anything more than a joke, however, and I'm surprised as hell that Mark bought it and made the picture, which ended up doing no business, because, as I keep saying, the Public isn't that easily fooled. To coin a phrase, they know the real illusion when they see it.)

Other things I know about writers: They all have unusual hands, I've never met one who didn't. Hands that are soft and delicate, fingers long and often sculptural. (Do they fingerfuck? Do they spend a great deal of time staring at their hands?) Mostly they steal, as I say, from each other. Beginning writers are the easiest marks—they have no idea about protecting their material. Writers who do know are typically second- or third-generation, the sons and daughters of Industry writers. They grew up being sworn to secrecy in their own houses. (They weren't allowed to mention their parents' ideas to anybody else for fear of being ripped off; they grew up believing that those ideas were like money in the bank—which, of course, they were.) Other things I know: Writers have the worst relationships with women of any of the creative people in the business. They can't seem to make up their minds what women should be, or what they *want* them to be. I know when Billy and Roy bring their wives over to my house on weekends, they look slightly embarrassed. The wives are nice, attractive but out of it. Most of them don't like the business and worry that their husbands will waste their talents. (This happened to my first wife; she hated the business and we fought many times over whether I should stay in it or not. Finally *she* left.) Writers have this basic problem, as I see it. They write something and immediately they want to be loved for it. They attack the system, just as I'm doing (even though I know I represent a large part of that same system, I'm the very thing I'm against), and they want the whole world to love them. Same with women. Writers want everything they say and do to be adored by women—or other men—and when it's not, when they're rejected, they suffer. I hate to see that happen, I hate to see writers become casualties of the Industry and suffer.

I know one writer who suffered tremendously. Bob Blackman came out here years ago—he'd had a successful career as a playwright in New York (good notices but no money). Well, he couldn't adjust to the climate, the freeways, the necessity of living inside a machine. Then he got involved in various Leftist causes, and before he knew what was happening, the Industry suddenly blacklisted him. Zap! He tried to get work (I gave him some writing assignments surreptitiously), but no one would allow him to put his name, his signature on a piece. People were scared—scared, as I think Orson Welles put it, of losing their swimming pools. They tried to ignore him, as though he didn't exist. They made him transparent. And Bob Blackman changed. For many years I felt there was a tiny man inside him, the last remaining vestige of his former self, who was desperately trying to get out and become large again—but couldn't. His was a tragedy worse than anything these young Kid Writers have ever ex-

perienced, or will experience. (The Kid Writers
come to me saying they can't get a script I com-
missioned them to write finished, they're "blocked."
I ask them, very coolly, if they've ever been *against*
anything, if they've ever felt angry or outraged by
what they see around them, by some injustice . . .
and they just stare blankly at me . . . as though they
didn't have the vaguest idea of what I was talking
about.) You see, I grew up thinking that writers
came along in society for a purpose—*not* to appear
on Johnny's show—they came along when there was
a particular need, maybe the need for an opposition,
when they could articulate the mood and feeling of
that opposition.

Anyway, I'm beginning to think . . . that if I
can get Irv to agree to having the Kid Writers
write the script of *Studio,* maybe I can get Bob
Blackman to *rewrite* the Kids. . . . It'd be a terrific
credit for him and a chance for a comeback . . .
or, as Norma Desmond put it in that Billy Wilder
picture: "I hate that word—it's *return."*

I'm not sure of the title now, I don't know why
but I'm not. Should we change it from *Studio* to
something else? (This always happens, by the way,
during the early stages of a project; you get panicky
about the title and change it around a half-dozen
times, often to the very opposite of what you started
with.) Yet the boys in the Tower keep insisting on
titles that are literal, titles that are "instantly identifiable," as they tell me. If we make a film about
high school (and we did), they say we should call
it, obviously, *High School* (we didn't, but that was
only because the director fought us like crazy), or
one about airplanes we should call *Airplane,* a
train, *Train,* a car, *Car.* And so on. They say the

audience then knows right away what the picture is about; no guessing involved, no mystery. Very direct, blunt. The boys say you can market and advertise a film better that way—which is one reason why we're making so many goddam sequels now. Mark feels that after *Airplane* or *Train* or *Car* or *Studio* becomes a hit, he can make a sequel and call it *Studio, Part II,* and everybody will know exactly what it is. "Half your work is done for you already in terms of the marketing," he tells me. The audience sees the ad, and presto! you've established identification. (So they say.) Maybe we should keep the title for now. Tomorrow I'm sure I'll change my mind.

Now if Billy and Roy write the script and Bob comes in to rewrite . . . well, I've forgotten the director. He or she may come onto the project and demand that both the script and rewrite be thrown out! Jesus Christ, most of these directors have so much ego at stake in a project that they can't shoot the script the way it's written. No, they have to bring in their "own writers," or start tinkering with it themselves. (Unless these guys started out as writers, the results are always disastrous.) How do I deal with that? I hate to see a script written and rewritten until all the juice has been sucked out of it. I remember one project where a dozen writers wrote a dozen scripts for a dozen different producers, drafts piled onto drafts, and then a dozen directors wanted a dozen new scripts and the whole process was repeated. . . . Happens all the time. (Fortunately, the picture was never made.)

Speaking about directors, I want to say a few things. I want to say that, frankly, I'm tired of all the adulation directors receive in the Press. I'm tired of this Cult of the Director. Because a Truffaut or a Bergman or a Fellini can make his own movie in Europe, that doesn't mean we have the same system here. We don't have *auteurs* in America. It's a ridiculous notion that the *auteur* is responsible for everything that gets up on the screen. It just doesn't happen that way in American film. Besides, only a handful of people, mostly *stars* and not directors, get the Cut on a picture. What's on celluloid is the product of many people's efforts, and not all of them are "collaborating," as the Press would have you innocently believe. If anything, every person on a film is *fighting,* at one time or another, with every other person. When the director is in control, that means he's a better fighter than anybody else, or he's got certain things in his contract (which he fought like hell for) giving him the power to do what he wants.

Anyhow, I don't like the Director-Star system, and I'm glad it's changing. The Director-Star system, which was in vogue a few years back, meant that the director commanded the same salary as the star (over a million dollars a picture). Which is excessive. Too, with that kind of directorial ego involved (the director thinking of himself as a culture hero), there was hardly any room for other talents, like the producer and the writer. And there wasn't much room in the budget for anybody else, either. (A million for the director, another few million for the stars . . . and what's left over?) Some of these Director-Stars got so egotistical that they wouldn't allow anybody to work on a project, they had to do it all themselves. Often, the results were big, lavish flops. Thankfully, the system has changed (for the moment) and directors are getting back to normal (and true) size in the picture-making process.

Of course I have to admit to a prejudice on the subject. I don't want the director to be larger than I am. I don't want him always to get what he wants. I know that's the way the Industry feels about, say, Francis Coppola. They resent his being the Golden Boy so long and doing whatever the fuck he wants. They want him to fail. (Personally, I admire the way he, like Stanley Kubrick, makes the kind of pictures he has to make, risking his own money and controlling all aspects of the production.) Rather than wanting Coppola to fail, I think we should want him to take over one of our studios and show us how to make pictures (because clearly most us have forgotten). In fact, Jake ought to look to him as a possible successor.

As for the choice of director on *Studio,* I fear Mark will pick some hack from our stable of television directors. Most TV directors I know are similar: They make tons of money but suffer. The medium is so confining, so limiting, that every TV hack hungers to get out of it and direct *just one feature.* But a lot of them never get the chance because they've been branded forever as TV boys. (Same thing happens with a lot of actors who are forever typecast.) So they suffer, and work out their suffering through drink or dope, or both. It's pathetic to see talent used up like that. But I don't think the studio minds. Hacks, after all, can be controlled.

There *is* one promising director to come out of television this year—Johnny Ray Lombardo. I think he'd be perfect to direct *Studio* (and make the nearly impossible jump to features), but I bet Mark won't go for him. (I ought to mention his name to

Irv and get Irv to exert pressure on Jake, so that maybe Jake can persuade Mark.) Johnny is better than he really knows. He can get performances out of his actors and that's something for TV work. He makes terrific choices in terms of storytelling. (Those are the only two things I look for in a young director: Can he tell a story? Can he work with actors?) I've been trying to get BB to meet him, but she wants to work with one of the big-name directors in town. I've been trying to get Daphne to represent him, but Johnny is scorned because he comes out of television. (Nobody wants to recognize his talent.) I keep telling the Suits that he's terrific but nobody wants to listen. Johnny's pictures are *"wet"* as we say (they flow)—which is almost impossible for television. He's a character: wears hunting jackets and cowboy outfits. Likes champagne and caviar (but drinks Welch's grape juice most of the time). Talks for hours about his guns—Purdeys and Perazzis. Runs old gangster movies at his house in the Canyon. Likes to work at our studio because we have "no pretensions to art" and we're in business "for entertainment and lines around the block." (He's wrong: All the majors are in business for lines around the block—some are just more upfront about it.) Johnny drives a Japanese car with a phone in it, and talks incessantly. (One time, he told me, he cruised the freeways all day talking on the phone and got more business done than if he'd come into his office on the lot, in the building across the street from the Tower.)

I love the story of how Johnny got his first break. He was going to film school but wasn't learning anything he didn't know already. So he dropped out and began looking for work at one of the seven majors. He knew Hitchcock worked here, so he picked us. Well, the first time he drove up to the main gate in his old American clunker, Benny wouldn't let him in—he looked too grubby and didn't have an appointment to see anybody. Johnny tried a couple more times but still couldn't get in. He noticed, however, that guys wearing suits and ties and driving black cars were automatically allowed through. So he cut his long hair, got a dark suit and painted his car black. And drove up to the main gate again. "Here to see Mr. Steinman," he said, in his most authoritative voice. "I'm his nephew." Benny said, "Yes, sir," and waved him through. He drove around the lot until he found an empty space and parked. (Several days later he painted a sign with his name on it and placed it on the space.) Soon he started coming to the studio every day and parking in his own space and hanging out on the sets of various features and TV shows in production. Whenever somebody asked who he was and what he was doing, Johnny would say without hesitation, "I'm an unofficial observer." Of course, they didn't know if this meant he was the nephew of Jake Steinman or what, so they never bothered to check on his credentials. He took notes, met people, and learned more than he'd ever learned in film school. One day he decided he needed his own office. He went into the Tower, saluted the bust of Uncle Max in the lobby and took the elevator up to the seventh floor (like Francis Coppola, seven is his lucky number). He had no idea what was on the floor (we don't have a directory in the Tower lobby). Just took a chance. Sure enough, the floor had a number of empty offices. He found one and moved in. Nobody seemed to notice; they all just went matter-of-factly about their business. Every day Johnny came into his office (always saluting

Uncle Max—he swears that one time Uncle Max saluted him back). He made phone calls and talked to people about various projects and began writing film scripts. One day about six months later an Efficiency Expert (our studio is very big on efficiency) happened to be on the seventh floor, checking up on things. Well, of course, he found Johnny's office—but couldn't find any record of the studio ever having hired him. He was so astounded that he didn't know what to say. Finally (after conferring with some Suits upstairs) he said, "Keep it." The next day a Suit offered Johnny a job at the studio.

I talked to Irv and pitched Johnny to him. He said, "Jake isn't committed to any one director now, but he's thinking about Hitch." (Jake and Hitchcock are old friends.)

"It's an inspired choice," I said.

"That's what I think."

"But if Hitch is in the picture—the terrorists hold him hostage—and he's also got to direct, it might be too much for him to handle."

"Jake is worried about that," Irv said.

There was a long pause.

"Oh, by the way," Irv filled the gap, "Jake liked your treatment."

I didn't say anything. Jake and Mark and their boys never "like" or "dislike" anything—they just want something that works. So I was surprised by the comment; didn't know what to make of it. (Most of the time in this business when people tell you they "liked" or "loved" your piece of work, it's their way of getting out of any involvement with it. "I loved it," they tell you after reading your script, "but I can't see making a movie out of it.")

"And Mark? What'd he think of the treatment?"

"He didn't say anything."

"And for choice of director?"

"Mark wants a guy from TV."

"He won't go with Johnny?" I pressed.

"No."

"Johnny's the best."

"No."

"He's a helluva talent."

"No."

"Come on, Irv. What is it?"

"Mark's afraid of him."

Another long pause.

Irv said, "Think of somebody else."

I'm thinking . . . Coppola? He writes his own scripts, makes his own pictures. Same for Kubrick. Bob Altman? He's great—a genius—but not disciplined enough. Besides, he doesn't make scare pictures. Billy Friedkin does, and he might be a good choice for *Studio*, though I'm pretty sure he's not bankable after his last disaster. Bogdanovich? Pass. Polanski could do it and make it scary as hell, but Roman has other problems (I'll say he does!). . . . Hal Ashby? Too sweet. De Palma? He can scare but he needs lots of blood to do it. Mike Nichols? I wish he would go back to making comedy. George Lucas? He's terrific, but after his last hit he can do whatever he wants. Same for Spielberg. John Boorman? You've got to be kidding. Arthur Penn? Maybe, maybe not. Peckinpah? *Studio* isn't a Western, is it? Sam sure needs to work more, I wish the Suits would allow him to. Mazursky? He's wonderful and I love his pictures but he's not right for this one. Norman Jewison? Norman can do blood 'n' guts, but I don't know if he can scare. For that matter, can anybody scare? John Schlesinger can, but only when he wants to. George Roy Hill? He works here and has his own projects going and he's bankable. Maybe . . . How about Billy Wilder? Now there's a flash. John Milius? Whatever happened to him? Nick Ray in a comeback? You're on. John Huston? Kazan? Frank Capra? Howard Hawks? Are you ready for this? Orson Welles.

I'm thinking . . . nobody accepts your first choice immediately. You've got to make a list of fifteen and eliminate them one by one . . . until you come back to your first choice. I'm thinking . . . if I run through the list with Irv and Irv runs through it with Jake and Jake . . . Hell, I'm going to call Johnny and see what *he* thinks.

Hitch made the scariest picture of all time at our studio, right here on the backlot, about a hundred yards from my building. I was working out of this tiny office on the other side of the lot. He made it for Jake. He shot it in thirty-six days, including retakes, with one of our crews that we use on television shows. I had a deal to produce three pictures at the time. He shot it purposely in black and white because he didn't want to show blood running down that bathtub in vivid color. "That's the photography of violence," he told me. I can still see that brutal murder in he shower, still see it in my darkest dreams . . . still hear what Tony Perkins said, "We all go a little crazy sometimes." Every day I pass by the set from that picture, this three-sided house, "backless," which is a fixture on the Studio Tour. And its eeriness still pervades the scene. . . .

Johnny called me. He'd read my treatment and liked it (Billy and Roy had passed it on to him thinking he'd be the best choice to direct). "I want to make this picture," he said. So he decided to see Jake about it. He walked into the Tower, saluted Uncle Max's bust in the lobby, and shot up the elevator to Jake's office on the top floor. By chance Jake was in between meetings, and he got to see him. (The secretary didn't want to let him in at first because, of course, he didn't have an appointment. "All I'm asking is one minute of the chief's time," he said.) Well, Jake was delighted to see him, he'd been thinking about him (he said) and was glad he came up. Johnny began talking about the picture. He talked and talked, very fast, very loudly, telling Jake with great passion that he, Johnny Lombardo, was the man to direct *Studio* and why. "I'm doing this *for you*, Mr. Steinman," he said. And after thirty minutes in his office, Jake said, "All right, kid. You got it." (Now I know why Mark's afraid of the kid.) They shook hands, it was a deal.

So . . . what Johnny was calling me about was to see if I wanted to produce the picture.

I fell over in my chair.

"It was Jake's idea," said Johnny.

Jake is so smart, he thinks of everything. He knows I'm real high on Johnny because Johnny's a comer—and that I want to work with him. He knows I'm also the ideal person to produce *Studio* and get it right, indeed kick the hell out of it, because I know more about how this studio operates than anybody else working here. But it puts me in a bind. If I accept the offer and agree to produce, I play right into Jake's hands: He controls me and has a way of taking my criticism (I can't see making *Studio* any other way except as a critical document, and I'm sure Jake knows this) and turning a profit from it. In addition, it'll be his final picture, his farewell movie before naming his successor and retiring forever. . . . *Studio* then becomes his triumph. The Industry will love it, as will our stockholders if it becomes a hit, and Jake's methods and the system he's developed over the years for running his "factory," as everybody calls it—this machine—will go unchallenged. The system will win out because it was able to absorb all criticism of itself and *still* make money. You can't beat that, can you? Nothing more ingenious has ever been devised for manipulating criticism for your own end. (History will render Jake and his successor Good Guys because they maintained order and stability and tolerated, if not encouraged, criticism.) But . . . if I *don't* accept the offer, the odds are I won't get another shot like this again, a chance to say what I want to say, what I have to say. If I don't produce *Studio* and make it into an instrument for my own criticism of the system—which is undoubtedly what Jake wants me to do—then I'll look like a fool for having passed up the opportunity. Jake knows this. He and all the other Jakes in our Industry and all the other industries in America know the same thing. Survival is a two-way street. I need them (to criticize) and they need me (and my criticism) to turn a profit. So what do I do?

I'm going to the Beach right now to think about it. I'm calling BB and telling her that I'm coming out. I need time to plot a counterstrategy *before* Jake makes the formal offer tomorrow. (He just planted the seed with Johnny and knows Johnny told me and wants to see what kind of a counteroffer I come up with.) So I'm going to the Beach.

I ought to call Bob Goldsby, my best and only friend (the business doesn't permit friendship, so this is rare). Bob is my lawyer, he's handling my custody case to get Jason. I know I can trust him, I know it. Of course, Jake has made the game even tougher for me, because if I go to my "friends" (Bob and Irv and BB and Daphne) and explain "my problem," they'll all know I'm disillusioned. They'll see me, rightly or wrongly, as somebody who wants to defy the system. Maybe they'll see me as somebody not to be trusted. I risk exposing myself and my unhappiness with the way things are by telling my "friends." Jake knows this, too.

Tomorrow I'll know, tomorrow I'll have an answer. I live in tomorrow. I rarely talk about what I *am* doing, always what I'm *going* to do. Tomorrow—I talk a pretty good tomorrow, just as most people do in the Industry. I'm preparing for and organizing Tomorrow....

I came home instead. Cinnamon is here, pouring me a Coke. I talked to Bob and he said he'll come over later tonight. I'm going to call him back and tell him not to. BB wants me to drive out to the Beach, but I'm too frazzled after all. Daphne thinks I ought to get out of the deal with Jake. Says, in the end I'll get screwed. "I'm still thinking about it," I told her.

I'm nervous as hell about the whole thing.

I can't seem to relax.

I can't seem to relax in my own house. I live in this big house up in the Canyons that once belonged to Garbo's second husband (but now belongs more to the banks than me), and I can't relax. I've *never* been able to calm down here, yet that's why I bought the house in the first place—because I thought I was Buying Calm. The house has a lot of rooms and most of them were done by a decorator (who's moderately famous) and his army of assistants. I paid him a princely sum to give the place a "contemporary look." They bought me all these pieces. I have your standard novelties: antique pool table, espresso machine, two pinball machines, old Wurlitzer jukebox, hot tub, sauna, Jacuzzi, and meditation platform. And yet, I don't feel anything in the house truly reflects any part of who I am.

There was more of me in a cheap pink stucco bungalow where I used to live years ago, in the ratty part of town.

Cinnamon is trying to calm me down.

Perhaps I've blown this out of proportion, perhaps I'm not seeing very clearly.

The house feels so empty now, so devoid of all life.

(It's very well maintained. I have a Japanese gardener who comes twice, no, three times a week to keep up the landscaping. My maid cleans up twice a week. I have phones in every room and flowers next to the phones.)

Yet I'm not comfortable here, it's not me.

And I pay too much for it—this façade, this fantasy. Bob, my lawyer, tells me I pay too much, but I don't know what to do—except try to make more money to keep up with property taxes and maintenance costs and keep making more money to support this fantasy.

Which isn't calm, which isn't me.

Cinnamon thinks I should produce *Studio*, she wants another shot at a big hit. She wants all the excitement, the incredible rush that comes from a big hit. She reminds me that none of the films

I'm producing now have that kind of potential excitement. The films are like the rest of our studio Product—they star machines—and the only excitement comes from building these infernal beasts and then making the damn things work right. Of course, *Studio* stars a machine . . .

One picture I'm preparing (which Nick Benvenue wrote) stars this giant rogue elephant. Well, the elephant goes berserk in Africa, terrorizing a small village where the natives are too superstitious to do anything about it, because the elephant is sacred to their tribal culture. A small boy and a white hunter (I'm trying to get Charles Bronson for the lead) go after the elephant—which is a machine we're constructing on the backlot, in total secrecy, with a team of British special effects experts. The elephant is thirty feet tall and eighteen feet wide; it moves just like a real elephant, head and ears and trunk. It can wink, smile. It can even lift its leg and take a piss. At any rate, Bronson and the boy hunt the elephant down and capture it alive (they use a special tranquilizer gun during the mission). And bring the creature back to America. They keep the elephant in the San Diego Zoo, and the boy develops a wonderful friendship with the beast. One day he wants to release it from captivity; the zoo trainers refuse. So secretly he frees the animal. And it goes on a wild rampage through the streets of San Diego. Bronson is immediately called in to help. But he's powerless against it. He has to persuade the boy to return the elephant to the zoo. The boy agrees, but only on the condition that it's sent back to Africa afterward. And he wants to go back with it. In the end . . . I won't spoil it for you.

The second picture is about an engineer who one

day, mysteriously, begins receiving boxes and boxes
of electrical parts in the mail. He doesn't know
where they come from. The boxes include a set of
elaborate instructions. Out of curiosity—just for the
fun of it—he starts to assemble the pieces, and
working day and night, he soon completes the
project. It's a robot. Yet the robot, whom he calls
Howard, doesn't seem to work. Nothing happens,
Howard doesn't move or light up, and the engineer
can't figure out what's wrong. One day his son
begins talking to the robot, and the robot talks
back.

"Surprised?"

"No."

"I'm Dan," says the robot. "What's your name?"

"Johnny."

"Pleased to meet you, Johnny."

"Robots can't talk. My dad says they can't."

"What do parents know?"

"My dad calls you Howard."

"I'm Dan and I'm coming to get you."

"You don't scare me."

"That's the spirit, Johnny. I like kids who aren't
afraid."

"I'm only scared of my dad."

The boy and the robot become good friends. One
day when the father threatens the boy because he
hasn't done his chores, the robot decides to get rid of
the father. The robot zaps the engineer (his creator,
really) and turns him into a mechanical man sub-
servient to the boy. Soon the robot begins sys-
tematically wiping out all the parents in the neighborhood—and turning them all into robots at the
command of the kids. The kids take over. The
parents clean the houses, go to work, while the kids

. . . You'll have to watch it in the theaters to see how it turns out. . . .

The third picture I'm preparing is about a family, a mother and father, their teenage son and daughter, who live out in the country on several acres of land. The family is obsessed with cars. Each person has one, plus the son has twenty-five or thirty of them sitting out back—old wrecks, some working, some not. Dad drives a truck and loves trucks. Mom drives a station wagon, the son a jeep, the daughter a sports car. (Dad met Mom in a drive-in, and she lost her virginity in the car, but not to Dad. For a wedding present, Dad gave Mom a white Thunderbird. At the birth of their first child, he gave her a Corvette. And so on. Instead of trading in these cars on new ones, they decided to keep them. The kids grew up playing in them. The kids gave each car a name. The cars were named Buster, Sam, Mervin, Frank, Louise, Ginger, Sparky, Muscles, Yum-yum, Thumper, Crank, Rod, Matilda, Moses, Punch, Perky, Sunshine, Toot, Miles, Rodney Junior. . . . The kids learned how to fix them up, learned about the history of each—whom it belonged to and when it became part of the family.)

One night Dad wants to teach his son all about cruising. So he takes him into town cruising on the local gut, the strip where everybody hangs out. Meanwhile, Daughter meets her boy friend and they also go into town, cruising. . . . The boy friend is a punk who loves to hotrod. He takes the hot rod and drags against another punk, as the father and son are watching, and crashes the car. Which goes hurtling off the road at high speed, flipping over several times and exploding in flames. The daughter is killed, along with her boyfriend. The parents decide to have the funeral at the house and bury the wreckage of the cars, with the bodies still inside, out in their backyard. At the funeral they talk about the punk boyfriend—what a bad kid he was. The wrecked car, nonetheless, is buried.

Well, one night the parents and the son hear sounds coming from the backyard. Sounds of the punk's hot rod, its motor revving. . . . They check it out but find nothing. Same thing next night. And the night after. So they stay awake the following night and, sure enough, it happens. The hot rod is revved up and moving. . . . They see the boy friend at the wheel and their daughter sitting next to him. Dad and Mom and Son run out of the house and jump into their own cars. A battle begins. All the old wrecks and clunkers, once belonging to various members of the family, now begin ramming into each other. The hot rod goes after the parents, smashing into their car and killing them. Only the son manages to escape, as this orgy of destruction continues through the night until the house is completely demolished. . . . The son escapes into a field. The other machines come after him—but to no avail. The son watches his house go up in flames. . . . In the morning, as the sun comes up, he finds himself mysteriously by the side of the road leading into town, bleeding, bruised, yet still able to walk. He stumbles along. Sticks out his thumb. Shortly, a white car comes to a screeching halt . . . and the driver offers him a ride. The son gets in, barely able to see, and turns to the driver. The driver looks exactly like the punk boyfriend. He's very proud of his new white car, he revs up the engine and speeds off. The driver talks a mile a minute, as the son sits there paralyzed with fear. Then . . .

* * *

All three pictures are about machines, all three don't require stars (except maybe Bronson in the first) and therefore can be made on lower budgets. All three should make money, maybe one will be a hit. (One out of four movies makes back its negative cost, though, as Jake says, negative cost is something of a joke because it doesn't include advertising and distribution charges.) I don't think any of those three pictures "says" anything, or has "content." I'm sure they'll each be consumed right there in the theater—and forgotten the moment the audience steps out onto the street. I doubt that people will talk about them, except maybe for a performance here, a car wreck there. I will spend about one year on each picture, maybe longer. Doubtless there will be one crisis after another, starting from the day we sign the contract with the studio to the day we deliver the release prints to the distributors. Actors will demand more money; writers will turn in bad scripts. The director on each picture will think he's an *auteur* and try to be "artistic" and go over budget and fuck things up. There will be featherbedding on the set during the shoot and fights with the unions; they'll want over-time and God knows what else. The scores (music) will be junked, the dubbing a mess because the man who's doing it, the mixer, doesn't care. The cutter will come through at the eleventh hour, but the labs will fuck up the prints. Before release, the studio will demand changes, and I'll have to fight them all the way to preserve the integrity of the film. The distributor (in collaboration with the studio) will fail to give us an honest accounting. A picture delivered at a negative cost of two point five million will have to make eight million at the box office just to break even. That means at least two, three, four million people, mostly kids, will have to pay to see the picture—just so we make the Break. And in the end, the critics will rip us to pieces, destroy one of those three pictures, and rank them on their ten-worst-pictures-of-the-year lists. But it's fun.

It's fun, and just because three out of four pictures fail (or six out of seven, depending on how you interpret the statistics), that doesn't mean, necessarily, the studio loses money. We make money because we get all of what a picture makes up to the break-even point, which is about three times the negative cost. And we get at least *half* of what a picture makes after reaching its Break. Let's say that it costs three million to make a movie—about average these days, maybe even a bit low. That three million may include a million, or million-five in "above the line" costs, that is, talent (stars, director, and cast) and script. (Say the script costs three hundred thousand, the director two hundred, and the star, along with cast and crew, a million.) So we've spent a million-five without shooting a single foot of film. We spend another million-five on the actual shoot.

To raise that three million, the studio borrows money from the banks and charges to itself at least one-third of that budget for studio "overhead," meaning the use of the facilities on the lot: the casting, props and wardrobe, sound, cutting, and special effects. So we shoot the film for three million, okay? Surprisingly, we come in on time, within budget. Now we have to spend another three million, perhaps closer to four or five, for the prints, distribution (often inflated), and advertising. That means seven or eight million to hit the Break. And that's the risk, the gamble you're taking.

Yet the studio is way ahead because we've received a million already just for overhead, and we get, as I say, *all* of what the picture grosses up to seven or eight million, plus *half* of whatever comes after. (Selling it to TV accounts for a million-plus, and we can expect to equal our domestic gross on a picture when it is released abroad.) So, if you follow me, the system tends to favor bigger budgets. It favors making the twenty- or twenty-five-million-dollar picture because, if it's made and financed through the studio, more and more people will get a piece of it along the way. (Everybody gets a bigger cut.) There's also the feeling that big budgets mean more production value, getting more for our money up there on the screen (since millions have been spent on sets and location shooting), and a chance to have Product that really gets up and runs away, really excites the mass audience in large numbers. The system favors bigger budgets—and upward failure.

Cinnamon went home.

It's a warm night, the phone keeps ringing.

I don't want to answer it.

I want to *shtup* Daphne.

I'm with Daphne and BB at the amusement park. Daphne wants to take a ride on the roller coaster. I tell her no. I'm trying to hide my fear of the machine. I buy Daphne popcorn and BB cotton candy. I squeeze Daphne's breasts and kiss BB gently on the lips. Daphne kisses BB. Cinnamon says I have a phone call. "I'm thinking . . . ," I tell her. Jill McCorkle appears. She says she wants a ride on the ferris wheel. She promises me . . . I buy two tickets from the man at the gate. The man is Jake Steinman, dressed in a George Raft double-breasted suit with a white tie. "Step right up!" he shouts. "One for you, one for us." We sit on the wheel, the motor starts up. I see points and percentages in red lights. I try to kiss Jill but we go round and round. . . .

I drink another Coke.

The night air is still warm.

I can feel a Santa Ana blowing, I can feel how crazy it's making everybody.

I miss the East. I miss the seasons, the clear sense of fall and winter, spring and summer. (There are seasons here, too, but the changes are so minute —you have to be a native to really detect them.) I get tired of the same climate, month after month. I remember going to school in the snow, trudging along with my books and thinking, "One day I won't have to do this." Now for some reason, I want to go back. I know I can't but that doesn't stop me from trying. . . . And it's not the same thing—going back for a visit. Visits are painful reminders to me that nothing truly changes. Ever. The East is always the same, permanently fixed in my memory. The East is a reminder of what I was and could never be. Had I stayed, I'd be forever locked into the neighborhood where I grew up, among the Poles, Italians, Greeks, Czechs and Jews.

When I fly back to see my mother, who is now in her eighties (Dad died a dozen years back), I have trouble. I get nervous and edgy.

"Are you happy, Tony?"

"Yes, Mother."

"My son, I want him happy."

"I know. I am."

"Smart boy. And how's your wife? You never talk about her to me."

"Fine."

"You never tell me how she is."

"She's fine, Mother. We're divorced. The divorce went through. She has Jason."

"You tell her I am sorry."

"I will."

"Promise you tell her."

"Promise."

I meet my mother's friends, all of whom remember me as the young Tony Schwartz. I don't know what to say to them. They're so connected to the past; they seem to recall every detail of their lives. They talk about the Old Country (they each had different ones) and their childhoods, the dresses they wore and the boys who courted them. They get together and drink schnapps. The past is as immediate to them as anything in their current lives. They are jealous of each other; each one of them trying to be the center of attention. I don't stay very long, maybe at most a couple of days. At the end I pack quickly, quietly, and write out a check to my mother. "Too much!" she yells at me as though I were a kid. "I don't need it."

I leave and catch the first plane back to the Coast. On the plane I have three strong drinks and try to forget. Maybe the East is just something that's forgotten, or something I need to forget. Maybe it can't be very well remembered living out here in the Canyon. Maybe the East is lost forever.

This is the sixth or seventh place I've lived in out here. I like to move around, though I'm not sure the places have gotten any better. The last house I lived in was worse than the one before but cost me more money. (The house was modern, poorly made, and overpriced—I was paying for the location—ten minutes from the Beach.) This place is larger, more spacious than any of my previous houses. The property taxes are exorbitant. And, as I say, there's less of me here than any other place I've lived. Out front I have a security gate. Inside, a security alarm system—after that wave of gruesome murders up in Benedict Canyon a while back. Often I'm afraid of coming home at night, afraid of stepping in the door and finding some mutant, standing there, ready to cut my throat. The house is vulnerable in spite of the alarm system, and I know it. Somebody could get inside if he really wanted to.

There's less of me here because, physically and mentally, I'm always someplace else. I'm either driving the freeways or working in my office at the studio. Mainly I'm on the phone, and in Tomorrow. When Billy and Roy come over to see me, they say they don't feel "any of me" in the house. "You're like a visitor in your own house," they say. And they're right—I don't really *need* the place except for show, as a symbol of success, even if it truly belongs to the banks and, indirectly, to the studio. (Without the work at the studio, I lose the house.) Or else . . . it belongs to the ghost of Garbo's second husband, who died in here. . . . At night . . . when I'm alone . . . I get high on the possibility of ghosts.

The only place I remember liking was my third apartment. (The first was a cheap hotel filled with hookers and pimps. The second? Even worse than the first . . .) My third place was in the ratty part of town, in the flatlands. Stucco bungalows, in cheap pink. I drive by it every now and then just to remind myself that I actually lived there once. (It's right around the corner from the local bijou where I used to go and see pictures all the time, sitting always in the same seat, nine rows from the big screen, dead center.) The landlady is still alive, a sweet old lady in her eighties who claimed to have had psychic powers. She still remembers me, even though she's a bit senile, and always asks, "When you movin' back?"

"I'm not."

"What'd ya say?"

"I'm not."

"Place is ready. Got it all fixed up 'n' painted."

"That's nice."

"So you're movin' back."

"No."

"Glad to have ya."

"Sorry, but I'm not."

"What'd ya say?"

Legend has it that Cecil B. De Mille kept the stucco bungalow as a stable for his battalion of horses. When he gave up horses and moved on to women, he converted the stalls into a different kind of stable: one for young starlets constantly begging him for parts. He kept the starlets there, in what came to be known as Cecil B. De Mille's Whorehouse. (There were nights sleeping there when I imagined Jean Harlow and Carole Lombard coming to bed with me, or Mae West whispering something obscene in my ear.)

The bungalow court housed all manner of show people: actors with crooked noses, stand-up comics turned alcoholic, a fortune teller who read everybody's palms and told us, "Tomorrow is your lucky day, kiddo," and so on. I got involved with a set of twins who lived next door to me. Had an affair with one, which caused me to move out because her sister grew unbearably jealous. At various times there were stunt men specializing in car crashes, writers who played backgammon day and night and never wrote, an animal trainer from Nebraska, a man who always walked on his hands, a musician making an instrument that had never been heard before, an old Communist whose room was filled with leaflets and propaganda, an actor who parked cars for a living, a starlet who wore nothing but gold, a poet who shaved his head every morning, a doomsayer who told us, "Act wisely, as the end draws near," a man who wrote pornography so that he could make money and then lose it at the crap tables in Vegas, a man who slept with his TV set on at night because "I like the hum," a woman with a pet snake, a woman who was a writer's groupie but hated writers, a man who collected Eisenhower buttons, one Bette Davis look-alike, one Joan Crawford look-alike, two Marilyn Monroe look-alikes . . .

Often I wonder whatever happened to those people. One time in New York I ran into an actor who used to live there. Yes, he remembered the period but didn't want to be reminded of it very much. "Too many weirdos," he said. He was now "in the liquor business," which is what actors tell you if they've become bartenders. And he had.

My room there had more of me than anyplace I've lived. It was empty, except for some books, a wooden desk, a bed, a cane chair, and my clothes scattered all over the place. Yet the room looked like me, even *smelled* like me. I wrote long letters there, sitting at that desk. I wrote to my family and my buddies back East (most of the letters went unanswered). I wrote to Jill McCorkle—and remember waiting anxiously each day for the mailman to come with her reply. Of course it never came. . . . I ate out of tin cans in that room, I drank beer in bed. . . . If somebody next door was having a fight (usually some actor trying to get starfucked without being a star), I'd yell at the top of my lungs, *Shut up! I'm thinking!*" And pound my fist on the walls, which were thin as cardboard. (Now I'd never think of pounding on the walls of my own house, for fear of setting off the burglar alarm.)

On the overstuffed, creaky sofa, I got laid a lot. Before the twins there was this salesclerk in a fancy department store, an actress hoping to be discovered. She had long legs and wore cherry red lipstick. I was passionately in love with her and told her we'd get married as soon as I got a break and made enough for the two of us. (I wonder whatever happened to her; I can't imagine her still working in that store, but maybe she is . . .)

I worked as a messenger boy, then as a sorter in the mailroom at the studio. Nights, I worked on my first script. I remember lying on my living room floor, face down, scribbling on the backs of envelopes and paper bags, I remember stealing a typewriter from one of the writers who played backgammon and never wrote. . . . The script was about a guy living back East who wanted to be somebody and impress a certain girl with his worthiness, but who couldn't find a legitimate way of doing it. So he started stealing Valentines from a department store and sending them to her every day. She sent them back. One day he steals a car, this beautiful sleek machine. Drives up to her house and honks the horn. She comes out, she's curious. Well, before too long she falls in love with him, and they take off together in his machine. . . . In the end, the cops go after them and he gets shot and she gets away. The script sold but was never made into a picture. Nevertheless, I was on my way. I sold a script, I had money under my belt—it was Disappearing Money (which is what most writers are paid in), money you spend faster than you make. . . .

The sun is coming up over the mountains to the east. I haven't slept at all. I want to eat something before driving out to the Beach. The trades are here, but I don't want to read them. I better shave and take my hot-cold shower. . . .

I'm in my German car, driving down the Canyon, my house just a blur in the rearview mirror. I have on a T-shirt and swim trunks, that's all. I like this city in the morning. You always feel like something will happen . . . if you follow a hunch, play your cards right, keep looking for clues. . . .

There are so many permutations and combinations of the Possible, so many things that could happen, and that's why the city comes alive in the morning.

I'm driving fast, yet smoothly. I'm in no hurry. It's about a half hour's drive to the Beach. I see cars, Japanese cars, French, Italian cars, American cars, large and small, old and new, and it's miraculous how they shift from lane to lane, each driver knowing exactly when to change, knowing intuitively, almost like a great dance of machines, a ballet of metal and glass and rubber. . . .

You know, I think I'll take Jake up on his offer, which I'm expecting this morning, and produce *Studio*. Hell, what have I got to lose. I need the money, don't I? Of course, I don't know whether it's the *right* decision or the *best* decision, or what.

You have to change lanes sometimes. The game is so fast that you have to make *a* decision or risk having people lose interest in you. In other words, you have to keep generating *heat*.

I made it. I'm here at the Beach. BB is coming out of the house to greet me. She has on a bikini and looks terrific, beautifully tanned. I need a tan, too. My face has no color to speak of. There's nothing worse than getting pale, ghostly like this. From the Beach I'll come back to the studio all sunburned and healthy. I got to have a good tan.

PART 2

Jake made the offer.

He offered me a flat fee (in six figures) to produce the picture, plus ten percent of the net profits. Instead of bringing in Daphne or Bob Goldsby to negotiate the deal, I decided to negotiate it myself. I counteroffered: no fee but a percentage of the gross. He looked surprised. I wasn't asking for any money on the front end; if the picture failed I'd end up with nothing for a year of my life. How much of a percentage? "Nine points," I told him in the conference room on the top floor of the Tower. (If the picture hit big, each of those points could be worth a million dollars.) "Five," he said, pure ice. I countered with seven, and he walked out of the meeting. Negotiations had broken off.

When they resumed the next day, he said he'd agree to seven if I'd agree to a "pay or play" deal. Which meant, in this case, delivery of the picture in time for a Christmas release or, if I was late, a loss of my points. I said yes. *But* he'd have to agree to Billy and Roy writing the script for *Studio* from my original treatment. Negotiations broke off again. (Billy and Roy would have to be pulled from the war picture they were doing for S/D, and, Steinman/Dalton would be pissed about that because it'd set back their schedule at least six months, and they'd scream bloody murder/blackmail at Jake and Mark for the delay.)

When we got back together, Jake said he'd agree to the Kid Writers if I'd agree to having *Irv* pulled off the project completely, with no producer or executive producer credit. (Goddammit, this was a hard one because, after all, it was Irv's concept film—he'd proposed the idea for it—and he was my friend, somebody to whom I felt a measure of loyalty, and I didn't like fucking him over. Besides, if *Studio* became a hit and I scored on all those points, he'd probably kill me. What could I do? In every way, it was a no-win situation. I needed the Kid Writers, I needed Irv's friendship as a means of survival in the studio system. Obviously, I couldn't have both.) I agonized over the decision for several days, I took long walks along the Beach (where I was now living with BB in her house) and talked to the sea gulls. I threw rocks out into the ocean and watched them die in the foam. I called Daphne and Bob and got their opinions (which were split). I began thinking about what was really happening. . . . *Irv was being sacrificed.* Probably Mark thought I'd conspired with Irv against him in order to get Johnny as director (which wasn't exactly true, because Irv was pushing for Frank Shelby until he realized that Johnny was the better choice). Probably this was a form of retribution. Or, perhaps, Mark was afraid that if I teamed up with Irv and this project really began to take off, we'd pose some kind of threat to his power at the studio. . . .

One morning I agreed to pull Irv off the project. And closed the deal with Jake on *Studio.* When I told Irv (and Mark asked me to break the news to him), he was mad as hell. Called me a prick. A son of a bitch. A *momser*. Accused me of selling him out for my own advantage. He was so mad, in fact, that he called up a trade reporter and complained to him about the "impossible conditions in the Tower" and the "ruthlessness" of those running the studio. But succeeded only in damaging his cause. The story appeared next day in the paper and there it was, in black and white, STUDIO EXECUTIVE RIPS INTO STEINMAN'S ENTERTAINMENT EMPIRE. Jake was not happy. And Irv tried to correct his error by doing a song and dance about how he'd "misspoken" himself in the Press. I felt sorry for the man, I hated to see him flounder like that, although I knew others didn't exactly feel as I did. (I was sure Mark Fowler and probably Roger Dalton—who'd been eyeing Irv's position for a long time —took a perverse pleasure in the man's misfortune.) Speaking of Dalton, he was furious at me for luring away the Kid Writers from his war picture; he claimed the war project was now doomed. (Curiously, his partner, Michael Steinman, didn't seem that upset by the loss of the writers. I ran with him one morning on the Beach—we jogged for about a mile not far from his house— and he told me he wasn't so keen to make the film anyway. He had "no special attachment" to the war project, he said. "Roger's baby," he added. I tried to run with Michael every morning and get on his better side. For I could see a split developing between them, with Roger aligning himself with Mark's forces . . . and Michael striking out on his own. . . . I wanted to do everything I could to encourage the split and maybe, in time, win Michael over into my camp.)

At any rate, Jake wasn't happy with Irv. So he sent him on assignment to Europe. Irv was to scout locations for one of our action-adventure pictures and look for fresh talent, particularly young actresses on their way up. He took on the assignment with relish. And once there, he sent back a barrage of telegrams with lewd comments about all the starlets he'd *shtupped* in Paris and Rome and London on his "talent search." The starlets all thought he was ten years younger because of his face-lift. (That's what he said when he called me in the middle of the night.) As for Frank Shelby, the Suede Man, he bitched about being passed over for Johnny Lombardo. Again, Jake didn't like to have anybody at his studio unhappy, so he gave Frank a lot of work directing episodic television. Frank threw a tantrum at first, but Jake told him bluntly, "Take it or leave it." Frank took it.

With the deal closed, Jake was all sweetness and light toward me. He had my office moved from the first to the third floor of the Producer's Building, my white ziggurat. He gave me an extra parking space, he ordered cream-colored stationery for me embossed with my monogram. He had the office decorated with Louis XIV chairs, a dark brown Chippendale desk that once belonged to Uncle Max, and a Moroccan leather sofa. Emblazoned on the door, in ornate lettering, was *TS Productions*. (I felt like one of the old signature producers.) He called me every day to ask how things were going. (Again, the calls only lasted thirty seconds—the longest Jake ever talks to anybody on the phone —but his voice instilled confidence in me. In fact, with every call I was growing less and less afraid of him.) He was extremely generous with money to develop the script (which excited the Kid Writers), because he wanted, he said, to get a story that "everybody could believe in."

Part of my agreement in producing *Studio* was, of course, to develop the screenplay from the treatment I'd written. That would take money (which I had) and time (which I didn't). For the moment I had Billy and Roy working away on the script. I figured I'd get a better script if I could offer them some incentive beyond the money. So one night I told them: "You do a good job on this for me, and I'll get you a deal to produce and direct your own picture." Apparently, it was just what they wanted to hear—because they worked like crazy on the material (late nights, many cups of coffee, not too much time with the wives). I figured, too, that they'd turn my treatment into an action-adventure thriller with some artful suspense and lots of violence (which they were especially good at), including a bizarre chase sequence (mandatory) and a stylish apocalyptic finish (optional). I wanted them, above all, to capture a sense of the irrational, of the ways in which our Industry (not unlike other industries) is paranoia inducing. So one day I hired a private detective to follow the writers, to listen in on their phone conversations. The day after, I told the writers what I was doing. "Simulating paranoia," I said. They freaked. (And their wives hated me for it.)

For my part, I began to take on the personality of the main character, called the Actor. I didn't shave in the mornings, I popped pills to stay awake all the time. I drove the freeways in a '57 Chevy painted in psychedelic colors. I tried to understand the sensitivities and tolerances of my machine. I practiced speeding, cruising, hobbling along in traffic. I hung out at Jimmy Ray's, the actors' bar in town. I mingled with actors who were desperate for breaks, any break, no matter how small. I started collecting (and dealing) guns. Pretty soon I had a .44 Magnum, a .38 Smith & Wesson Special, a .32 revolver, a Colt .45. I tried to imagine liking guns. I shot at practice ranges, I shot holes in the car. I slept with them. (BB was scared out of her mind when I took one, then two guns to bed.) Each of these experiences I told the writers about. I fed them details, sensations—everything as precisely as I could remember—for I wanted the script to have texture, nuance. I wanted the script to be personal.

Yet I was afraid the Kid Writers wouldn't be able to create three-dimensional characters. If that was indeed the case, I'd bring in Bob Blackman for the rewrite. Bob could come in, elevate the characters —flesh them out, make them believable. (Bob hadn't lost his sense of the tragic, stemming from his blacklisted days, and I could take advantage of that.) In the end, he'd split the screenwriting credit with the Kids, and I'd get credit for the original story, which was something I wanted very badly —just to leave my mark on the picture beyond the producer credit.

In several long memos, I told Jake that I was doing everything possible to get the story right because without the story, what have you got? In my opinion, the story is king. You can execute it well, badly, or indifferently, but if it isn't right from the beginning, I don't think you can save a picture on the shoot, with endless retakes and "coverage" (multiple cameras shooting all the action simultaneously) or, later on, in the cutting room. Jake also was aware of that. From day to day, I told him what we were doing and how things were progressing. He was very curious.

I liked the large new office with the antique furnishings. I liked the private patio outside, beautifully landscaped with wisteria, bougainvillea, and honeysuckle. I liked sitting out there from time to time, working on my tan—which was getting darker every day, though still nowhere near as dark as Jake's. I liked the stroking calls from Jake and his boys.

Of course, I was being seduced. I knew it but didn't really let it bother me at first. (Jake was providing a custom-fit of the Golden Handcuffs.) Daphne thought it was terrific; BB said that it was "the best thing that could've happened" and that my success had improved our sex life "*easily* one hundred percent." Cinnamon loved it because there was some excitement in the air again, and she thrived on that.

My power was on the rise, and the true measure of that came one day when Frank Shelby called me (for no apparent reason except to tell me that he thought we should make *Studio* into a disaster picture), and I told him, in this deep voice that came out of nowhere, "Fuck you, Frank!" And slammed the receiver down, feeling very good about it. In this Industry, your power is measured by the number of people to whom you can say, without missing a beat, "Fuck you."

I suggested we hold a press conference. (I wanted —well, if not to ballyhoo the picture at least to let the Industry know we were going ahead with it.) The studio commissary seemed as good a place as any in which to stage the event. And Jake liked the idea. I suggested, too, that we pull Uncle Max Schumacher out of retirement for the occasion. (As it turned out, he wasn't quite up to it—I can understand, the man is over a hundred. Still, Uncle Max told me over the phone that he'd be there "when the picture's finished, okay?") I suggested Hitch appear and talk about the old days and then give us a tour of his three-sided house, the set from the scariest picture of all time, which he shot here. I suggested Jake preside over the ceremonies.

So we held it—on a Thursday, the day Hitch and Jake traditionally eat lunch together at the commissary. The press turned out *en masse*, reporters from all the local papers as well as a number we'd flown in from out of town. We offered a "studio lunch": hot and cold sandwiches, all the Coke you could drink, plus copies of the trades. We got Hitch to tell stories about making pictures in the early days. He was wonderful. Then Jake came on, looking almost statuesque, in his dark blue suit, his hair silvery, his tan deep and rich. The room went silent. (I was sitting at a corner table and couldn't get over Jake's presence in a crowd, the amount of space he took up, like a Bogart or a Cagney.) He told a funny little story about the day he first met Hitch and how Hitch had frightened him. Everybody laughed. He told the story about the midget who tried to steal the bust of Uncle Max in the Tower lobby because "he wanted a souvenir" from his trip to glamourland. And while he was telling it, he looked at me the whole time. Yes, the midget was my uncle Saul. Yes, he came out for a visit one year with my mother and dad. Yes, the studio guards caught him just as he was leaving the main gate. Everybody laughed again; I tried to but couldn't. Then Jake delivered his pitch for *Studio*. He announced that the film would be a "family chronicle" from the earliest days of the studio to the present, based on historical fact but "peppered with a lot of fiction." It concerned, he said, the rise to power of a studio chief during a period of change and turmoil, when a group of terrorists try to take over the studio complex by holding a certain famous director (he didn't mention Hitch by name) hostage. The film, he went on, would be a "monument to the courage and valor of the Industry in an age where anarchy and terrorism prevail." Budgeted at many millions, it would feature roles for "stars, superstars, and great character actors." Casting would begin next week, Jake concluded, for a start on the first day of summer. Which meant that we had less than a few months to get a decent script, decent actors, and make all the preparations that were necessary for the shoot. (What usually happens is that there's this Trajectory of Enthusiasm: You close the deal, start high, and then, as time passes, you come down and try like hell not to fall into a tailspin and get killed.) I didn't know how flexible Jake would be about meeting that date. In the past, whenever he'd set his mind on something, there was nothing stopping him. He was the most decisive, determined man I'd ever known, and probably that was one of the keys to his success in the business. Once he'd made up his mind, wild horses couldn't change it. Which was his great strength—and great weakness.

When the conference was over, I felt pretty good. I knew we had something, I knew we'd aroused the curiosity, if nothing else, of the Industry. My only hope now was that we wouldn't kill all the life in the project ourselves. I could feel certain forces at work, and I feared for the numerous fights ahead. (Everybody would be fighting to gain control of the picture.) The first fights would be with the writers. They'd get angry at me for insisting on changes in their script. I'd seen it happen many times before. "It's not there," you tell the writer after reading the script. The writer looks at you in total disbelief: "But I did exactly what you told me to do." Which is . . . exactly the problem. Yet with Billy and Roy, chances were that, if I kept feeding them material and provoking them, I'd get a ballsy script, one that took some shots at the studio system and *delivered*. That, at any rate, was my bet. The next round of fights would be over casting. (Johnny feels that seventy-five percent of a picture is made just in the casting. I happen to disagree but . . .) I could see some major battles ahead with the boys in the Tower over which parts should go to whom. (I knew there'd be a strong push to use as many studio players as possible. Or else actors who were once stars long ago, as we used Joan Crawford in our monster picture—because they're hungry to work again, come pretty cheaply and will do as they're told.) Nevertheless, I knew we'd just have to go to the outside for some of the parts. . . . The final round of fights (in preproduction) would obviously come over budget. Budget—I hate that word, but it's the thing, as a producer, you worry about most of all. This was a period of extreme cost control at the studio, I knew that. Yet I also knew that Jake would pull out the stops in making this picture *with his studio* as the big star. He'd spare no expense in Getting It Right. So budget wasn't something I was too worried about, though things could quickly change, who knows? (Mark was, as I said before, a devil about watching costs, accounting carefully for every penny by computer. But I didn't think he was in a strong enough position to intervene if things got out of hand and *Studio* became Jake's lavishly expensive ego trip.)

So far at least, very little was said to me or to Johnny about budget. I was pretty sure that if Jake and Mark and the other boys in the Tower were going to fight us, they'd do it over script and casting. It was paradoxical in that we were known as the most cost-conscious studio in the Industry, and here we were preparing to spend millions . . . and nobody was saying a word about budget. . . . Perhaps they felt Johnny and I weren't worthy enough as opponents in the Budget Wars, and it was *just more fun* to fight us on the creative choices (script and casting). . . . I don't know.

The next day a front-page story appeared in the trades. MAJOR STUDIO PLANS BIG BUDGET SPECTACLE ON SELF. STEINMAN OVERSEEING PROJECT PERSONALLY.

Same day I called Sandra to tell her I was canceling my weekend visit with Jason. I just didn't have time right now to see my boy.

I knew I forgot something. I forgot to send a birthday card to my daughter back East. Damn, I'll get her a card and a present later.

I seem to have less time now for my past life, the one that belongs to my first and second wives.

I haven't set foot in my house up in the Canyon for weeks. It's an eerie place—all those alarm systems. Maybe I don't want to go there because I'm afraid of finding Tony Perkins, in disguise, just as he was in the scariest movie Hitchcock ever made.

I've been neglecting my two German cars. (I bought a terrific old Chevy for my reenactment of the Actor's life—and prefer driving that.) The

German cars must know I've been neglecting them. One didn't start yesterday and had to be towed (the mechanic still hasn't told me what's wrong). The other blew a tire at high speed on the freeway last week. At first I heard this explosion but didn't think it was the car. Then I felt the front end collapsing, vibrating madly, thumping, bouncing . . . But the machine somehow held steady, and I was able to bring her to a halt without losing control. I felt very lucky; a close call. Maybe the machine was trying to tell me something. . . .

I have two Coke machines in my office now. So I don't run out.

My strategy, then, was to get a good script with a minimum of fighting. In the meantime, I'd throw out some names of actors I wanted to see in the picture . . . names I knew Jake and Mark and their boys would never buy. I'd do it as a tactic: They'd reject the names and I'd allow them the illusion of a first victory. Then I'd retreat for a day or two (in faked anger) and suddenly come back with a "compromise solution," only the "compromise" would be the stars I wanted for *Studio* in the first place. Unless they confronted me with their choices, I might be able to persuade them of mine. The next ploy would be to convince them that the picture was totally under their control—when in truth it belonged to us. This would take a real sleight-of-hand. Jake and Mark and the other Suits could never suspect that another force, another intelligence was at work here, because if they did, I'm positive they'd fire us from the project instantly. The big question was, how critical could the film be of the studio when the studio was spending millions for us to indulge our fantasies? How can you be a critic of the very thing that feeds you?

Our studio had an incredible capacity to absorb all criticism of itself, and still come out ahead. Self-perpetuation was all it really cared about. The Industry was the same. But I figured at least this time there was a shot at doing it differently, and that's all you could ask for. . . . If I could control all the elements and produce a film that was authentic—its own movie—I'd have something. On one level I'd have an action-thriller with a set number of audience-grabbing devices to insure its commercial success (if the Kid Writers and Johnny did their jobs). On another level (which Jake would want) the film would chronicle the birth of this studio, and its rise to preeminence within the Industry. But what the film would really be doing, if it were authentic enough, would be making a statement about power and control and the horrible need to perpetuate illusion in America. . . . Meanwhile, in my fantasy, the film would enjoy both artistic and commercial success, money and good reviews—the criteria of Ultimate Achievement in our Industry. The Suits would look at the grosses coming in hourly off the computer and shake their heads in amazement: "This *must* be right if it's making all that money. . . ." Other people (perhaps a little wiser) would know that I'd pulled off a feat of daring—using this dream factory, with its enormous resources and power to shape thought in America, for purposes of making a statement about what was—what happened—and what is. I'd be applauded loudly for my *chutzpah* and be free to do whatever I wanted.

That was my fantasy. I wasn't sure if I could pull it off and hated to think of the consequences if I didn't. . . . I knew, of course, that Jake wanted the film to be critical of the studio system, but I also knew he didn't want it to be *too* critical. He'd allow us to have our fun making the picture, but then . . . if he didn't like what he saw, he'd turn all the fun into misery. . . .

For a while there, I kept the fantasy to myself. I went to the studio each morning at the same time, in the same clothes, with the same expression on my face. I talked to the same people every day and said the same things I'd said before. I ate the same food at the studio commissary and called the same people after lunch and said more of the same things I'd said before. I told no one, not BB, not Daphne, not Cinnamon.

But one day I told my lawyer. We were talking on the phone, Bob Goldsby and I, about the merits of my case to win custody of Jason. I don't remember how it happened but I just blurted it out. "I want to make *Studio* a critical statement and this is . . ." Bob didn't really understand what I was talking about . . . an infallible way to beat the studio at its own game . . .

How lucky I was, because as soon as I'd said it—given him a piece of my fantasy—I knew it was the wrong thing to do. For if you tell someone your dreams, they'll take them away from you.

The next morning I met with Johnny.

We sat outside my office on the patio, in the hot sun, drinking liquid. He drank his Welch's grape juice, I drank my Coke.

"Hey, I'd like to see violence in the picture," he said.

"Make it sex *and* violence."

"The main character, he should be a psychopath."

"I want a revolutionary."

"The Tower's gotta blow up in the end," he said.

"I want a fire."

"Hey, yeah, the fire sweeps across the lot, yeah, burning out of control."

"Maybe."

"I figure I can make it in forty-five days," he said.

"Make it in thirty-six, Johnny."

"That's not enough."

"Shoot for it anyway."

"Listen, I want final cut."

"I'll give you first director's cut."

"How do you see this picture?"

"I see it," I said, "as an ice-blue thriller about people we know and love."

"Can you give me a budget of five million?"

"Do it for three."

"I want stars."

"I want stars and unknowns."

From that point on, I knew we were perfectly matched as a producer-director combination, because we didn't agree on *any*thing.

I also knew that, when it came right down to it, Johnny was mainly in this for the ride. He didn't think of *Studio* as anything more than a routine commercial picture, perhaps at best a thriller with class. (This didn't bother me, however.) He knew, though, I was hungry for something more. . . . He could see it written all over my face. (At some level I wanted to make a love story out of the picture, a man-woman story, which women love to see and end up bringing men to the theater to see.) For Johnny, this was a chance to move out of episodic television (where he'd paid his dues) and direct real film. . . . Jesus, he'd certainly earned the opportunity—convincing Jake as he did that day in his office.

"I really want to gas the audience," he told me.

In particular, he was looking forward to working on the special effects.

Our studio has the best special effects men in the business. Men who can do anything. Blow up buildings. Trash cars. Set people on fire. Build mechanical apes and sharks and elephants. Build humans that are also mechanical: lifelike dummies of little girls possessed by the devil whose skins are made of Lasmer (a liquid plastic) and whose heads can be operated electronically by remote control—capable of swiveling 360 degrees on command, for maximum shock. Recreate any period in history. Invent any future you care to imagine. They're true craftsmen, these guys.

I hoped in any case that Johnny would stay within budget (I figured we'd make it for closer to five than three, which was my number) and get good performances out of the actors (which isn't easy because a lot of actors are lazy and don't want to work very hard). I doubted whether he'd make any but the most cosmetic changes in the script or try to impose his own vision on the picture. (He had no pretensions about being an artist, and for that I was grateful.) After proving to the studio, as well as the Industry, that he could indeed make a thriller, Johnny would move on. He'd make a side-splitting comedy next, or perhaps even a musical. That way he wouldn't get stereotyped as just an action director or a guy who could only do violence.

He knew all this, had the system down pat. Once you got a break and made your first feature, your choices were simple. You could lay back and wait for the picture to be released. (If it was a hit, you could do anything you wanted next—commercial success enabling you to direct at least three more pictures, all of which could be flops, before losing your power. If it missed . . . well, good luck getting another project off the ground.) The other choice was to start work immediately on your next feature, even before releasing your first. (Bob Altman does this.) That way, by the time the first was released, you'd be moving toward completion of your second. In effect, you'd be one step ahead of the game, one step ahead of all the people (and I'm afraid there are many) who desperately wanted to see you fail.

Later in the afternoon Johnny and I walked the studio lot, still drinking Welch's grape juice and Coke, respectively. It took us about three hours to go from one end to the other, and by no means did we get to see everything. We were scouting locations (sort of), looking for possible camera angles. In the main I wanted to get a sense of how Johnny saw our dream factory in operation, with its twenty-four production units at work simultaneously, and what he thought usable for *Studio* and what not. . . .

I doubted whether he had any idea of all the changes that, over the years, we'd gone through. While other studios (in the wake of a stringent cost-reduction program not too long ago) had bulldozed over their Western towns, European streets, Transylvanian castles, and frontier train stations, and sold at auction whatever they had in their prop and wardrobe departments, Jake had done just the opposite. He'd *added* sets to the backlot and charged admission (just like Uncle Max in the early days) for a complete, three-hour tour. Millions of people came each year to see our full-scale mock-ups of the machines used in our film Product. From a recent picture there was a roller coaster that crashed through a gate, exploded, and hurled bodies (dummies) into space. Tourists leaning out of our trams always shrieked when they saw that. (The action took exactly two minutes and ten seconds; then the whole thing—this gigantic contraption—was rewound like a clock and set to go again.) Upon leaving, tourists saw a billboard that read: LOOK FOR ROLLER COASTER, PART II. COMING SOONER THAN YOU THINK.

In addition, there were mock-ups of a jumbo jet, an ocean liner turned upside down, black cars once possessed by the devil, a gigantic white buffalo (mechanical), two robots made to look perfectly human, with plastic smiles and period clothes (from a picture about two smiling, lovable con men who salute each other by running their forefingers across their noses). My favorite mock-up, though, was of a huge white rocket. The rocket rises many stories upward into the hot Valley sun and is a marvel of special effects engineering. It was used in a remake of an old science fiction film that we did a few years back. (In the film, Earth is threatened with destruction by a star called Bellus. The star is headed on a collision course with Earth. Something must be done. A group of scientists and engineers goes to the mountains to build a spaceship that is supposed to take a select crew of people to the safety of the planet that orbits Bellus. The space "ark" is to be launched from a long ramp like a ski jump, down the side of the mountain. Soon Bellus approaches, causing gigantic tidal waves and flooding; indeed, New York City is entirely wiped out. Just in the nick of time the space "ark" takes off, with its crew of survivors, and lands on the newly discovered planet, which resembles Earth, to start a new life in a new world.) Oh, the picture was very successful and rekindled interest, once again, in the space program.

Anyhow, Johnny surprised me. He had more of a feel for the texture of life at the studio than I'd expected. He understood how interconnected everything was, especially in television production. He knew why we made pictures that could be turned into movie sets on the tour. And how, in turn, the tour reinforced audience identification with our Product. Everywhere you looked, from the commissary to the Tower, you saw stills and posters plastered on the walls. Stills and posters of our stars, our Product. . . . Most of the activity on the lot, these days, was television. Film people would come and go on a project (and most of the features would be shot on location anyway), but television was always shot here, six days a week, in the big sound stages and on the various sets. Without it, there'd be no tour, and no chance for visitors to catch a glimpse of the stars from our numerous TV shows.

I never understood why they wanted to see them in the first place. Our TV stars invariably played humans who'd suffered in some horrible accident that left their bodies all mangled. So these "humans" had to have their arms and legs replaced by synthetic limbs made of Teflon, Dacron, and steel, their veins replaced by miles of plastic tubing, their eyes with sensitive photoelectric cells, their hearing with miniature amplifiers, their brains restructured, somehow, to function as if computer programmed, thinking forever in ones and zeros, always controlled by somebody else, "humans" who ran on atomic power and were indestructible—at least from week to week on television. These were our "heroes," but I could never figure out why.

Bob Goldsby called: Did I want to play tennis this weekend? For a hundred dollars a game?

Mark called: Where was the script? What stage of development? Did I know I was responsible if we were late on the picture and missed our starting date?

Irv called (from London): Would I mind playing a dirty trick on Mark? "Just for the fun of it," he said. Tell him that he, Irv Steingart, had secretly tape-recorded all the initial meetings when the concept of *Studio* was being discussed. Tell him that he was now playing these tapes back "for friends."

Daphne called: She wanted to represent Johnny at her agency. Would I be so kind, darling, as to put in a good word for her?

Roy and Billy called: Could they perhaps get the next installment on the money I was paying them to develop the script? This week rather than next? They were "running low."

BB called: Would I bring home milk, butter, a dozen eggs (extra large), grapefruit (because she was dieting), two loaves of dark rye, and all the yogurt I could find in the supermarket? (We'd been living together now for several months, and *I* always ended up doing the shopping—at Ralph's.)

The mechanic called: Nothing was wrong with my German car. The bill: fifty dollars, "for inspection."

Benny called: a man at the main gate who didn't have an appointment but wanted to see me. Should he let the man in? The man's name: Bob Blackman.

A reporter called: She thought the press conference was "fabulous." Could she interview me for a piece she was writing about the "new breed of producers" in the business?

Mark again: Why didn't I put more pressure on the writers to turn out the script? What was taking so long?

A man from Jake's office: Bobby Crazy had just gone crazy again on the set of his cop show. Would I go out there and try to calm him down? Jake would certainly appreciate it.

Michael Steinman: How come I wasn't jogging on the Beach anymore? "See you this weekend," I told him.

Nick Benvenue: Well, he'd just written this new script and thought it was a "hot one" and wouldn't I be the first to read it for him?

My source in the Tower: Jake isn't happy with Al Lucky, Jr., the Sleeper, who's vice-president in charge of marketing, and wants him out. Mark is opposed, however. There could be a confrontation. We'll know more in the next few days. Use the information to your advantage. "Don't forget where you heard it," says my source, reminding me that one day I'll have to return the favor.

Of course, everybody manipulates everybody else at one time or another. Perhaps the Industry is *built* on manipulation, I don't know. I'm not a very good manipulator, even though I know all the rules of the game. (You have to in order to survive for any length of time.) I know that you never do anything as an end in itself. You never write a screenplay, for instance, because it is something that burns inside you, something you feel passionate about and can't rest until you bring the characters to life. On the contrary. You write a script as a means toward an end: You need the money or want to impress people with a sample of your work, or get a shot at directing or producing. If you meet somebody in town, it is never for the purpose of becoming his or her friend. You meet somebody *to see what they can do for you.* (That's probably why I have no "friends" in the business, with the exception of my lawyer Bob Goldsby, and indeed *can't* have any friends.) If you go to a party, most of the people there stand around and say nothing. They don't say anything because they already know what they can get from you and you know what you can get from them. So what *could* you possibly say? If somebody new arrives, a fresh face on the scene, I introduce myself to that person asking, in the back of my mind, "What can he or she do for me? How can I manipulate them?"

The way I manipulate is probably no different from the way that everybody else manipulates. I approach someone with a product or an idea and try to convince them of its usefulness *to them.* (People have to believe that you are really doing something for them and not just for yourself. Which, invariably, takes a lot of work, as well as a *total belief* in what you're pitching.) They'll play the game with you so long as they feel they stand a chance of getting more out of it than you. Other ways of manipulating: You make an offer on the promise of future reward. Do this for no money up front and I'll get you a fat percentage of the profits. Or, if you really have power: Do this for me or you'll never work in this town again. Still other ways: You become all things to all different people. (Mystery is a source of power; nobody knows where you stand on certain issues.)

Interestingly enough, the young lawyers and

producers now coming into the Industry seem to think that in order to succeed, they must manipulate coldly, without emotion. Which just isn't true. Johnny Lombardo is the classic example. He's a terrific young Player—and he's *very* emotional. I've seen him negotiate a deal where he goes into a meeting with the Suits and gets all worked up, fiery, impassioned. He starts out by telling you about his personal life and problems, where he grew up, and how the girls in high school never liked him because he was such a jerk. He cries on your shoulder, and pretty soon he's got you identifying with *his* problems. You never stop to think that his life can't be all that bad. I mean, he's young and a real comer. But he's got you right where he wants you. If you resist his charm, his pitch, his personal problems, and *disagree* with him, he'll walk right over you. He'll whip out of his pocket the latest miniature Japanese tape recorder—he loves gadgets—and he'll talk you to death about it.

The one thing I can't do when I manipulate is tell the truth. (I always tend to lie in order to get what I want.) And because of that I'm a poor manipulator. (The best manipulators *never lie,* they always tell the truth—the truth is more powerful than any lie you can make up.) Most people lie, I'm convinced, because they're afraid or desperate. Yet lying can be a very tricky business, for once you start, you have to keep covering up. Typically, you build this gigantic scaffolding of lies—and the larger the scaffolding, the greater the chances of the whole thing collapsing under its own weight, coming apart under stress. For example, you manipulate a person by telling him lie after lie. And just as you're about to get what you want, another person comes along and says one small thing in passing, an offhand remark, a tiny detail that doesn't match, that's inconsistent with all the lies you've told, and suddenly . . . this huge edifice you've erected is threatened with imminent collapse.

So lying is dangerous—and God knows I've tried to stop doing it. But it's such an accepted practice, a common occurrence—all day long people lie to you about themselves, their work, their private lives—that it's hard to break the habit. I'm hooked, addicted to lying. I've tried more and more to tell the truth, just as I'm doing now, but it's not easy. Sometimes you revert. (I keep asking myself, "What's the point? Why continue to lie when you can manipulate people just as easily and indeed more effectively by telling the truth?") I stopped lying for about a month last year when I went on vacation, but started again the moment I came back to the studio. I wish somebody would realize the gravity of the problem—families built on lies, neighborhoods built on lies, industries built on lies within lies, and pretty soon the whole country built . . . Maybe they ought to set up a Stop Lying Clinic, much like the Stop Smoking Clinics you see advertised in the papers (on such-and-such a date you will stop lying), so that all of us could kick the habit of lying to everybody . . . all the time . . . about everything.

The next weekend I wanted to be alone. Usually, I hate being alone, hate being by myself. After a while I don't know what to do. I get bored. I start to eat, I eat everything in sight, cookies, candy, anything sweet. I drink one bottle of Coke after another. I start to smoke again (a habit I never quite gave up years ago). I comb the house looking for butts that guests might've left in my ashtrays.

(I'm too afraid of buying a pack because I know I'll smoke them all, one right after the other.) I chew Vitamin C tablets by the dozens to counteract my hunger for smoke. I chew B_{12} tablets because they're supposed to enhance your capacity to dream, though I'm afraid to dream. I think up plots for new movies, but never get very far with them. (I'm not your creative artist, I reach a point in the plots —when the guy meets the girl—beyond which I can't go.) I change clothes all the time just to kill the boredom. I watch television, switching channels constantly (nothing satisfies). I play music, mostly classical, but can't listen to it for very long. I'm still bored. I want to get laid but not by any woman I know very well.

On Friday night BB flew back East for her father's sixtieth birthday and I *was* alone. I fixed myself a strong drink and watched the sun go down over the ocean, the sky turn from red to pink. Out there I saw a woman walking alone on the Beach, her white dress fluttering in the cool evening breeze. I couldn't make out who she was. (I'd lived on the Beach now for several months and thought I knew its inhabitants pretty well.) She kept walking and there was something about the way she walked . . .

I didn't want to see anybody, talk to anybody, think about anybody. Mindlessly, I watched the Eye until midnight when I crawled into bed. I slept on the side of the bed that BB sleeps on.

In the morning I woke up fast and realized that BB was still there. I could feel her presence in the house—she didn't want to go back for that birthday.

I went from room to room, opening and closing doors, talking to her presence.

"It's okay," I said, trying to coax her gently. "You can go back."

In the kitchen I said, "He wants you to be there."

In the dining room, "He's your father, he can't always be your friend."

In the living room, "He can't hurt you. Nothing to be afraid of."

I went on like that for several hours, coaxing, prodding, nudging . . . until I could feel her gone at last. And I was *really* alone. I didn't like it, as usual.

I called up my lawyer friend Bob Goldsby. Could we get a tennis game this morning?

"Okay," he said. "For a hundred dollars a game?"

"Sure."

A half hour later we met at the Canyon Club. The Club sits on a ridge high above the city, above even the smog line. On Saturday mornings there is a good crowd of people at the Club, mostly lawyers and doctors, executives and actors. In one way or another, everybody is connected to the Industry: the attorneys handle our lawsuits, the doctors our ulcers. And while waiting for a court people talk shop. The lawyers and doctors and actors all live nearby, practically next door to each other. Their wives know each other, and their kids all go to the same schools. They tend to look alike and talk alike— and play tennis alike. They hit the same kind of forehands (sliced) and the same backhands (also sliced). They slice and chop and chip the ball low —and fight like hell to win each point. They smash their serves (nine out of ten go out, but it's a way of showing off their power). They scramble for shots, they hit balls on the run, they try to look flashy on the court. But their games are makeshift at best, without rhythm or structure. They really don't know *what* they're doing out there, or what they *should* be doing. Just as long as they're mean and aggressive in their play, they figure they'll win some points and the points may add up to a game and the games to a set and the sets to a match.

I used to play the same way.

I'd smash my serve as hard as I could and come charging up to the net behind it and try to put the volley away for a winner. I used to play with my racquet as though it were a club, a tomahawk. I'd clobber the ball with all my might and win every point outright. I didn't care about stroking or touch or consistency or depth to my shots. I'd swear if I missed a shot, I'd sneer at my opponent if he made a good one. I hated to lose and the more I hated to lose, the more I kept on losing.

One day I changed.

I started doing it differently. I came onto the courts with a different attitude: I wanted to enjoy playing, I just wanted to keep the ball in play. It didn't bother me if the ball came back. In fact, I didn't want each rally to end. I hit all my shots crosscourt—without thinking about it. I played for process instead of results. I wanted each point to last forever. I figured that if I could get the ball back more times than the man across the net, I'd win.

I began winning.

Anyhow, Bob was there, along with all the Club regulars.

We got on quickly and played a set.

Bob is a contradiction in terms. He plays exactly the opposite from the way he practices law. He plays recklessly, with abandon, taking wild chances all the time. He rushes the net on poor approach shots, he aims for the lines, the corners, and goes for them. His game is all topspin, all attack. In law, he's cautious, very conservative. He's known me for years, seen my first marriage dissolve, then my second. Both times he's been there to help, extremely supportive. Bob himself is something of a womanizer, and I don't think his own marriage is going well now. Which is why I hate like hell to beat him in tennis. (Besides, he now has a piece of my dream, my dream of beating the system, and while I trust him because we've known each other for so long and count him truly as a friend, I wonder . . . Goddammit, the business makes everybody so paranoid!)

He's up three-two in the set.

On the court next to us is someone who looks like that woman I saw last night walking along the Beach. Is she an actress? She's in a white tennis outfit; she's playing with the wife of one of the doctors. She has good strokes. She looks a little like Jill McCorkle. I like her long dark hair pulled straight back and pinned.

I'm coming back. Three-all, four-three . . .

I "win" the set six-three.

"You son of a bitch!" Bob says.

"Bad luck."

"I had you three-two, forty-love, and then you reeled off four straight games. That's humiliation."

"Sorry."

"You're a prick, Tony."

"You're not so bad yourself, Bob."

"Tell you what. I owe you three hundred dollars, right? I'll take you flying tomorrow at one hundred dollars an hour."

"Let me go by myself, Bob, and we'll call it even, the bet settled."

"You're on."

"Okay, it's a deal."

"Tony, be gentle with her. She's an old plane."

She was old, all right, but fabulous.

She wasn't afraid to show her age.

I'd only heard about her, read about her, and seen pictures.

Her wingspan was thirty-two feet.

Her wing area: two hundred and seventy-three square feet.

Her weight empty: sixteen hundred pounds.

Her engine: a two hundred and twenty-five horse-power Jacobs.

Her maximum speed: one hundred and seventy-five miles per hour.

Her cruising speed: one-fifty-two miles per hour.

Her landing speed: forty-five miles per hour.

Her climb with a full load: eleven hundred feet per minute.

Her service ceiling: fifteen thousand feet.

Her power loading: fourteen pounds.

She was a biplane, meaning that she had both an upper and a lower wing.

She was designed by Walter Beech (along with Ted Wells), tested and built in 1934; the B17L Staggerwing.

They called her the Staggerwing because her lower wing was thrust farther forward than her upper. This enabled her pilot to have a much better view than more conventional biplanes; it also gave her several aerodynamic advantages (too complicated to mention) and allowed her landing gear to be wing mounted.

She was about the best airplane you could fly, said all the old-timers.

She was the Learjet of her time (and, in fact,

Bill Lear bought one in 1935). She's credited with ushering in an era of corporate aviation.

Every pilot who ever flew her noted that she had a particular "feeling" like no other plane he'd flown.

Her successor, the A17F Staggerwing (one of many), was once owned by Howard Hughes, a pilot of some repute. He flew her at two hundred and fifty miles per hour—faster than some military planes in the Thirties.

She was by all accounts revolutionary in design, outstanding in performance. She set the stage for efficient, economical private air transportation to come.

I couldn't believe her when I got to the airport and saw her. In beautiful condition, expertly restored . . . she looked almost sensuous with her long, smooth cowl around the engine, her sloping windshield, her fuselage tapered back so gracefully. . . . Her skin was painted in two-tone: black and white, with silver wheels. I was dying to get inside her.

I checked her out mechanically.

She was fine.

I let down the flaps and took the blocks from under her wheels and untied the wires anchoring her.

I hadn't flown for a long time, I didn't know why. (Years ago I'd learned to fly and loved it and logged a lot of hours, but then suddenly . . . gave up on it, like you suddenly give up on a marriage for reasons you don't quite know, can't quite explain.)

I got inside, and she made me feel totally at ease.

I had no fear.

So I contacted ground control, got the report on weather conditions—winds westerly (not too high velocity), visibility surprisingly good (you could see for many miles in every direction).

I checked out the instruments. Fine.

I brought up the flaps and taxied down the runway.

Full stop. I did my "run-up": both feet on the brakes—I revved up the engine. Okay. Everything checked out.

I waited now for the control tower to give me clearance, my go-ahead. She was throbbing underneath me. . . .

I got it, and I was off.

She came up almost immediately—I couldn't believe her responsiveness. I was up and making my first turn. She handled beautifully. Old Walter Beech knew what he was doing, all right. . . . I pulled the throttle back and made another turn. It felt like my first solo years ago—the exhilaration of doing it for the first time on your own. The Staggerwing brought it back to me vividly. I felt this renewed sense of freedom, this rush. . . . I shot up to twenty-five hundred feet and leveled off. That's where I'd stay (I couldn't go below two thousand or above three), just maintaining a steady speed. I could feel a sense of calm, cruising along. . . . I set my course: due east.

Below me I could see the entire anatomy of the city, its bones and muscles, arteries and skin. I followed the veins of the freeway system for a while and watched them converge downtown, at the Interchange, and then spread out again. I watched the monotonous pulse of Sunday traffic, I took out my binoculars and looked for fast cars. I saw one jumping from lane to lane—it looked exactly like my old Chevy. For a moment, I thought somebody had stolen mine. I descended for a closer look and zoomed in with the binoculars. I couldn't make out who was driving the car, except that I saw a long scar running down the man's face. I followed it from one freeway into another freeway into another, but suddenly lost it when I looked out my window and saw a 747 jumbo jet slash by me at three o'clock. I almost panicked because I could feel my plane begin to flip—from "wake turbulence," as it's called. And if that continued, you could be corkscrewed right to the ground. So I straightened her up quickly and got out of there. I'd completely lost the clunker on the freeway. It didn't matter.

I flew over the cheap pink stucco bungalow where I used to live in my early days, in the tacky part of town, and saw my sweet old landlady out front, watering. I flew over the Kid Writers' house (rented) just over the Hill. I was sure they were popping Dexedrine and working away on the script. Outside the house I saw the private detective I'd hired to "simulate paranoia" just sitting in his car, waiting, watching. I flew over Sandra's house—and through the binoculars saw her (that tiny little woman who once took up so much space) and her actor-boyfriend sitting by the pool, both naked, sunning themselves. But I didn't see Jason anywhere (after circling the house several times) and wondered what they'd done with him. I got angry all over again. Soon I flew over Daphne's house and saw Johnny's Japanese car parked out front. I wondered if he was *shtupping* her. . . . I flew further east and saw some drive-in churches; cars parked as in a drive-in theater, the preacher delivering his sermon to all the cars out there.

I made a long, loving turn and took her in another direction. She responded smoothly, almost as if she knew what I wanted her to do. I flew over

Mark Fowler's house in the Canyon, a large modern job on struts, with a deck and pool, that the studio had partly financed. I saw no signs of life there, only a gigantic antenna on the roof Mark had reportedly installed himself, beaming signals of some kind (for what reason, I have no idea) in all directions. (Mark was a mystery to most of us; didn't socialize at any of the spots around town, a very private man.) I flew over the Boulevard and saw hordes of people lined up at Grauman's Chinese Theatre, waiting to see the Sunday matinee (I think it was one of our machine pictures). I flew over Norma Desmond's mansion and saw rats in her empty swimming pool; I wondered if Erich von Stroheim was still inside, with Bill Holden writing that comeback picture for "Madam," as von Stroheim called her. I flew over Uncle Max's estate, this sprawling Bavarian castle (earthquake-proof, like the Doheny mansion, with steel-reinforced walls) on several dozen acres of choice property, immaculately groomed—all the beds of flowers, huge fountains, terraced waterfalls, and the like. I wondered what Uncle Max was up to. I felt this terrific sense of loss. . . . He was indeed a showman, and there was none of his breed left in the business. . . . I saw the billboards on the Strip, promoting this rock star or that, monumental works of op 'n' pop art . . . and thought, "These guys think they own the town." I flew over Jake's house—his estate (not as large as Uncle Max's) on the other side of the Hill. I focused the binoculars and saw a garden party in progress, with guests in black and white, standing there, holding drinks, chattering. I saw servants passing drinks on silver trays, I saw a small orchestra playing music in the background (I couldn't hear the sounds). There was Jake, in a black suit, a group of people huddled around him. His wife, who'd decorated my office, was standing nearby. And I saw Bob Goldsby—I'm sure it was he. He also had on a dark suit, was standing by the pool. Next to him was a woman dressed in white; I couldn't make out her face. I saw Jake suddenly look up at my plane—stare for the longest time, then disappear inside the house. I pulled away and headed east. Very soon I came to the studio. There was that old Chevy I'd seen before on the freeway! Parked in my space at the Producers' Building! I couldn't believe it. Parked in my space! I got mad. Then I thought: "What could be more preposterous than to get mad about somebody parking where you park?" I circled the studio a couple of times—the place looked deserted (it was, after all, Sunday). I saw from the air what Johnny and I had traversed by foot just the other day. I saw the Tower (with an antenna on top), the sound stages, the "backless" house from Hitch's movie, the sprawl of Western streets and European streets, the sets from various pictures, the rocket, the roller coaster . . . I remember thinking, "My little studio." And feeling, somehow, very proud.

I climbed higher.

I pulled back the stick, turning, banking. I whispered to her, nudged her along. I tickled the stick, then held her tightly. She responded beautifully. I took off my shirt and coaxed her: "Come on, baby." She was pure music, purring smoothly. I felt at one with her.

Soon I turned her around and flew west as far as I could fly. I flew to the Beach and saw the ocean and realized there was no more West. I looked up and down the coastline, but the West stopped in both those directions, too.

I didn't want to land her and she didn't want to come down, either, I had the feeling. I whispered to her again and told her everything was "peachy keen," she could trust me. Finally I took her down. Nose up, wings billowing . . . I laid her down on the hard, flat runway. A perfect three-point landing. She came to a quick halt, silver wheels screaming for a moment, then burning to a stop.

I called Bob Goldsby.

"I love your plane."

"Welllllllllllll," he slurred, sounding a bit drunk. "I'm glad."

"I wanna buy her."

"She's not for sale."

"I'm prepared to make a decent offer."

"No, she's not."

"Listen, Bob." I tried to be more authoritative. "This was the first time I've flown in three years, and it was like soloing all over again. I think—"

"Three years!" he interrupted. "You're a crazy man, Tony! You wanna get yourself killed or something? Jesus, if I'd known that. . . . You could've gotten me in a lot of trouble."

"I want her, Bob."

"I told you, she's not for sale."

"If we sat down and talked it through, I know we could come to terms. Be reasonable."

"Sorry."

"Why?"

"She belongs to Jake."

The next morning I ran on the Beach with Michael Steinman. He was very friendly. He asked about BB, asked how the script was coming along on *Studio*. Invited me over to his house for breakfast. After shaving and showering, I went over, and a strange woman answered the door to Michael's spectacular though theatrical house on the Beach. She looked like the same woman I thought I'd seen at the tennis club and before that, walking along the Beach. We went into the kitchen where she was preparing a breakfast of eggs and bacon. Her name was Deirdre and she'd just started work as a reader in the Story Department at the studio. Michael came in, toweling off his head. We all sat down for breakfast (just as everybody does at this hour all over town) and talked business, deals, money. We talked about the power structure at the studio. I liked him. He knew more than I thought he knew.

Toward the end of breakfast, I remembered that Michael was obsessed with cars and that every time I saw him he was driving a new one. Would he want to take one of my German cars—the one that my mechanic "fixed," though he said nothing was wrong—would Michael want to take it for his collection? "Take her off my hands for a while," I said. "Get her to start, okay?" He was delighted.

The next morning I called Johnny and put in the good word for Daphne to represent him. "You know her pretty well already, don't you, Johnny?" He was surprised.

The next morning I called the Kid Writers and asked how things were going. They said they hadn't gotten their installment check yet. I told them I'd have Cinnamon hand-deliver the check to their house, with the agent's fee already deducted. "Not to worry," I said. "It'll be there pronto." For I knew it was absolutely essential to keep the writers happy.

(How do you get a good script? You keep the writers solvent, you coax them along gently. Most of all you *allow* . . . you allow whatever is going to happen to happen. That way you stand a chance of getting something that's *real.* . . . Too bad Mark doesn't know that.)

I told the writers that I was pulling off the private detective whom I'd hired to follow them.

"We'll miss him," said Billy.

"He was a lot of fun," said Roy. "We'd make faces at him through the window—and one time we saw him fall asleep in his car. So we sneaked out the back door and crept up . . ."

". . . and let the air out of his tires." (Billy always completes Roy's sentences; he says that collaborating as writers on a script is like "having a marriage without sex.")

"We even used him in *Studio,*" Billy said. Or was it Roy?

"Oh."

"Yeah, we named him after you."

The next morning I called Irv in London and told him that instead of pulling the dirty trick he suggested, why didn't we try something bolder? He was intrigued. I said a reporter was going to interview me for a story about the "new breed of producers" in town. Well, halfway through the interview I'd tell her, "Oh, by the way, did you hear about Mark Fowler? No? Now this is strictly off the record—you don't know where you got this, okay? Fowler is on his way out." The reporter (and I trust reporters, though not all the time) would promise not to name me as a source. She would then call up her contact in the Tower to verify the rumor. Had he heard about Mark? Of course the contact would be too embarrassed to admit that he had *not* heard because that would mean he didn't know what was really happening in the corridors of power. So to save face, he'd say, "The rumor is partially true." Then the newspaper story appears, speculating about a shakeup in the Tower. Mark's name is whispered. Soon the rumor spreads, and it becomes fashionable (insider gossip) to know that Mark is on his way out. And with each passing day, more and more people think the same thought, and the odds begin to improve on Mark's actually getting fired. Rumor (admittedly the ugliest thing in the business) turns into self-fulfilling prophecy.

Irv laughed when I told him of this dirty trick.

"You know that can't happen, Tony," he said confidently, "because there's continuity of management. Nobody gets fired."

"I guess you're right, Irv."

The next morning I called Mark and told him the script was coming along fine, yes, sir, we'd have it right away. I didn't want to make my next move until I had the script.

The next morning BB came back from New York. How was it? She walked around the house.

"It doesn't feel like I was gone," she said.

The next morning I promised Bob Blackman a shot at the rewrite.

The next morning I had a script.

"STUDIO"

SCENARIO BY BILLY DE WITT AND ROY HOTCHKISS
FROM AN ORIGINAL STORY BY TONY SCHWARTZ

Exterior of the Studio in the Valley at night. Shots of the main gate. Parking lot. Sound stages. Commissary. Producers' Building. A red bus marked:

Studio Tour. Empty. The Studio is cold, deserted. Nothing moves. There is total silence. Main title superimposed. Credits come on. Shots of the Tower, rising twenty-five stories, lit up in a checkerboard pattern. A full moon.

Interior of the Tower, night. Silence continues. The top floor, a suite of offices, empty. Thick carpeting. Rich, elegant antique desks and chairs. Office of the Studio Chief. A large metal desk, clean. Except for a collection of old scrapbooks, with sepia-colored photographs of the Chief as a young man, handsome, tall, with thick-black hair combed straight back, wearing a double-breasted suit, no tie. Shots of the young man against the backdrop of the Studio in its early days, smiling. The young man standing next to once-famous movie stars. The young man in the company of beautiful women. The women are wearing slinky black clothes. A series of old newspaper clippings about awards won by the Studio. The camera pulls back slowly as the scrapbooks and old photographs fade. Shot outside the office window. The full moon. Camera picks up, miles in the distance, the silhouette of a car in the moonlight. On the Freeway. Moves in closer. Credits end.

The car, cruising the Freeway, early morning. The car is an old clunker, a piece of junk, with many dents and bruises, undefinable in make and year. Rock music is heard on the radio. The man driving is the Actor. He is thirty years old. Rugged yet somehow frail in appearance. Wears a blue flight jacket, collar turned up. Has on mirror sunglasses. There is a quickness in the way he moves his hands, turning the wheel, shifting gears when he wants to pass. He is at one with the machine. An M14 rifle lies on the front seat, along with a box of ammunition. He punches the radio, picking up snatches of news, weather, sports, music. He turns off the Freeway, braking, clutching very smoothly. Cruises a tacky part of town. Shots of pink stucco bungalows, cracked, peeling. People watering their lawns, as the sun comes up.

A Spanish restaurant, later in the morning. The Actor walks in, carrying the M14 over his shoulder. Waitress asks what he's doing with the rifle. "For a movie," he says. "It's a prop." He eats breakfast at the counter, reading one of the trades. Several men appear, slap him on the back, and ask how he's doing. "No work," he says. The actors laugh loudly and kid each other, in an effort to hide their own desperation. The Actor leaves.

The car, on the Freeway. The Actor drives with one hand and points his rifle with the other at cars passing by, like moving targets in a shooting gallery. A highway patrol car shoots by him in hot pursuit of another car ahead. He quickly puts the rifle down and turns off at the next Freeway exit.

The Studio, day. A black limousine, chauffeur-driven, arrives at the main gate. Camera picks up the profile of the man in the back. He is aging yet handsome, with graying hair and a deep tan. He is the Studio Chief. In the car with him is a young woman, dark-haired, extremely attractive. She is the Actress. She kisses him. He steps out. Limousine drives off with her inside. He enters the Tower. At every step of the way people greet him, show him respect. He takes the elevator to the top floor. Steps out. Immediately executives in black suits approach him with reports and papers, asking him to make decisions. He goes into his office. Sees the old scrapbook open. Closes it, tucks it in a drawer. Then picks up the phone and says, "Get me—" Looks out the window. What he sees is the backlot filling up with people. Much activity. Trucks. Tour buses. Crews. Down there below the camera picks up the Actress as she steps out of the black limousine and walks into a building marked CASTING. The Chief watches, lighting a cigar, then picks up the phone and starts talking almost in a whisper.

A state unemployment office, later that day. All manner of people—freaks, weirdos, cowboys, dwarfs, lovable eccentrics—stand in line, waiting to collect their checks. The line looks endless. At the end is the Actor. He's anxious, impatient. When he finally gets to the counter, the woman tells him, "This is your last check." He nods. "I know." Picks it up, leaves. On the way out an actor bumps into him. He knows the man. The man tells him, "Hey, I got a part in a picture. I play a sadistic cop. I knew I'd get a break; just knew it, if I stayed in there long enough." The Actor smiles, says nothing. Outside, he opens up the trunk of his car, pulls out a neon sign reading PRIVATE TOURS. Attaches the sign to the roof of the car. Drives off.

A row of tourist buses, on the Boulevard, day. The Actor pulls up. Stops. Gets out. Approaches the tourists clustered nearby. Delivers a pitch for his own private tour of movie star homes. Tour bus driver sees him, gets angry. "You again." The Actor gets into a fight with the driver. Exchange blows. The driver hits the Actor in the left eye. The Actor knocks the driver out cold.

The car, packed with a load of tourists, cruising the homes of the stars, late afternoon. The Actor is pointing out the sights. He has a black eye. The tourists chatter among themselves like schoolkids on a picnic. They're having a ball. The Actor stops at a huge mansion in the Canyon. The home belongs to the Studio Chief. Everybody gets out. Walks around. A small kid throws up in the front bushes. Sees a black dog, runs away scared. Dog growls through the side gate. Everybody piles back into the car. The Actor drives off just as the black dog comes chasing after the car, barking viciously.

The Studio, a conference room in the Tower, afternoon. The Chief is meeting with a team of writers, other executives, and the Director, a short, stocky man with a black beard, who is wearing rumpled corduroy clothes. Chief tells them that he wants to find a vehicle for the Actress. "A love story," he says. There is quiet resistance in the room, a few mild protests. The Chief grows furious. Pounds his fist on the antique conference table. Asserts his power. The writers reluctantly agree to develop a property for the young Actress. The Director refuses to go along. He argues with the Studio Chief, says, "I'm the knife in the back of this Studio."

The main gate at the Studio, day. The Actor's car pulls up, still filled with tourists. The guard refuses to let the car in, so the Actor crashes through and gives the tourists a joyride around the backlot. Security guards go chasing after. Call other cops into action. The Actor drives through sound stages, around the Tower, over the exhibition marked: ROLLER COASTER. Noise, commotion. Sets disrupted. People gather around to look. Cops from TV shows appear. The Actress, working in a sound stage, comes out and sees the Actor's car. "Oh, my God!" The car ricochets off a bus transporting props, and spins out the main gate with the security guards still giving chase.

The car, parked in front of the original tour buses, early evening. Tourists get out and thank the Actor for a swell ride. Some give him extra money for the trip. The Actor gets out, too. Takes the sign off and tucks it under his arm. He abandons the car and tries to thumb a ride. He sticks out his sign. A car out of nowhere stops and picks him up. In the car, he looks back in the rearview mirror to his own beast fading in the distance. "I'll miss that machine," he mumbles to himself.

The Studio, night. Security guards are talking among themselves about that "crazy car." One swears, "We'll catch the son of a bitch!" Shots of people leaving the Studio. Upstairs in the Tower, the Chief is screening old movies. "Roll it again, Charlie." The movie is a classic Western, with Indians attacking a cavalry fort, circling on horses and shooting with rifles. The soldiers in the fort pick the Indians off one by one, as though they were taking target practice. The Chief has fallen asleep. The film ends. His secretary comes in, tries to wake him. She tells the projectionist to stop the film. "He's seen it at least a hundred times," says the projectionist.

A low-rent apartment, night. The Actor sits in the living room, drinking beer. He lives in an old hotel now converted into apartments. Mostly actors live there. The place is a mess: beer cans on the floor, ashtrays knocked over, clothes scattered everywhere. Some clothes are hung up as costumes. A military uniform. A three-piece suit. T-shirts with the photographs of old movie stars emblazoned on them. On a makeshift table is the neon sign: PRIVATE TOURS. The Actor sits in a big overstuffed chair, then gets up. Goes to this large mirror. Does an acting bit in front of it. Impersonates people. Mimics the Studio Chief. The black barking dog. The tour bus driver. The people. Contorts his face in various ways. Mugs.

Grimaces. Cries. Laughs. Finally splashes cold water on his face, on his black eye. Tries to wake up. In the mirror he sees the blurred outlines of somebody. Can't make it out. He reaches for his M14. Grabs it. Pivots on his heel, points the gun at the person, his face dripping with water. It is the Actress. He knows her. They were once lovers. He is still in love with her. She asks about his black eye. "Oh, nothing." She asks what he was doing at the Studio, crashing through the gate and taking everybody on a roller coaster ride through the backlot. He says he's giving special tours these days. He laughs. She asks if he needs any money. He pulls out a roll. "I'm okay for a while," he says. "But I don't have a car no more." In passing, he says, "What I really wanna do is work. Fuck! That's what I want." She says she's got a couple of parts at the Studio. He asks if she's making it with the Studio Chief. She admits that she is. She prepares to leave. He tells her that he's still in love with her. "It's over," she says. He tries to embrace her one last time. She rejects him. "Hey, don't forget who you are," he says as she leaves. After she's gone he put his fist through the mirror, cutting his hand badly in the process. He bleeds.

The Actress' sports car, driving on the windy canyon roads, night. Strange music on the car radio, dissonant sounds. The Actress is distraught. She has trouble focusing, drives badly. A black dog leaps out of nowhere onto the road. She hits it. Cries, whimpering. The animal in pain. She stops, brakes screeching. Then steps on the gas. She speeds.

The sports car, jammed in traffic, cruising the Strip, still night. The Actress grows angry, frustrated. Honks impatiently. Then looks at herself in the car mirror. Begins applying makeup in the slow-moving traffic. Paints her face. Looks pleased with the mask.

The sports car, stopped in front of the Studio Chief's house, late night. The Actress sees a light upstairs. An older woman standing at the window. The woman sees the sports car. The Actress immediately drives off, laying rubber. Camera moves in close to the window but not inside. The Chief appears. The woman and the Chief argue. We can't hear what they're saying. The woman, we conclude, must be the Chief's wife.

The Actor's apartment, late night. The actor, with a black eye and cut hand, is lying in his bed, still awake.

A drugstore, on the Strip, morning. The Actor walks inside. Browses around. Looks at a postcard stand. Quaint cards with photographs of life in the city. Shuffles through them. Buys a dozen. Writes a note that he's doing well as an actor in the movie business. Adresses them to his parents in Chicago.

Montage of postcard shots of the Studio. The Tower. The Main Gate. The Tour. The Producers' Building.

Interior of a small apartment in Chicago, day. A haze fills the room, very dreamy. A tall man, the Actor's father, is reading the postcards aloud to the Actor's mother. The father looks exactly like the Studio Chief. Same features, only poorer clothes. The same actor who plays the father also plays the Studio Chief. "Our boy, he's going to be famous," says the mother.

*   *   *

The Studio, early morning. There is a flurry of activity on the lot. Trucks. Film crews. Actors arriving along with executives. In one office a team of writers is trying to dream up a story for the young Actress. In another office, the Director associated with the same project marches back and forth, shouting obscenities. He asks himself why he ever got involved in such a project and tries to figure ways of getting out. In the men's room, two executives stand in front of the mirror, talking negatively about the Chief and his plans to make the Actress into a star. "We ought to do something," one says. The other says, "Yeah. He must be out of his mind. She has no talent." One suggests putting a private investigator on the case. "See what he can dig up."

The Freeway, Actor cruising in another car, day. The car is an old white Cadillac with tail fins. On the roof again: PRIVATE TOURS.

The Actor's apartment house entrance, day. A man in a white suit who identifies himself as Mr. Schwartz is talking to the landlady. She is hard of hearing, so he shouts at her. The man is a private investigator. "Yes," says the landlady. "She used to live here. With her boyfriend. Then moved out. He's still here, though. An actor. Not much luck, poor guy."

The Actor's car, cruising the Freeway. The Actor glances in the mirror and suspects he's being followed. The private investigator isn't too far behind. Bears down on the Actor's car. The Actor tries to elude him. He weaves through Freeway traffic at high speed. Shifts abruptly to the right lane and gets off at the next exit. He shoots up the Canyon. Looks in the mirror. The private investigator's car is gone. He pulls up to a modern glass house on huge stilts, overlooking the Canyon below. Goes to the door. Rings the bell. The Actress comes to the door. Won't let him in. "They're out to get me," he pleads. "I don't know who." She lets him in. "Can I stay here for a few days till this whole thing blows over, baby?" Outside, across the street, the private investigator is sitting in his car, watching discreetly.

The Studio, day. The Chief is giving his own private tour of the lot to a group of executives from the East. He points out the various departments. Introduces the executives to some of the TV stars and contract players. The scene dissolves.

The Studio, as remembered by the Chief in the early days a half century ago, day. The Chief is a young man, wearing a double-breasted suit. He stands at the main gate, trying to talk his way in. "All I want is a break," he keeps saying over and over again. We recognize the Chief as the Actor. Same features, different clothes. The Actor plays the Chief as a young man.

The Studio, present, day. In the office of one of the executives there is talk about the Chief's fitness to run the Studio. A call comes from the private investigator. A report on the connection between the Actor and the Actress. The executives see this as an opportunity to take over, to oust the Chief from power. "He's too old to run this show anymore," one says. They talk strategy. One suggests the computer. They run their data through the computer. The machine feeds them a series of answers. They are delighted with the options.

A high-class restaurant, inside, the corner table, night. The Chief and the Actress are talking about the Actress' career. The Chief promises to make her into a star. They toast to that.

The Actor's apartment, night. He is cleaning his rifle when a couple of other actors come in, drinking beer, talking loudly about who's getting what parts in movies being made. They chain-smoke and chug beer. The Actor overhears that his ex-girl friend, the Actress, is going to get the lead in a vehicle the Studio Chief is preparing especially for her. He doesn't believe it at first. Gets angry and kicks the other actors out of his apartment. The room is still full of cigarette smoke, thick as fog.

The Actress' house on stilts, night. The Chief and the Actress are undressing, preparing to make love. She runs through the house suddenly, flinging off her clothes, piece by piece. The Chief chases after her. Catches her. They are about to make love when they're interrupted by a phone call. It's the Actor. He thanks her for letting him stay there. Warns her about getting too involved with the Chief. "He's dangerous," he says. She hangs up. Chief wants to know who it was. "My cleaning girl," she says. "She can't come tomorrow."

The Actor's apartment. The room is still full of smoke. The Actor sits in his overstuffed chair, cradling his rifle, totally awake.

The Tower, top floor, day. The Chief is in his office, meeting with other executives. The two executives who hired the private investigator and programmed the computer are there. They sit quietly, say very little. An assistant comes in with a stack of computer readouts. "One of the programmers found this," says the assistant. It is part of the strategy to oust the Chief from power. He grows disturbed, leaves the office. The meeting ends.

The Studio, a sound stage, day. The Actress is rehearsing a part with the Director. She keeps blowing her lines. The Director is calm, imperturbable. "Take it again from the top," he says. He continues working with the Actress. A phone call interrupts the rehearsal. The Chief wants to see the Director on the double.

An Acting School, downtown, day. The Actor wanders into the School. Greets some of the actors, who are busy doing improvisations. They know and recognize him. Watches an old man with white hair and a beard directing the actors in the class. This is the Old Actor. He's demanding, a total professional. The class breaks. The Actor approaches the old man, who recognizes him. They embrace each other. They talk. The Actor says he can't find work. The old man says, "You can't live with rejection. That's your trouble." The Actor wants to take classes again at the school. The Old Actor says his classes are full right now, but maybe in a couple of months . . . "I don't have a couple of months," says the Actor and walks out.

The Tower, Chief's office. The Chief fires the Director, who is sitting in a green chair stroking his beard nervously, from all film projects connected with the Studio. Tells him that he wants him to lock up his office, hand in his resignation, effective immediately, and leave. The Director is stunned.

The Chief's black limousine, traveling on the Freeway, later that day. The Actress is being chauffeured home. She sits in the back, putting on makeup. A car moves up alongside the limousine. It is the Actor's. He rolls down his window and yells something, inaudible, to the Actress. She sees him but turns away. "Step on it," she tells the chauffeur. The limousine speeds off, leaving the Actor's car way, way behind.

A gas station, in town, late at night. A black Cadillac pulls up. Attendant comes out. Pumps gas. Checks the oil, wipes the windows. Another Cadillac pulls up. Then a third. Men get out and go inside the gas station. Tell the attendant to take a walk. Sit down. The men are executives from the Studio. We recognize the two who programmed the computer for ways to oust the Chief. The third man is the Director. They talk. Debate various strategies to take over the Studio.

First day of shooting, on the backlot, day. The picture starring the Actress is being made. Things go badly. The Chief appears to oversee the production. Grumbling among the crew. The Actress blows her lines again.

Fifth day of shooting. More difficulties. A stuntman is hurt badly in a simple fall. Equipment breaks down. Somebody appears to be sabotaging the film. The Actress looks unimpressive in the rushes. The Chief is worried.

Twentieth day. Nothing seems to work. The production is plagued with all kinds of problems. The Chief knows he is being pressured by the Opposition Forces to close down the film. He meets with the Actress. Explains that he wants to halt production. She is outraged and won't stand for it. She walks out and isn't seen for several days.

The Actress' house, late at night. She is lying in bed awake when the phone rings. A man claiming to represent the Opposition Forces has a proposition for her: Get her ex-boyfriend, the Actor, to "take care of" the Studio Chief and then she'll be allowed to finish work on the picture she's making. She rejects the proposition. "Think about it," says the man. She hangs up. Tries to fall asleep, can't. The phone rings again. She doesn't answer. On the tenth ring she picks it up. It's the Actor. He wants to talk. She tells him to come over now. Hangs up.

The Actor's car, traveling on the Canyon roads, night. The Actor is driving fast. He's on his way to the Actress' house. Rock music on the radio. Suddenly a black limousine goes through a stop sign and the Actor slams on the brakes. Not in time. He crashes broadside into the limousine. The tail fins are knocked off his white Cadillac. Both cars are bruised but not too severely damaged. The Actor gets out. What he sees dimly is the Studio Chief sitting in the backseat with the private investigator who'd been tailing the Actor before. He panics. Runs back to his car. Drives off. In the damaged car, he tries to say something but can't.

The Actress' house, same night. She is lying on the bed naked, reading a book on politics. She reads with large round glasses. Thick frames. Doorbell rings. She gets up, goes to the door, still naked. Answers it. The Actor stands there, shaking. He keeps looking over his shoulder, afraid the private investigator has followed him there. He regards the Actress, who looks seductive. Steps in. He grows confused. Sits down. Tells her to put on some clothes. She says no. He paces the room nervously. She asks what's the matter. He thinks he saw the same man again who was tailing him. She tells him not to worry, everything will be all right. She has a proposition for him.

The Studio, a conference room, day. The Chief is having a meeting with his top executives. He announces that he's closing down, temporarily, the production involving his Actress-girl friend. Looks of surprise among the executives. Then he announces that he's purging the ranks. Names the people he's going to fire. The Opposition Forces aren't among them. There are mild protests. The Chief walks out of the room, crushing his cigar in the gold ashtray in the shape of the Tower, in miniature. The crushed cigar is his signal that the meeting has officially ended.

A montage of shots. The Actor driving on the Freeway, turning off into the tacky part of town. Stopping in various bars and hangouts. Seeing his old actor buddies. Slapping them on the back, being friendly.

The Actress going to the hairdresser, getting done in a beauty salon. A complete facial.

The Actress talking to her agent on the phone, angry.

The Actress shopping in a supermarket, buying bottles and bottles of Coca-Cola.

The Actor in his converted apartment house, knocking on doors. Talking to one actor after another. Going from room to room. Actors of all kinds appear. Old, young, tall, short, good, bad. Dwarfs and cowboys, vamps and flakes. Circus music is heard.

The Actor at the old bus stop, talking to tourists. Offering them a private tour in his dented white Cadillac.

The Actress in front of a mirror, naked, caressing her shoulders.

A loud crash, the Studio roller coaster set, day. Screams, shrieks. Shots of the Tower in the background. Camera floats. Picks up the Chief coming onto the lot in his black limousine. Up in the Tower, inside one of the executive offices, two men are pounding their fists on the table. One says, "I don't like it, Harry. We're going too far in this." The other: "There's no turning back now." First one: "She said she would do it." Other: "Yeah."

The Chief, getting out of his limousine in front of the Tower. He is met there by the Press. Questions thrust at him on the recent corporate shake-ups in the Tower. He has no comment. Pushes his way through.

In his office, he calls the Actress. Says he has a surprise for her. Tells her to meet him for lunch. She resists, but then yields. They are to meet for lunch at noon at the Studio. End of conversation. The Chief calls in one of his top executives. Tells him that he's planning to resume the film he's producing as a vehicle for the Actress, now that "the air has cleared a bit." The executive asks, "Does she know?" "No, I'm going to surprise her." He walks out to the window. Points to the factory below. Camera pans the Studio lot, floats out to the Freeway. Picks up, way off in the distance, a tourist bus. Follows the bus on the Freeway.

The Actress, at home, in the bathroom, putting on makeup. Then dressing in a sexy outfit. The phone rings. She answers. We recognize the voice as belonging to one of the Opposition Forces. "Yeah, he's on his way. In a bus," says the Actress.

The bus, pulling up to the main gate, being checked by the security guards. The driver is the Actor. Behind him in the bus are all the actors from the apartment house, in strange costumes. The bus is allowed through. The crazy actors from the apartment house stick their heads and arms out of the windows. The Actor begins to drive slowly around the lot. At the main gate the Actress pulls up, goes through. Stops at the Commissary. Sees the Chief coming out of the Tower. They meet in front of the Commissary. The bus stops there, too. The driver lets everybody out. The actors appear as if they've just been let out of the loony bin. The Actor is the last to get out. He has on a military uniform. Carries a rifle over his shoulder. Nobody pays much attention to him. He appears to be an extra from some film in production. The crazy actors swarm around the entrance to the Commissary. Several of them leave to find Hitchcock, whose office is nearby. The Actor moves in close to where the Actress and Chief are standing. He winks, then sneers at them. Repeats it. There is a large crowd of tourists and executives and secretaries on their lunch breaks. The Actor reaches the Chief and sticks his rifle up the Chief's ass. Tells him to march on over to the Tower. "What's going on here?" the Chief demands. Actor says, "Shut up and move. You, too." He tells the Actress. She looks scared but it's a bad acting job, she's not very convincing, though the Chief doesn't know. Meanwhile, the crazy actors return with Hitchcock and join the Actor. As they move to the Tower, the crazy actors form a circle around the hostages. At the Tower, security guards see what's happening. Fire a couple of warning shots. The Actor fires back. Everybody runs for cover. People scatter. The Actor, along with his crazy friends, pushes the hostages into the basement of the Tower. They jump into the elevator and shoot up to the top. The crazy actors scatter into the building, on every floor of the Tower. Security guards chase after them, fire more shots. Some crazy actors go down. Pandemonium breaks loose on the lot. Production stops. Shortly, a helicopter, then a small plane, buzz the Tower. Actors from TV cop shows appear to see what's happening. Police arrive in numerous squad cars. They try to disperse the crowds, yelling into bullhorns.

At the very top of the Tower. The Actor pushes the Chief and the Actress into a room filled with extremely expensive antiques. He commands the Chief to call off the police or else he'll be killed. The Chief picks up the receiver in the antique room and calls the security guards. Actor tells the Chief to have food and water sent up. He plans to hold them both hostage until his demands are met. Hours pass. Food and water come. The Actor next demands to see some of his favorite movies. They are sent up, too. He watches a Western but with the lights on in the room. The Western is the Studio Chief's favorite movie, too, the one he's seen over a hundred times. More hours of anxious waiting pass. The Actress grows restless. *"Well, when are you going to do it?"* she asks the Actor. "Do what?" "Shoot the man." The Chief soon discovers that the Actress knows the Actor. He learns of her collaboration in the plot to have him killed. He tells her, "But, listen. I'm going to start shooting on your picture. That's why I called you to the Studio today." "Sure, sure." She doesn't believe him. She doesn't believe a word he's saying.

I won't spoil it for you by telling the ending—you'll have to see for yourself. . . .

I called the Kids back and told them I thought what they'd written was terrific. But I didn't want them to get too cocky, so I said, "It needs a couple of changes." (In truth, the script was fine and could go as is, but you see, if I told them that, I'd lose some of my control over them. They'd think they knew more than I knew. So, for tactical reasons, I fabricated a few suggestions for change in the material.)

They weren't too happy about that (I wouldn't have been either). I said, "Get some sleep, fellas. Get off the Dexes."

Billy and Roy sounded surprised that I knew they were popping speed to write the script.

"Talk to you after you've gotten some sleep."

Now it was a question of names, whom to cast. . . . The choices were more complicated than I expected. For the part of the Studio Chief I could see William Holden. He has both weight and stature, and plays the older-man-falling-in-love-with-the-younger-woman role very convincingly. (Besides, it might be a logical progression from that terrific Billy Wilder picture where he played the failed screenwriter who gets involved with Norma Desmond, the once-famous silent screen star.) I could see Greg Peck in that role, too. He certainly has

the dignity, presence, and authority for the part.
Or Bob Mitchum—in a comeback. Make the Studio
Chief into this boozy, heavy-lidded man who has a
lot of charm, a kind of swank hero— Or Brando.
Come to think of it, I'd prefer Marlon myself. (Yet
I doubt that Jake Steinman would go along with
him.)

As for the part of the Actor, let me run down the
choices. McQueen? He doesn't *do* anything anymore, he just is. Yet he's a very strong male force
(more that than a good actor). Steve always can
be trusted to get a job done. Newman? We'd have
to rewrite the part especially for him. Paul is a
sweet brawler. He's macho but *cute* (those baby
blue eyes of his). He always looks like a Cowboy
in the Big City. You think of him, somehow, as
forever sleeping with his boots on. Bob Redford?
He's awfully pretty. But he can't play a guy with a
dark side. He wants you to like him—because he
looks as though he likes himself. (You see him and
think, "Gee, he's good-looking.") Eastwood? Clint's
basic function for the audience is to shoot people.
Which he does better than any other film actor I
know. Hackman? Gene is good at stalking people,
hunting them down, then hurting them. Gene's
function is to hit people. And he's terrific in parts
where that's all he's required to do. Bronson? Well,
as a film actor he kills people better than Clint or
Gene, in the sense that he kills them more authoritatively. And looks as though he may enjoy it. But . . .
I couldn't see him killing for love. He kills for the
sport of it, and as a means of revenge. Burt Reyn-
olds? I like the man personally, but he's good when
he can mock himself and let the audience in on it
and everybody, including him, can have a good
laugh. Pacino? He's terrific, one of our best, and he

could do this part so well . . . Al gets angry at people better than any other actor (stage or screen). He yells and screams and you believe it's really coming from his guts. He releases all the anger and frustration pent up inside us. He plays victims (particularly victims of social injustice) better than any other actor I know. God, if we could get him . . . Dustin Hoffman? I like Dusty a lot and think he's really talented. He plays the part of the Innocent extremely well. You're afraid for him because he looks so innocent, you're afraid he might get hurt, and that fear can carry you along in a picture. Ryan O'Neal? His basic function as a film actor is to cry for us, which he does superbly. (How many other actors can? But we don't need tears in *Studio*, or do we?) Warren Beatty? He's good, some say he's the best to work with. He looks like a man who is always about to get laid. He seems to live right on the edge of getting laid all the time. Jimmy Caan? He's terrific when he gets hotheaded. He's pure male energy—swift, impulsive, sexually charged. Donald Sutherland? I like him best when he's frightened. He has a bizarre look on his face (those big bulging eyes), and that's his function— to be scared for us. Nicholson? Now that would be a bit of inspired casting. Jack's terrific; he's so good he can do anything. What I think he does better than anybody else is . . . whisper. He's so intense, so involving that all he needs to do is whisper. Jack is riveting on the screen; you can't take your eyes off him. He could even be a clever choice for the Studio Chief, if we rewrote the part making the Chief a more offbeat, eccentric character. In the supporting parts, I could see Bob Duvall, Harvey Keitel, Keith Carradine, Bruce Dern. Also, as Studio Executives: Jason Robards, Jack Warden, and

Robert Shaw (Shaw could be one of the Opposition Forces, he plays Bad Guys supremely well). But . . . probably Jake Steinman will want Charlton Heston as the Chief, George Segal as the Actor. (Both are solid actors, not all that exciting anymore, yet not likely to offend very many people, either.) Well, if Jake wants Chuck Heston, then I'll fight for my first choice in the part of the Actor: Robert De Niro. Bobby could play it better than anybody else, he's perfect. He embodies the dark side in all of us; he's a street fighter. He can also be sick, twisted. Yet I also like him when he's funny, happy-go-lucky. I know he can be private, mysterious—as if he were holding something back from us. He's kinetic, attuned to what's going on around him. Very alert, driven. Most of all I think Bobby clings to this weird individuality (that which makes him unique, different from everybody else) —and fights against those who are forever trying to take it away from him.

Casting the female lead? I don't think we'll have a problem. I mean, the part of the Actress could be played by any number of talented women. The choice will be: Should we go with an established star or take a chance on an unknown? Julie Christie would play the part savagely—with devastating impact. She exudes more sex (fuckability) than any actress around. Opposite her, the Studio Chief would have to be a man worthy enough (sexually) for her. Jane Fonda could do it, though the part demands an actress with more cunning, more deviousness. Faye Dunaway? I could see her as one of the top Studio Executives, fierce and combative, yet not really fuckable, except as a woman on a power trip. (Fuckability is essential; the audience wants to imagine going to bed with the star.)

Karen Black? Possibly. She's very good in certain parts. Cybill Shepherd? The perfect bitch-tease. I could see her doing it. Candy Bergen? Possibly. She cries better than any other actress, but aside from that she's limited, as are a lot of women who start out as models, then go into film acting. They're too aware of the camera, they know that people are watching them. Shelley Duvall? God, she's terrific. Cissy Spacek? I don't know—her appeal is that of the child-woman. Diane Keaton? Comedy is her forte. Liza Minnelli? Maybe, maybe not. Raquel Welch? Perhaps in a supporting part. (I fear that her fans now come out to see how much she's aged.) Glenda Jackson? Excellent, yet not quite sexy enough for the part. Liv Ullman? She's so good, I wish we could use her. Lee Grant in a supporting part? You're on. Mia Farrow? Goldie Hawn? Marlo Thomas? Blythe Danner? I've had a crush on her for years. Talia Shire? Dominique Sanda? God, yes . . . but would Jake go for her? Jacqueline Bisset? Too vague in her presence, though she has fuckability. Charlotte Rampling? She's pure fuckability. Ali MacGraw? No. Farrah Fawcett-Majors? She's a fad, though who knows?

Names, names.

Names mean everything. They mean nothing. Some mean money in the bank—in fact, the banks have a list of "A" names and "B" names and "C" names, and you better pray to God that you're on one of those lists, because if you're not. . . . That the names attach to real people, people made of flesh and blood, is something we tend to forget. We think the names belong to us, we think we can do anything we want with them. Julie Christie is in the public domain, right? She belongs to us, rather than to herself.

Names made this business, and we made a lot of the names. Now the names get smaller and smaller each year. There are fewer of them, for one thing, though the demand goes up all the time. The Public is starved for names; we can't feed them enough—and don't. One picture can make an unknown actress or actor into a star—that's how hungry the Public is for names.

Now that we have the basic material (plot, characters, some dialogue) everybody will begin fighting for control of the picture. The writers will want their script to be shot as written. (They'll be lucky in most cases if sixty percent of what they've written gets used.) The stars will want the material to reflect their preoccupations. (Stars get to be stars by acting out in mythic terms—larger than life—the fantasies of the audience.) So they'll do everything possible to adapt the characters into characters that their audiences expect them to be. The director may resist and, consequently, fight them on that—though not with much success if the star is bankable. (Obviously, the studio will get rid of the director and keep the star.) The producer may have to fight the director in order to get the picture he wants, because directors have a tendency to change the original concept around until it bears no resemblance to how it started out. Meanwhile, the studio will maintain tight cost control and the moment they smell trouble—a few days over schedule, reports of fighting on the set—move in to take over the production. Before it's all over, I know I'll fight with the Kid Writers, with Johnny, with the Suits in the Tower, with the stars and character actors. And they'll fight with me. But it's fun. And we'll fight because we want to bring *this being* into existence, however imperfect.

I remember growing up back East and learning about street fighting. I learned that either you fight for what's yours or somebody else takes it away from you. I learned about territory, your "turf," and how to protect it.

I belonged to a street gang; I had to. Either you joined a gang or risked getting killed. Our gang was called the Black Cats, and we were violent, though not as violent as most. (Oh, we'd shake down kids for quarters. . . .) They called me Smart, as in "Hey, Smart . . . do us a favor and read another book." At which point they all started laughing because they knew I read—well, *books*.

Most of the kids in my gang became small-time punks and hoodlums. They lived on excitement, on the thrill of just being street punks and hoodlums. They liked to scare people, I remember, just for the sake of *seeing* them scared, seeing faces panicked and helpless and frozen with fear when those faces were threatened with violence. They got a big adrenaline rush out of that. I didn't because I didn't like to see people get hurt.

All my buddies wanted to be *known*. In a way, they wanted to be stars.

I haven't forgotten what I learned growing up on the street, just as Jake hasn't forgotten. (We both had the same choices: We could've become criminals.) I know, for example, that in this business you can't deal in a balance of power. (There was a time long ago when you could, but that's gone.) Either you deal in power, or not at all. Either you're in control, or somebody else controls you. And with more Players in the game now and fewer projects being made, the stakes go up incredibly. The hits are bigger, so are the failures. For all of us the highs get higher, the lows much lower than ever before. As a result, the game tends to make everybody more desperate (everybody wants his shot). So maintaining your power becomes the only way to survive in the plastic jungle. Commercial success, as I say, is the true measure of your power in the Industry, and you can't get it unless you're willing to fight like hell. Even then, it may elude you —if you don't have the luck on your side.

I had this hunch, I felt the time was right to make a move. The next round of fights would be over the script and casting. That's what Mark and his boys would be preparing for. (They'd demand changes in script, they'd push for certain favorites in terms of casting.) While this was happening, I could work on something else. . . .

I called Jake late in the afternoon (when he's most tired and therefore slightly more amenable to suggestions).

"You know, Jake," I said, after noting that the script was okay (that lasted five seconds), and, yes, I had my choices for casting ready for discussion (another five seconds), "I think we need a smart ad campaign to sell this picture. Michael and I were talking about it just the other day" (five seconds— only fifteen more to go). "There's a fellow at Metro who, along with his Protégé, has devised some of the most successful marketing strategies in our business. I think we ought to have him working for us."

"You mean Gray Cooper," he said, not tired at all.

"Yes."

End of conversation, my thirty seconds with the Chief were up.

Gray Cooper was in his early sixties, a handsome, distinguished-looking man with a shock of white hair. He looked like a movie star from the Thirties. He had a reputation for both creativity and taste in his advertising campaigns for various Metro pictures. I thought we needed a man with his taste very badly at our studio. To be truthful, I also thought I could suggest that he replace Al Lucky, Jr., the man about whose executive capabilities Jake and Mark disagreed. (I had nothing personal against Al Lucky—though his continual sleeping, on the job and in meetings, annoyed me.)

The days were surely gone when a group of executives could just sit around in a conference room and say, "Let's sell this exactly like they sold last year's biggest hit at the other studio." Marketing, I was convinced, now required a total handcrafting. You had to prepare well in advance for a campaign. You had to know what kind of strategy worked best in each part of the country. (New York doesn't respond to marketing the way Atlanta does.) And you had to realize that you couldn't just rely on television to promote your Product, because television isn't the great panacea that a lot of the marketing boys think it is. Of course, TV is the most effective way to reach thirty million homes in one shot, but the thing most executives don't realize is that advertising is a force that can work both ways. You can turn people off. Advertising on TV can kill a film, because there's no more effective way to convince thirty million people *not* to see your film.

By any standard, Gray Cooper was our man. If he

came aboard—and I was sure Jake could hire him away from Metro—we'd really have somebody of intelligence and taste (rather than Al Lucky) in our management group. It would be the smart thing to do, wouldn't it? Gray would bring his own staff, including his Protégé, the genius behind all those recent ads for Metro Product. I'd met the Protégé once at a dinner party. A tall man with short dark hair, big thick horn-rims, and Ivy League suit, I thought he was a straight corporate Suit. But he surprised me—he said he practiced yoga every morning in his office at nine o'clock and felt it "purified" his thoughts. He spoke of having "visions" —flashes for each ad campaign. He said that yogis had developed their perceptions to the level of imagining life as a dream and dreams as a part of their waking lives. He said we were moving out of a "reality period," one in which the film audience wanted "truth," and into a period where the audience wanted total escape (films with no statements)— fantasy—or an upper (films that were in some way affirmative). He said that right now there wasn't an audience for new work, but that one day . . .

So I made the move with Jake. He'd at least know that I'd back him all the way if it came down to firing Lucky and bringing in Gray Cooper and the Protégé.

I ran into Deirdre again. Her boss, the man who heads the Story department, kind of threw us together one morning. "Deirdre, meet Tony. He's a bright old producer." "Tony, Deirdre. She's a bright young reader."

"I'm not that old," I said.

"I'm not that young," she said.

I asked how Michael was. (I wasn't really sure

if Michael was living with her or just going out with her.) I asked how her backhand was, if she hit it crosscourt with top spin or not. I asked if she remembered walking along the Beach in a white dress one Friday night.

Michael was okay.

Her backhand needed work.

She didn't remember walking along . . .

I kept looking into her eyes as she spoke. They were very dark, with large circles underneath. Yet she looked refined. She wore expensive jewelry, smoked French cigarettes, and had the most elegantly lacquered set of nails I'd ever seen. I mean, her nails were *done*. It was hard to take your eyes off them, once you got a glimpse.

Strangely enough, she brought out a certain shyness in me that I try to hide, usually. (I don't like shy people, including myself; I'm afraid for them, afraid they'll get hurt. This business hurts shy people so easily.) Nevertheless, I found myself drawn to her—it's weird how people are attracted to each other.

I wanted to know more about her. She seemed to possess a history, I saw short stories written on her face.

I asked if she wanted to get together for a drink sometime.

"Maybe," she said.

Tomorrow, I meet with Jake and the boys to discuss script changes and casting. Doubtless Mark Fowler will be there, along with *his* boys. I expect a real clash of wills, the beginning of even bigger fights to come.

I can see them now, in the conference room, sitting on green leather, their faces implacable, eyes focused intently on me as I deliver my pitch for the actors I want in the film.

What will they be thinking? Looking for?

They'll be looking for any signs of weakness on my part. A hesitation in my voice. An untimely cough. A faltering in my pitch. A bit of nervous laughter. (The Industry cannot tolerate weakness of any kind: Those who are weak—which includes most of us—end up being devoured by the strong, or we devour ourselves.)

If for some reason I'm not firmly convinced of what I'm saying, if I don't reflect a *total belief* in the actors I want to be in this film, they'll detect it right away. And they'll eat me alive. For, after all, they're carnivorous.

The actors I want for *Studio* are Jack Nicholson, Bobby De Niro, and Candy Bergen. Tomorrow, I'll propose different names because I know they'll reject my first choices automatically. Yet I'm taking a big chance—in trying to convince them (unconvincingly) of names I don't want. I've done it before, however, and even have my own name for it: the Black-Shoe Shuffle.

Tomorrow, I wear my only pair of black shoes for the meeting.

Tomorrow, I see that woman reporter who's doing the piece on the "new breed of producers." Maybe I'll plant the rumor that Al Lucky is on his way out, to be followed by . . .

Tomorrow, I run two miles on the Beach instead of one. I need to get in better shape.

Tomorrow, I call Sandra and make arrangements to see *my* boy. I'm afraid he'll forget who I am. . . .

Tomorrow, I see four movies. I see the new Jack Nicholson picture, the new Bobby De Niro picture, the new Candy Bergen. The fourth? A love story (now forgotten) that I produced years ago.

Tomorrow, I send scripts of *Studio* to each one of those stars, as well as their agents.

Tomorrow, I buy that present I've wanted to buy for my daughter's birthday, which I've forgotten. The present? It's a secret, I can't tell you now.

Tomorrow, I send money home to my eighty-year-old mother, along with a note promising to come back East for a visit.

Tomorrow, I send a check to my charity. (Everybody in the Industry has his or her own charity.)

Tomorrow, I make love to BB like I've never made before.

Tomorrow, I meet Deirdre for a drink.

Tomorrow, I put money into my bank account. (I'm always overdrawn. One day I have money in my account and the next day I'm overdrawn —bouncing checks all over town. Money goes so fast here, making everybody rich and poor at the same time.)

Tomorrow, I refill my Coke machine.

It's a cool night. I'm cruising the freeway in my ancient Chevy; I'm talking to myself. I've had two Cokes already and feel refreshed. My teeth sparkle, lips burn from the Coke. I'm taking it slow, handling the wheel gently, letting my beast float. The night air has a certain *sting* to it, I can feel it in my lungs.

Daphne called—she thinks she can help me with casting. She wants me to come over tonight. "Just like old times, darling," she said in her siren's voice. I'm tempted, I haven't *shtupped* her in a long, long while.

God, I'm hungry, my stomach's growling. I need nourishment. . . . One freeway flows into another freeway, into another, into another, into . . . I don't know where I'm going, my beast is driving itself. She's devouring the road ahead, mile after mile, burning up fuel, killing time.

Before too long I'm turning off the freeway, I don't know where. The streets look vaguely familiar, it's a tacky part of town. I'm stopping at a restaurant I used to frequent years ago. I remember it as being the only "real" place in town, one which wasn't an imitation of an imitation of an imitation.

The restaurant is run entirely by ex-convicts. They serve as cooks, waiters, cashiers. I used to know the owner. He served a lot of time before starting the business.

Tonight, he's not there. I wait for a table; I'm growing hungrier by the minute. I like the decor, it's stark yet somehow warm, "real." Checkered tablecloths, in black and white. A long-stemmed rose in a wine bottle on each table.

My turn comes, I sit down. Immediately, the waiter brings several loaves of fresh bread. The place smells of bread. I order wine and a simple dinner of steak and baked potato, with a large tossed green salad. I eat slowly, savoring every mouthful. My waiter is a tall man, extremely thin, wiry. He wears a uniform of white. I notice his hands are peeling, reddish. I'm finishing the bottle of wine when I see out of the corner of my eye Daphne's carrot-red hair at another table. It looks like Daphne Jones, yet I'm not sure. She has on very tight-fitting jeans like Daphne wears. Sitting next to her is a man who startles me as I look at him. He has short-cropped hair, wears a blue flight jacket, dark shades—I can't see his eyes. Strapped over his shoulder is a hunting rifle. I keep staring at him. He stares back, as though he knows who I am.

I finish the wine quickly and get out. I leave no tip.

Back on the freeway, cruising, night. I speed, then slow down. I look for music on the radio, can't find any sounds I happen to like. The midnight news comes on, I don't care what is going on anywhere else. I feel drunk from the bottle of wine, but not sleepy. I can't sleep. I don't want to go home, I should go home. Wherever my beast wants to take me, I'll go.

My beast takes me to Deirdre's house. It's past midnight when I arrive; I ring the bell and she doesn't want to let me in. I apologize profusely for the lateness of the hour and my unexpected arrival, but tell her, "I think I'm flipping out."

"Come in before the cat gets out," she says, opening the door.

The cat gets out.

"Ja-a-a-a-a-a-a-c-c-c-k-e-e-e-e-e!" she yells.

"The cat's name is Jackie?"

"After my sister."

I sit down, she offers me a cigarette from a Chinese box within a box, containing her French cigarettes.

"Thanks, but I don't smoke."

I take one of the cigarettes anyway, and light up.

"I'm seeing things, Deirdre. It's weird."

I explain about seeing the Actor from the script of *Studio* sitting in a restaurant that I used to frequent years ago.

"Maybe you've multiplied."

"Multiplied?"

"Yes. Maybe there are just more of you around."

I notice her living room is stacked, almost from floor to ceiling, with movie scripts. The scripts are in every color of the rainbow, some stapled, others bound. She sees that I notice.

"Oh, these."

"It's just that I've never *seen* so many scripts in one place."

"Well . . . can I offer you something to drink, by the way?"

"A Coke would be fine."

She disappears into the kitchen for a moment, and her cat Jackie suddenly jumps onto my lap, purring. How'd it get back in?

"You see," she says, handing me a Coke, "everybody in town is writing a script and I like to read them and collect them. Come on, I'll show you."

We walk into the study and I see scripts stacked from floor to ceiling again.

"Somebody has to keep them," she whispers.

"I suppose so."

"I've been for years. They're like all the dreams of all the people who came out here and made pictures."

We walk back into the living room, and I can't take my eyes off those beautifully lacquered nails of hers.

"How's the picture coming?" She smiles.

"Well, I meet tomorrow with the boys to discuss casting."

"Who's going to play the female lead?"

"You." I couldn't resist the opening.

She laughed.

"It's a really big question." I turn serious.

"Go with an unknown," she says, "a woman you could imagine men fighting over."

"Where do we find such a woman?"

"She's here."

"That's what I'd like to think."

"You'll find her."

"And what about the part of the Actor?" I'm probing.

"Oh," she says, without hesitation. "He's De Niro. Nobody else."

"And the Studio Chief?"

"Anybody you like," she says. "Could be John Houseman, Kirk Douglas, Robert Mitchum, Gregory Peck, Robert Stack, William Holden, Brando, Nicholson . . ."

"Kirk Douglas?"

"Sure."

"Any one of those actors?"

"Well, some are sexier than others. . . ."

"What has that got to do with it?"

"The Studio Chief, you see, has to be sexy enough to look like a young actress could fall in love with him."

I keep thinking I'd like to sleep with Deirdre, sleep with her now, but I know it's not right, I just know . . . so I won't even try . . . this time.

"How do you know so much?"

"I'm a child of the movies."

Tomorrow came suddenly.

My meeting with Jake and his boys was supposed to begin at nine o'clock sharp, so I arrived early, though, as it turned out, not early enough. Mark Fowler was already there, with Roger Dalton sitting next to him at the far end of the room. For today, Roger was sporting thick black horn-rim spectacles. Mark's twitching assistant, this bone-headed man whose only function (I was convinced) was to make you nervous just watching him twitch, arrived shortly after me. Didn't say a word, just sat down. And twitched. Soon Al Lucky, Jr., appeared, looking very well rested. Plus a couple of boys from production. They were all there, with the exception of Jake—the headfuckers of the business (the men who control thought and make decisions and shape the future)—yet somebody was missing—a woman? I couldn't figure out who. . . .

Johnny came in, wearing a Cowboy hat and boots. I waved at him but said nothing.

Scripts of *Studio* were floating on the conference table like dice from last night's crap game.

I yawned, then yawned again. I wanted to appear half-asleep. (Meetings like this served no purpose other than to allow for some headfucking among the principals. One had little to gain from them; in fact, they were designed to take things *away* from you. You'd go in believing you had a fine property, a worthy script, and the talent to make an exciting picture, and you'd leave after they'd chopped it to pieces, shattered your belief in the project, and taken away your ownership—and control—of it.) Under the circumstances, my strategy was to yawn a lot and appear totally nonthreatening. Then, at the appropriate moment, stand up and do my Black-Shoe Shuffle. . . .

Jake arrived, several minutes late. Two of his boys were with him, one from marketing, the other from production.

I didn't know exactly what to expect—one never does—though my greatest fear was that Jake, under Mark's influence, would decide to bring in Roger Dalton on the project and make me a *co*producer with him. If it happened, it'd be a brutal bit of surgery because I'd end up only being half myself.

Mark, the most accomplished headfucker of them all, stood up. "I'm not satisfied with the script," he said. "I don't see enough action."

Roger nodded in agreement, twirling his black horn-rims.

"We need more violence in the last part in order to make it work and to sell it to the public," added Mark.

Jake said nothing.

Roger stood up next and echoed Mark's sentiments. He delivered a pitch for "developing a whole new screenplay with new blood on the project." I tried to yawn but couldn't—I was seething. When he finished I could see Mark cracking a faint smile.

"Tony," Jake looked at me. "How do you see this picture?"

I got up and walked slowly around the room, glancing down from time to time at my black shoes. I grabbed Johnny's Cowboy hat, putting it on. I stopped by the tiny window in the conference room and looked out at the studio below. I spoke very, very slowly.

"I see this picture as an ice-blue thriller about people we know and love."

That was all, I sat down.

The expression on Jake's face was unchanged. He stubbed out his cigar, the signal that the meeting was over, and got up and left with his boys in his wake.

The faces at the table stared at one another knowingly. They also got up to leave. "Hey, what's the matter?" Johnny asked, taking back his Cowboy hat. "Later," I said.

On the way out, Mark told me, "I do think you ought to consider adding more scenes of violence in the last sequence. Perhaps some falling bodies from the Tower as sacrificial lambs—symbols of appeasement—you understand?"

I said nothing.

"Will somebody tell me what's going on?" Johnny insisted.

A few moments later, one of Jake's boys came back to tell me, "Mr. Steinman wishes to inform you that he thinks you're terrific and that he thinks we've got a winner on our hands."

Johnny and I had lunch together about an hour later in the Lounge of the Pink Hotel, the one with the Brazilian pepper tree outside. By some stroke of luck we were able to sit at Table Three, which faces the entrance and is therefore the most advantageous place To See and Be Seen.

"Jesus, we didn't even talk about casting."

"You're young, kid," I told him. "You don't understand—we won the first round. Jake is telling us in his own peculiar way that we can do anything we want."

"Come on. The Chief didn't say anything."

"Jake is an intuitive person, he lives by hunches. If something strikes him a certain way, he jumps. You can tell if a picture's a hit or not just by watching if the man jumps in his seat."

"Yeah, okay."

"And he goes with *people*. That's the bottom line for him. He's got to believe he's chosen the right people on a project."

"All right. So what's the next round?"

I told him of my plan, in elaborate detail, for gaining control of the picture. He nodded and nodded but pretty soon I realized he wasn't there. He was staring at a woman with carrot-red hair sitting at a table nearby. It was Daphne. She was lunching with the actor who ran off with my second wife. She pretended not to see either of us.

We drove back to the studio in the afternoon, and as soon as we stepped into my office Cinnamon said there was a message for us. Call Jake's office. I called and his secretary said that Mr. Steinman would like to see us immediately. Pronto, no time to prepare. (I should've known what was coming; Jake had done this before. He lets you win the first round, then surprises on the second, catching you with your guard down.)

We went up to his office. I couldn't believe how clean his desk was—not a scrap of paper in sight.

"Now tell me who you have in mind for the cast."

It's just Johnny and me against him. Mark and Roger are momentarily out of the picture. Jake seems to want to make it a fair fight.

And fight we do. I propose all the names on my "A" list, and he nixes every one. No, no, no, no, no. Johnny looks on in amazement; he doesn't know quite how to respond to this flat refusal to consider any of the top stars in the Industry.

"Now," Jake says, authoritatively. "Get some unknowns. I don't want to hear about big stars for this picture. Unknowns. Just one big star to carry the picture and the rest unknowns. You understand?"

"Unknowns, yes," I say, backing off.

"Get them," he whispers, like Jack Nicholson whispering.

"It may mean a lot of, well, *test*ing."

"I don't care what it means," he commands. "I want unknowns to back up the star. I want the public to discover an unknown the way they used to. That's what this business is all about, isn't it?

Discovering people who've never been discovered before."

"Yes."

"Making everybody believe they've got a chance to be a star."

I didn't hear a word from Jake or his boys for almost a week after that. Johnny, in the meantime, conferred with the writers over the script and decided to keep it pretty much intact—without massive revisions, as usually happens the day the director steps onto the project. (The writers were ecstatic.) Mark, however, tried to intercede. Every day he sent me memos with suggestions for more violence in the picture. (Goddammit, I wished I had Irv here to get Mark off my ass.) Mark's memos, which I framed, ran like this: KILL BY TYING BODY TO RADIATOR. SLOW BURN. KILL BY TAKING DRY-ICE BATH. KILL BY SHOOTING OFF EAR FIRST, THEN SPRAYING WOUND WITH SHOTGUN. DEATH ON STUDIO ARC LAMP. HELICOPTER CRASH INTO TOWER. BLADES CHOP UP TERRORISTS. DEATH BY KLIEG LIGHT BLINDNESS. IMMEDIATE DEATH BY PENCIL INSERTED IN EAR.

Where was this man coming from? He started to scare me again. He didn't have the power, fortunately, to impose his memos on the script, but he could demand, as head of film, that we have a number of violent scenes in order to insure the commercial success of the picture.

Was he trying to "motivate" us in his own twisted way? Trying to make us aware of the fact that he was watching our every move?

I found out one morning next week when I saw this distinguished-looking man with a shock of white hair. Gray Cooper. Jake had hired him against

Mark's wishes and also canned Al Lucky, Jr. I felt great.

Until Jake called me and said, "I told Mark that you suggested Gray Cooper."

Thanks a lot! No, I didn't tell Jake that.

It was obvious that Mark was unhappy with me because I'd gotten Jake to do something against his, Mark's, will. I could see a real power struggle on the horizon, with Jake sitting back and watching it all happen, just as he watches that favorite Western of his when he *really* wants to enjoy himself. . . . (He has a projectionist run it every couple of days in the top-floor screening room.)

While I was fighting with Mark, I was also fighting with BB. She wanted to know if I was seeing a lot of Deirdre. "Only a couple of times," I said. And what had happened to *our* relationship? "I don't know," I told her. "It's a difficult time, I'm under a lot of pressure." Was I sleeping with Deirdre? "No." She didn't believe me, even though it was the truth. Would I have a part for her in *Studio?* She wanted a definite answer. It was a no-win situation for me: If I gave her a part, she'd be terrible, and if I didn't, she'd kill me. I told her, "You'll have to wait for your definite answer." And was I seeing Daphne? "Yes," I said, jokingly, "in all the wrong places." BB didn't understand. So I explained about the two occasions on which I'd seen her. One, with a man who looked like the Actor in the script. Two, with my second wife's boyfriend. Okay. And who else was I seeing? "An airplane," I told BB. She got mad and looked ready to hit me. It was the truth—every now and then I'd stop off at the airport and take a peek at her: the Staggerwing I'd flown—Jake's Staggerwing.

"Let's not see each other for a while," she said.
"Come on, BB."
"I mean it."

Of course, we saw each other two days later at a party in the Hills. The party was a fabulous affair in this imitation Normandy mansion not too far from Jake's, hosted by a man I'd known for years —an agent who loved to entertain "casually." (So casually, in fact, that he'd often appear in dirty tennis sneakers, wearing a mink coat with nothing on underneath.) I hadn't been to his mansion in ages, and despite all the work before me on *Studio*, I didn't want to miss this party—in honor of a Swedish director who'd signed a contract with a rival studio. Anyhow, I got there with Deirdre. The agent greeted us at the door, drinking champagne. We were ushered inside and served champagne, the very best. For a moment, I did a double take. Something was missing here. Then I realized: There was no furniture in the house— not a chair, a sofa, a table, nothing. The entire house was blank, completely empty. The kitchen was the only place where there were *objects*. And every room was painted white and off-white. Yet nobody seemed to mind the barrenness of the place—the atmosphere was very pleasing. "I'm sure this is about the hundredth time you've been asked," I asked, "but what happened to all your furniture?"

He looked cheerfully at me. "Got rid of it. Looks nice, doesn't it?"

"Very clean." I was unable to resist the opening.

I looked around, Deirdre looked around. We saw BB, with Michael Steinman. We both looked at each other and laughed. (It was the first time I'd laughed in months.)

I waited for a while before saying hello to BB, Deirdre did the same with Michael. All I needed was for Daphne to walk in.

Daphne walked in, followed by Sandra.

Which was *more* than I needed.

I couldn't believe it: Deirdre, BB, Daphne, Sandra. I thought my love life was on parade. They looked at one another, and I looked at them. I thought they'd take turns ripping me to pieces. I said something idiotic, like, "Well, I hope everybody's having fun."

Just then a man swept by me, with a frizzy-haired woman clinging to his shoulders. It was the Hairdresser (which is what everybody I know in the business calls him, with more than a little contempt). And the Born Star. (The Hairdresser produced the last picture for the Born Star, and it made tons of money but neither of them is a very happy person.) And right behind them, the Swedish director. The Swedish director had an international reputation as a *shtupper* of beautiful women. There was some quality, uh, that people spoke of . . . some sexual magnetism that this man possessed . . .

Well, he cleaned out the room. Once Deirdre, BB, Daphne, and Sandra saw him, they marched out in his wake. I stood there alone for a moment until Michael Steinman appeared. He smiled at me. "The Swedish Shtupper," I mumbled.

Thank God, he happened to pass through. . . .

Back at my place Deirdre and I made love for the first time that night. We left the party early and drove up the winding Canyon roads leading to the house, in my old Chevy. The clunker wasn't as speedy as my German cars (one of which Michael still had—and, indeed, was growing very fond of, he said), but it was a nice ride.

I'd wanted to sleep with her from the moment that I'd first laid eyes on her—but felt guilty about doing so because of BB. (BB and I had grown close in the time we'd spent living together at the Beach.) Deirdre was strange, mysterious. I didn't really know who she was. And making love to her was, I suppose, another way of finding out, another way of knowing. . . .

In the kitchen (for some odd reason) we stood naked in front of each other. She was pure darkness: dark hair and eyes, dark skin and lips. Ouch! I could feel the jolt of the cold tile on my feet. She didn't say anything to me, yet I seemed to know more of what she was about. . . . She wasn't a starlet (like BB)—she had too much poise and self-respect for that (a luxury most starlets could hardly afford). She wasn't a film groupie, a hanger-on. She wasn't a career woman, ambitious and strong-willed—determined to make it big in the business. (Which is almost impossible anyway, because this is a business largely run by men—who are women.) *And she didn't want anything from me.* Quite a relief in a town where twenty-four hours a day somebody is either trying to sell you what he's got or take something away from you. At the same time Deirdre had the *looks* of a starlet, *liked* being a film groupie to the Swedish director and was doing *well* in her job with the studio. Maybe . . . she wanted *some* . . .

So she was all of those things and none of those things. Hence the mystery.

She scratched and pawed and dug her beautiful lacquered nails into my flesh. She ran them up and down my spine. I felt for her breasts and squeezed them gently. I felt the largeness of her nipples; I licked them. I ran my hand down from her shoulder (which was quite round, sensuous) to her pubic hair. I probed for an opening and quickly found it. But waited before going inside. We were on the cold tile, our bodies like ice on its black-and-white checkerboard pattern. I waited to learn more, to feel more. . . .

I went inside and stayed for as long as I could before letting go. She came and came—I think we connected at precisely the same moment. Zapped! It was incredible.

You know, I think we'd all screw until we died of screwing—if we had the chance. I think we'd behave just like those monkeys in the experiments they conducted a while back . . . those monkeys whose tiny heads were wired with electrodes connected to the pleasure centers of their brains. Press a button on a machine and the monkey experiences supreme pleasure (to the point of orgasm). Show the button to the monkey and he learns very quickly to press it . . . and keep pressing it . . . and pressing it . . . and pressing it. Until he's dead.

So we find substitutes for all the screwing we'd like to do, all the buttons we'd like to press (including the one to end it all). And out of those substitutes, I think, we've managed to build this society . . . this dream machine. . . .

The next morning I woke up with the shakes. I could barely dress myself I was shaking so hard. My hand, my hips, my whole body. "I'll call a doctor," Deirdre said.

"No-o-o-o. No. It's al-l-l-l-l-l right."

Deirdre wrapped me in a thick blanket and walked me around the living room, pumping me up with coffee. I knew I'd picked up something—not the flu or a cold or anything like that. It was a seismic tremor, a physical manifestation of a quake of some kind, a disturbance I was connected to. Something had gone wrong. Bad news. I'd been through this before; could recognize the signs.

"Ca-l-l-l-l-l-l."

"Yes."

"Cin-n-n-n-a-a-a-a-a-a-mon."

I was right. Cinnamon had been trying to reach me all morning. She'd called BB and Daphne and even Sandra. Oh, Christ, I thought, I'll never hear the end of this. She didn't think to call me at my house.

"Listen," she said, anxiously, "we've got trouble."

"Wha-a-a-a-a-a-t?"

"Jake wants to see you. There's competition."

"Oh, my G-G-G-G-G-God."

"Well," said Cinnamon, "get your pants on, dearie, and move it over to the studio."

(She didn't have to say that.)

I snapped out of it suddenly. Told Deirdre to find Johnny and tell him to meet me at the studio pronto. Dressed quickly, ate nothing. I had a hunch that a certain Harry Cohn III at Columbia was behind this, and sure enough, when I picked up my copy of the trades, I saw the full-page announcement: HARRY COHN III AND COLUMBIA STUDIOS PROUDLY ANNOUNCE PLANS TO MAKE *STUDIO CITY,* THE MOST THRILLING ORIGINAL MOTION PICTURE EVENT OF ALL TIME.

Harry Cohn III was not, of course, the original Harry Cohn but his grandson from his third wife (in other words, his third wife's son's son), who was now preparing to take over that studio. I wondered how it happened . . .

Probably Harry called Jake at four in the morning and told him that Columbia was going to make an epic film based on the history and life of his studio and that, yes, an ad to this effect was appearing in the morning trades. (Columbia has always had delusions of grandeur, wanting so desperately to compete against us.) I bet Jake nearly had a heart attack when Harry broke the news. For *Studio* had been heralded in the trades as Jake's "farewell picture" to the Industry. I'm sure Jake couldn't believe that here was this young kid, this imitation of the imitation of the original Harry Cohn, telling him, Jake Steinman, of Columbia's plans to challenge us, to make a fight of it. But, in a sense, we were cornered.

Two separate films on virtually the same subject will split the audience for both. It would come down to a battle to see whose film could be released first. But what about combining our efforts with Columbia, as several studios have done in the past? It wouldn't work. Whose studio would a band of crazy actors terrorize first? Would they go to Columbia and then over the Hill to ours? Though we're cornered, I know Jake will fight back with incredible ferocity.

Probably, to go back a bit, Harry Cohn III got hold of a copy of our script and read it through and said, "Hey, this is terrific stuff! Why don't we do it, too?" So he went to his boys, and all being Yesboys, they said, "Yes, Harry." And Harry thought, "Okay, we'll do it." Not thinking that he was risking open warfare with Jake—competing for the same dollar—something Jake would never tolerate.

In any case, it's a bind. If we try to back out,

we'll look ridiculous in the eyes of the whole Industry, spineless and chicken shit. If we make the picture and Cohn makes it, too, we split the dollar and risk turning out a loser, no matter how good it is.

The meeting with Jake lasted well over an hour, the longest time I think I've ever spent with the man. Mark was there, along with the twitchy man. So was Gray Cooper and his Protégé. This was serious business: Not many games would be played. Johnny got there late and sat down, minus his Cowbay boots and hat, panting. (Had he *shtupped* Daphne last night?) Before he had a chance to catch his breath, Mark started right in, putting pressure on Johnny. Would he commit to making the picture on an accelerated timetable? Did he think we could beat out Harry Cohn III and his boys? Did he realize that our studio's reputation depended on his ability to crank it out fast? (Which was a lie. I wish Mark hadn't said that to Johnny, because Johnny, like me, hates authority trips. He likes to be his own boss, keep things loose and have fun. And it's dangerous to put pressure on him— he's liable to say, "Fuck you! I'm going elsewhere.") When Mark was finished working Johnny over, I was ready to punch the son of a bitch in the mouth. Instead, I tried to stay cool.

"Wouldn't it be smarter," I suggested calmly, "to *accept* Cohn's challenge? And try to *outclass* him—produce a better Product, one with quality?"

Jake was listening carefully.

I said that if we accelerated production and tried to produce it at breakneck speed, we'd also increase the chances of fucking it up. So what would be the point? Just because we were first out with our *Studio* wouldn't mean that we'd necessarily do all that much better at the box office. If we were first out with garbage, and Harry Cohn got a picture out about his studio that had class, we'd be the laughingstock of the Industry. Not only would we look like fools for trying to beat out Cohn, but we'd also have a Product that made *us*—the entire studio—look bad. We'd end up making a piece of shit about ourselves, and, "Frankly, I'm not going to go for it."

"You mean you'll quit the project?" Jake wanted to clarify.

"Yes," I said, without hesitation.

(I could see Mark smiling gleefully, trading knowing glances with the twitchy man.)

I think Jake was thrown by my remark. Probably he thought he could get me to do it no matter what.

"So how do we get class?" he said.

I had him now—I could do anything I wanted for just this one moment. *Jake Steinman was asking me how we got class!* I'd never have a moment like it again.

I don't know what prompted me to say the next word—I hadn't thought about it much before—and as soon as I said it I knew it was wrong.

"Brando."

Jake went silent, almost as if he'd stopped thinking, stopped maneuvering, stopped wielding all that power of his. All eyes focused on him. The twitchy man stopped twitching. Jake couldn't just say, "We'll think about it." Or could he? Suddenly he got up from his leather chair, stubbed out his cigar —the meeting was over—and walked out. Mark followed after him, and I saw them conferring for a moment. Mark came back inside and collected his notes. I asked what happened.

"Awright, awright, you made your point."

I turned to Johnny and tried to keep from laughing. It was hard to hide my feeling of triumph. I got on the elevator with him and went all the way down, still trying to stop from laughing. Finally when I got to my office, I cracked up. I laughed and laughed. "What's so funny?" Cinnamon wanted to know.

The more I thought about it, I couldn't figure out what was so funny, either. Steinman had, in effect, agreed to use Brando in our movie—agreed to have Marlon Brando play *him*. (And I was convinced I could get Marlon, I just knew it. The price might be high, very high, but with the pressure from Harry Cohn . . .) So I called Brando's agent and sent him a copy of the script. The agent was very interested.

For about two days solid I went around high from the thought that we had Marlon in our picture. I knew that he was a great actor and all, but I also knew the moment you mentioned his name, you generated both love and hatred, often at the same time. Which was not unlike the feeling that our studio generated. . . . Brando embodied every contradiction of our time; he could be at once good and evil, loving yet despicable, saint and monster. . . .

On the third day, doubts began to surface: How much would he cost us? Two, three, four million for just a few weeks' work? Wouldn't his part as the aging Chief of the studio, this patriarchal figure, dominate too much of the picture? With his fee plus the fees for supporting talent, wouldn't our budget escalate beyond reason? Would we have to dilute the film's content and simply go for a straight action-thriller with lots of violence? Wouldn't the film audience just keep seeing Brando up there on the screen and never suspend disbelief? More and more doubts . . .

Late one afternoon I got a call from Jake. He didn't even bother to say hello.

"Fuck Marlon Brando," he began.

I didn't know what was coming but Jake's voice was so powerful, so resonant that it felt as if every word was being pounded into my head.

"I think he's terrific, but I don't want nobody playing me *but me*. You understand, Tony?"

"Yes."

"I'm playing myself in your fucking picture. At least Harry Cohn the Third or Fourth or Fifth, whatever he is, can't do that."

"I know."

"You with me?"

"Sure."

"Okay." He hung up. Right then I knew we had a picture worth making.

As far as I was concerned, Jake Steinman could play himself better than Marlon Brando could. Others might disagree, but I felt it would enhance the authenticity of the picture. There'd be a kind of "truth," if you know what I mean, to the material. Besides, I remembered back to that press conference in which Jake announced the project—and all the space he took up in front of those people. He wouldn't have to say much in *Studio*—he'd be *there*, doing what he does every day. . . .

When I told Johnny the news, he was jolted. For he'd been expecting to work with Brando and had psyched himself up for that first day when Marlon would appear on the set. . . . It's the most important day of the shoot because it establishes the whole pattern of your directorial relationship with the actor. . . . Marlon is clever—he gives you two different performances, though they look virtually identical on film, and then he asks you after you've seen the rushes, "Which one do you prefer?" And if your answer is wrong, if you pick the wrong take of his performance, then he judges that you're incompetent as a director and so, why should he, Marlon Brando, exert himself in the picture when you, the director, can't see the nuances of a performance? At that point Marlon decides to mumble his way through the part. . . . Johnny had been priming himself for that fateful day. . . .

I think he felt at once relieved and disappointed when he got the news.

"You'll get to boss around the head of this entertainment empire, Johnny," I tried to console him. "How many hot young directors even get to boss around their mothers?" He wasn't amused.

The next morning I got a call from Gray Cooper. Would I meet with him and his Protégé to discuss some ideas for the marketing of *Studio?* He said, more than slightly embarrassed, that his Protégé had had "a vision." We agreed to meet in fifteen minutes.

I had so many things to do.

I still hadn't called Sandra to make arrangements to see Jason. Tomorrow.

I still hadn't sent that check home to my mother. Tomorrow.

Or gotten my bank account in order. (I was still bouncing checks.) Tomorrow.

Nor had I allowed the reporter to interview me for her story on the "new breed of producers." Tomorrow, okay?

And my Coke machine was still empty.

But at least I'd sent my daughter her birthday present, however belatedly. The present? A gold necklace with a gold star. The inscription? In large letters: STUDIO.

I met with Gray Cooper and the Protégé. We talked for thirty minutes and I was really impressed with both of them. I think they liked me, too, because they'd found out, somehow, that I'd encouraged Jake to hire them away from Metro. (And when Jake hires you away from another studio, he doesn't do it cheaply. He doubles your salary—so both Gray and the Protégé were now making twice what they'd been making before.) The Protégé told me of his vision.

In that vision he'd seen a small man wearing a blue flight jacket, collar turned up. The man had on mirror shades, his face was unshaven, his hair cropped short. The man was standing in front of the Tower with a high-powered rifle aimed at the very top. In the foreground were a number of recognizable faces from our TV shows, people standing motionless, in cop and doctor uniforms, with guns pointed at the small man. High above the Tower a helicopter was stationary in the sky. Behind the Tower were the sets from our various pictures: the robots, sharks, roller coasters, rockets. In a window at the top one could make out the face of Alfred Hitchcock, almost as if it were one of his famous "signatures" on all his pictures. Superimposed on the scene were the words: WHO'S FOR

REAL AND WHO ISN'T? Below that, also by the Tower, was the title: STUDIO.

The next morning I agreed to be interviewed by that woman reporter (she'd been hounding for weeks). We sat outside on the patio of my office. Her name was Barbara——I missed the last name. She flipped on her tape machine.

What was I working on now?

"Well," I said, "I'm in preproduction with *Studio,* and I've got three other pictures that are in preparation. Excuse me for a moment, please."

The Coke man had arrived to refill my machine. I grabbed a crate of thirty-six bottles from him and carried them out to the patio. I offered Barbara one, but she declined. So I sat there, sunning myself and drinking one Coke after another and talking into her machine.

"So—where were we?"

Why was I working as a producer at this studio?

"Because of Jake Steinman. I admire him very much because he's about the best businessman in the film industry. Especially in a business like ours where, as somebody once said, all the assets go home at six o'clock." She laughed. "To a 'dependent' producer, the most important thing is decision making: the studio's ability to decide on a project quickly, without having to go to boards, committees, you know. Jake is very direct, decisive."

In what way?

"Well," I spoke slowly, "this industry is no different from any other industry—except that it requires a *sixth sense.*"

Which is?

"To know what to make."

And Mr. Steinman has that?

"Yes."

What accounts for the success of this studio?

"Its manpower."

How are scripts decided on?

"It's a gut-level decision. You ask, what are the ingredients? The cost? And if the film works, how do we sell it? We have to make films that will appeal to an audience, films that work at an audience level. But that doesn't mean they all have to be alike."

Explain.

"We're trying to do unique movies, not the nineteenth version of last year's biggest cop movie. We want to do one-of-a-kind pictures."

What about the audience?

"There's a danger in trying to predict the audience from one month to the next, because it changes so much. There are a few constants: The audience wants violence, they want to scare themselves, and they want to bust their guts laughing."

How important is the selling of a movie?

"As important as the movie itself."

Why Johnny Lombardo to direct *Studio?*

"As far as I'm concerned, I'd like Johnny to direct all our pictures. I think he's a bloody genius, he really is. Capable of doing much more than just action. People who don't know that just think of him in terms of the stuff he's done on TV with cars and trucks and boats and planes. He'll make *Studio* into a thriller with class."

What's the most important thing to have in the business?

"I don't understand your question."

What do you need to succeed as a producer?

"The subject. That's the one thing I've learned

from Max Schumacher and Jake Steinman, and it's been forgotten so many times. If you've got the subject, that's the whole ballgame. You can screw it up, but if you don't have the subject to begin with, no matter who you put in the damn thing—no matter how brilliantly it's done—if you've made a mistake in your initial move, which was the acquisition of the subject, you're doomed."

How do you see yourself?

"I'm a conservative gambler."

Tell me something about your personal life. Where do you live? What kind of car do you drive? How much money do you make? Who are some of the women you see?

"No."

Barbara looked very unhappy. She repeated the questions.

"No."

I didn't want to alienate her—she might be very useful to me later on in case my battles with Mark and his boys escalated. I wanted the Press on my side, I wanted the option of planting a rumor or two . . .

"Oh, I have a scoop for you, Barbara." She was just about to end the interview. "Jake Steinman will play the part of the Studio Chief himself. You're the first to know, Barbara."

She was delighted and thanked me for the item.

"You're welcome, BB."

"Barbara," she corrected me.

"Oh, sorry. What'd I say?"

"BB."

"Yes. She's an actress I used to live with. Very talented. You ought to interview her if you write any pieces on new acting talent in town." I finished my last bottle of Coke. "Oh, stay in touch. I may have some more news for you." I figured there'd be plenty of excitement ahead in the next few months while we were preparing *Studio* for a shoot on the first day of summer.

PART 3

I can't remember all the things that happened in the weeks before the shoot, and at times I wasn't sure if we were on schedule or behind (I faked it when asked), but somehow, against all odds, we managed to push forward, soldiers in the night, in what could only be called a monumental War of Egos. I knew there was a lot riding on this project —money, power, and prestige—certainly more than on any other film I'd been involved in. And not just for me . . . Our studio was making a picture about itself, and everybody connected with the project was only too aware of that. If the film wasn't right, if it failed to *move* an audience, failed to reflect truthfully what was happening, it would be tantamount to saying we didn't know who we were.

The pressure was on. We were aiming for a Christmas release, which I thought next to impossible for us to meet (three months to shoot, three to cut, mix, and distribute), unless we continued operating in high gear and risked burning everybody out.

Things, for me, were moving fast enough already. I'd moved out of BB's Beach house, to my place back in the Canyon. (But I missed running with

Michael Steinman every morning on the wet sand. And was out of shape.) Michael, incidentally, didn't really mind my spending time with Deirdre. "I like her, Tony," he told me, "but I'm just not that interested in her." And I made Deirdre one of my production assistants on the picture. (She was on loan-out from Story.) I thought she could really make a contribution to the project, yet everybody else thought she was just one of my groupies, clinging to me in order to get a shot at a bit part in *Studio.*

By this time I had Jake in my confidence. He liked the story I got that woman reporter to write about him (after I'd given her the scoop). And he liked the ad campaign that Gray Cooper and the Protégé had devised. Meanwhile, of course, the Industry had taken notice of his playing what everybody thought to be himself in the picture. There were news stories continuously, as well as much gossip in the Press. Some thought it was terrific, "the best thing that's happened in the business for a long, everlasting time"; others said we had ruined a good property in the casting and the picture would be "a disaster." Our company stock even fluctuated on the market. Up one day, down the next. Nobody was sure if it was a wise decision on the part of management or not. Yet everybody was . . . curious. The trades, in fact, assigned a reporter to cover the making of the picture, and he wrote exaggerated accounts of its making. As tends to happen, fiction aroused even greater curiosity than fact.

Jake handled all the attention with consummate ease. "I'm not doing nothing differently in the picture that I don't do every day, you understand?"

He knew all this publicity was good for the picture, because people would indeed come to see it out of ... *curiosity*, if nothing else.

One morning I persuaded him to go with De Niro in the part of the Actor. I think I'd been able to wear his resistance down after weeks of wheeling and dealing. "Okay, okay," he told me and slammed the receiver. Immediately, I called Bobby's agent. Yes, he was interested. I hand-delivered a copy of the script to the agent's office myself. And within hours of getting the script, Bobby read it, liked it, and committed to doing it. I was ecstatic.

Luckily, he had no scheduling conflicts (another feature he was supposed to make during the summer fell through at the last moment). And surprisingly, we had almost no trouble negotiating an acceptable fee with Bobby's agent. (Sometimes these negotiations drag on for months and things get very vain—you negotiate with agents for the color of the wallpaper in the star's dressing room.) Bobby's fee was a little bit more than he got for his last picture, plus points. (If the film hit big, those points could more than make up for a modest increase in salary on the front end.) Yet from all accounts Bobby wasn't in this just for the money: He genuinely liked the script and wanted to do good work. "A picture that lasts. A picture they'll be seeing a lot of years from now."

The day after he signed, he borrowed my '57 Chevy and repainted it in colors that he liked: bright orange with black racing stripes. He started cruising the freeways. He tried hustling tours of the stars' homes (contrary to the character in the script, he didn't have much luck at first). He began hanging out at bars in the tackier parts of town where actors, broke and out of work, tend to hang out. They recognized him but left him alone. He rented a cheap stucco bungalow. He stopped shaving. To develop a "sense memory" of the character, he asked me if he could wear my belt and my only pair of black shoes. It'd give him a "better feel" for the psychological dimensions of the man called the Actor, he told me. He developed a quickness with his hands (by juggling tennis balls), a peculiar walk (almost a hobble), and a certain crazed look (eyes glassy, lips wet, always winking, then sneering whenever he saw somebody). He skulked around the studio backlot, trying to stay anonymous. He wanted to know what it was like to be on the outside continually looking in.

One day he got an appointment with a casting director and appeared in her office (a squat building next to the Tower) for an interview. He had on mirror shades and a blue flight jacket—a toy rifle strapped over his shoulder. The director thought the rifle was real. Bobby tried to convince the woman that he was "a kid with a mile of potential" and that he needed work as an actor. She failed to recognize who he was and dismissed him as "a Robert De Niro look-alike."

"Hey, you're not gonna believe this but . . ."

Before he could finish, she kicked him out of the office. "Bye. . . . Try another studio."

The next day he sped through the main gate in my clunker, and took a joyride around the backlot, honking his horn at tourists, the old beast sputtering and farting loudly for everybody to see and hear. Benny and the other security guards were madder than hell.

"You goddamn punk!" they screamed, thinking

he was that TV actor (the star of his own cop show) whom we all know and love—Bobby Crazy.

So we had De Niro, thank God, and Jake was preparing to play himself, but we still didn't have a female lead. I agreed with Jake that she should be an unknown. But we were at a loss to find one. ("She's here . . . somewhere," I remember Deirdre saying. The more we looked, the less we saw . . .) Face it, she had to be a certain kind of woman.

One week Johnny flew to New York and tested over a hundred actresses for the part, and while he was gone I tested almost that number here. I'd never *seen* so many women in such a short period of time; they came to the studio every day and read for us. Some did improvs, others stuck closely to the dialogue in the script. They talked about themselves and, as a ploy, tried to get me to talk. (It was a common strategy among young actresses: You get the producer to start talking about *his* life, and out of the fifty women he's seen in one day, he remembers feeling good about you because, of course, he associates you with the talk he made about himself.)

I saw women in vinyl jackets, cigarette jeans, and chrome sandals. I saw hot-pink strapless jumpsuits and gold necklaces engraved SWEET BITCH and JEWISH PRINCESS. I saw one woman with a T-shirt she said was the "most gross" she could find; in big letters, it read: ARROGANT CUNT. I saw feather boas and silver lamé pants with spike heels. I saw white piqué dresses, blazers and ascot ties, Moroccan tunics (embroidered), long, slinky bias-striped dresses, gauze blouses and skirts, black velvet capes and sequined jeans, women with white mink jackets and dirty tennis shoes. . . .

Some women looked as though they were no more than the product of the most current fashion magazines; women who'd spent long hours at expensive department stores and beauty parlors. A lot of them, surprisingly, had little tattoos on their bodies—most commonly above the left breast—tattoos of hearts, flowers, butterflies, wild birds, horses, half moons, stars. They were very intricate in design. I saw beautifully painted faces with no character, sad yet attractive bodies that seemed to serve no function except to pose, bodies that somehow just stood still, incapable of doing anything. I heard about broken homes, desperate lives. I heard about wanting to make it as an actress or die.

And I felt for these women—they were subjecting themselves to almost certain rejection. I wanted to choose one at random, any one, it didn't matter who, just so I didn't have to see and hear any more of them, for they were giving me pieces of their lives, indeed their dreams, they were giving me emotions based on their dying fathers, and I was turning them away, one after another, rejecting them . . . as though they were failures.

You see, I was looking for a woman slightly out of her time. (All the actresses I interviewed and auditioned were so contemporary—they belonged to the present.) I wanted an actress who could play the *part* of an actress without being mannered or self-conscious. She had to have, I thought, a dark side and a vulnerability that she was forever trying to hide. She had to be believable as a woman over whom an empire is won and lost. In other words, she had to be a woman not just of beauty . . . but of mystery.

* * *

Suddenly one day things changed for no apparent reason. The Suits were on the phone to us with a list of demands:

Cut the shooting schedule back by ten days;

Aim for a PG rating;

Cut the scene at the end where the Actor drives onto the lot with a busload of crazies;

Eliminate all sex scenes and stick with violence.

I was furious. And convinced that Mark and his forces were behind this. They caught us by surprise. But I fought back with all the strength I could muster. Cut ten days? "Impossible," I told the Twitch (who was obviously Mark's mouthpiece). "We'd butcher the script." A PG rating? "Well, I can't promise you right now, but we'll certainly try." Eliminate all sex scenes? "That's totally absurd," I said. To show the Industry fully clothed, as it were, an industry built on bodies, on the selling of flesh, was "preposterous." Why cut out the last sequence with the busload of crazies? "It would set a bad example," said the Twitch.

"Well, what would set a *good* example?" I wanted to know.

"I have no control over these matters," he twitched, matter-of-factly. "I am not required to tell you what our standards are."

What the hell was going on here? Were they trying to kill the project even before it had a chance to breathe life? Had Mark's forces taken over? I didn't know, and my source in the Tower (who'd tipped me to the feud between Jake and Mark over Al Lucky, Jr.) was curiously silent.

I got on the phone to Jake. His voice sounded different. (He had many voices, depending on the occasion and what he wanted.) But this one was more reserved, as though he were holding something back. I protested the new demands, taking them apart one by one. He agreed with my criticisms, yet said, "I have to go with the majority on this, Tony." Then he quickly changed the subject. "Find anybody for me yet?"

"No."

"Keep looking."

When I told Johnny about the edict from the Tower, he blew up—smashing his phone against the wall. (Our connection was broken, and he had to call me back on another phone.)

"Ten days! They're crazy . . . *nuts!*"

"I know."

"Tony, they're screwing our asses."

"It happens."

"Hey, there's no way I'm gonna cut that sequence, you understand? The movie makes no sense without it, man."

"I agree."

I told him that, just between us, we'd shoot it anyway, in secret. I'd make the production arrangements and we'd try to sneak it through, okay?

"Okay."

"As for the PG, worry about it later—in the cutting room."

"Next thing you know," he said, half-jokingly, "they'll be cutting out our salaries."

"I wouldn't mind."

"Oh, yeah."

"Just so long as we keep control. To do what you want, Johnny, sometimes you've gotta do it for nothing."

And we still didn't have a female lead.

Days passed. We continued looking for her, we combed the town at all hours of the day and night, we looked on the Strip, up and down the Boulevard, in the Drugstore. And we kept seeing the same people—only in different costumes. (All the women in town, I was convinced, were actresses anyway, so it didn't really matter if they dressed like secretaries or starlets.) Yet none looked like the woman that I thought Jake Steinman would fall passionately, desperately in love with. . . .

De Niro joined us one day on the hunt (he had on his blue flight jacket and looked half our size— I'd forgotten how short he was). We wanted to see what *kind* of women he might attract with that raw, animal presence of his. We went around to some low-life spots in town, seedy places reeking of stale beer and broken promises, and found the women there (mostly hookers) strangely hostile toward him. Later at a party up in the Canyon, I saw women from the wealthiest families in the city making advances to him. But I wasn't sure if it was due to his inherent magnetism or because he was Robert De Niro, the terrific actor. (I suspected the latter.)

Meanwhile, I was still very much disturbed by the recent demands from the Tower. My plan to make the film a personal statement was in jeopardy. I had to find out what was truly happening.

One Suit told me, "It's just cost control. Everybody's running scared, not trying to chase last year's hit, y'know? They're trying to keep the budgets down."

I wasn't satisfied. I called up Barbara what's-her-name? I wanted her to do "a little favor" for me. "Some investigative work," I said. "It could be helpful to both of us."

The plan was for her to spend a week on assignment for her newspaper, interviewing the Suits in the Tower on the pretext of doing a story about the "new breed of film executives." I promised to set up some of the interviews and give her access to private documents and papers. She agreed to do it, but wanted to know what I wanted from her.

"Find out what's going on with Mark and his boys regarding production on *Studio*," I said. "That's all I want to know."

Well, the next week she arrived at the studio with her note pad and tape recorder. I gave her my notes and memos on the making of the picture, I introduced her to Billy and Roy, to Bob Blackman (the blacklisted writer), and to Michael Steinman. Then she met all the top Suits in the Tower and they took her out to lunch, wined and dined her. They looked after all her needs (and, as I understand, told her she could have a job with us if she "ever got tired of the pressures of daily journalism"—which was fairly unethical). Mark and his boys really did a number on her.

So she went back and wrote a nationally syndicated feature for her newspaper that was terrific PR for Mark and the other Suits. It made everybody look just great.

Except Jake. She painted him as this "autocratic figure" who was "partly out of touch with the realities of the film business," this aging executive who was "now going to try to convince the Industry that he was an actor as well."

I could've shot myself. Here I'd gone ahead and encouraged a reporter to dig up the inside story of the power struggle in the Tower and she'd written a puff piece on the Suits. My plan had completely backfired, because now Mark would have some more ammunition to use against me: "Well, the Press says we're great." And poor Jake. I'd made him look bad. And I still knew nothing more than before.

Until one day when I ran into Daphne. She was sitting at the corner table of the French restaurant that serves the best soufflés in town. The corner table is where all the "A" people in the business, all the heavies, like to sit. It's the only table in the place with a phone. I figured she must be waiting for somebody, but if she was she didn't say. I sat down and right away noticed that she looked different: very heavily made-up, her red hair in a frizzy natural, eyes somehow aloof, almost sinister.

"How's your movie?" she asked, blasé.

"Problems."

"Oh, really."

I told her all about the demands from the Tower and the unhealthy climate at the studio, knowing full well of course that, as an agent, she was aware of everything already. It was a ploy on my part—I wanted to find out what she *didn't* know and, ultimately, things I didn't know.

"Mark and I are seeing each other," she said, lighting a cigarette. (*That,* I didn't know.)

"Do you like him?"

"Yes."

"But he's married." (Mark had a wife and two kids, though nobody knew too much about them because he was so private.)

"Does it make a difference?"

A long pause. (It wasn't jealousy, but why did she have to make it with that creep?)

"I suppose not."

"He's a remarkable man, that's all."

"You mean he's powerful."

"What's the point of all this, Tony?"

"I hear he's planning a take-over of the studio."

A long silence.

"Well," she said very slowly, "Jake *is* getting on in years, isn't he, darling?"

The next day I got a call from the Twitch. What about Daphne Jones for the part of the Actress? Or perhaps we could rewrite the part and make her the Agent?

"No."

"What do you mean no?"

"Exactly what I said."

"But . . ."

"No."

I smashed the black phone against the wall; it split down the middle.

That night I had trouble falling asleep. I tried pills, I tried several glasses of wine. I walked the living room, I walked the kitchen. I lay in bed awake for hours. Heard strange noises outside, coyotes howling . . .

In the morning I crawl out of bed slowly and look into the mirror. Don't recognize myself. I see this man who looks older, face wrinkled, almost scarred. I'm sure it's an illusion, a trick of some kind that my mind's playing on me from a lack of sleep. I peer closer into the mirror, see the blur of another face. At first I think it's Daphne's, then the face dissolves into BB's, then Sandra's, then Deirdre's. Yet it isn't really any one of them. . . . I think it's a composite woman. In a moment it dissolves, vanishes.

I'm haunted by it over breakfast, I eat nothing.

At noon I drive out to the studio for lunch with Deirdre at the commissary. On the freeway I see a woman in a car ahead of me who resembles the composite. I catch a glimpse of her. She's dressed in white, she's driving a chocolate-colored German sports car, streaking through traffic. My lips are wet.

I lose her. Damn.

When I pull into the studio, I see her again, or, rather, the chocolate-colored car parked in the visitors' lot adjacent to the Tower. I go inside the commissary, look for Deirdre. She's sitting in a green leather booth at the back of the room, and next to her is that composite woman. I'm sure it's the same woman. She's wearing a white dress. I'm thrilled. I walk quickly over to the table.

"Hello."

"Tony, this is Jacqueline, my sister."

"Pleased to meet you."

"Hello," she says.

I can't get over it. She has BB's boniness, Daphne's mouth, Deirdre's dark eyes and hair, and Sandra's presence. She's Jill McCorkle, isn't she?

"Jackie's home from the East."

I'm speechless.

"Tony, we've ordered already. Are you going to have something to eat?"

"What? Oh . . . no, nothing . . ."

Several Suits from the Tower appear at our booth, wearing the standard uniform of black.

"How's your father?"

"Fine. He sends his best to everybody."

"If you have a minute, join us," says another Suit.

She gets up and walks over to a booth reserved, usually, for Jake and his boys. I see the black-suited men huddled around her, attentive, all eyes focused on her.

"Jackie wants to spend the summer in Europe."

"I don't think she will," I say, cryptically.

"What do you mean?"

"Tell you later."

I turn to stare at Jacqueline again, sitting in the white dress surrounded by that group of executives, some of the most powerful men at our studio. The tableau, for some reason, looks so familiar. I stare and stare. . . .

These are the same men as the ones I see at night, the men who keep saying, "We must control." And Jacqueline is the woman whose face I could never quite make out!

Soon she comes back to our table. "Oh, just some old friends of Daddy's, you know," she says.

"How's the East?" Deirdre makes idle conversation.

"Fine. I'm seeing a guy now who wants to be a screenwriter. He sends me flowers and valentines. He wants me to see his new car."

Her manner and gesture are uncanny. She's Jill McCorkle—*never aged*.

"Do you act?" I ask her, interrupting the conversation.

"Of course I act. Everybody acts—you know that, Mr. Schwartz."

"Tony. I mean, are you studying acting?"

"Oh, no," she laughs. "I wouldn't do a thing like that. Real actors are so—well, insecure."

"I'm going to say something that may shock you. It may even change your life."

Deirdre looks sternly at me. "What do you mean?"

"Exactly what I said."

"What?"

"Jacqueline, I want you to be in a picture we're making called *Studio*."

"Oh, heavens." She laughs. "I don't want to be in the movies. I grew up in a picture family, Deirdre must've told you . . ."

"No, she never did."

"I know what the picture business can do to people."

"But, your sister is in it—"

"Oh, she's doing some work for you and having a little fun. That's all, I'm sure."

"You're perfect," I said, authoritatively.

"Perfect for what?"

"The part I want you for—a young actress who seduces the studio boss."

"Mr. Steinman?"

"Yes."

"He could be my father."

"But he's not—"

"Why would I want to seduce him?"

"To advance your career."

"Seriously, you *must* be kidding. That's just the furthest thing from my mind that I can imagine."

"Well, *imagine*. That's all it takes."

"Tony, are you serious? Are you mad?" Deirdre intrudes. "She's never acted in a major feature before. I know she's attractive but you'd be taking an awful chance."

"I like to gamble."

"You really *are* serious, aren't you?"

"Very. Will you do it?"

Suddenly Jacqueline became extremely large. Her presence filled the room and heads turned down at the end where the Suits were having lunch. "I need time," she said, suddenly expanded, *"to think."*

It *was* a wild gamble, as I later thought about it. Stars just aren't discovered that way anymore. It's a myth—I never once in my life believed, for example, that Lana Turner was really discovered in that Drugstore. I thought it was made up by a dozen press agents working overtime. And yet, here I was perpetuating the myth! Offering an unknown the lead in a picture that meant everything to me! (Isn't that what Jake wanted?) Now all I had to do was convince Jake and his boys, Mark and his boys, Johnny and the studio casting director—and God only knows who else. Would Jacqueline herself turn me down? No.

To convince everybody and his boys, I made a ten-minute test of her, no sound. I got Johnny to shoot it (he loved her instantly and wanted her in the picture). In the test she is heavily made-up, almost unrecognizable. She sits in front of an actress' mirror, with rows and rows of light bulbs. You see her gradually taking off these layers and layers of makeup. Until you come to the real Jacqueline—possibly with a sudden blackout, so you're not exactly sure if it's the Jacqueline you know as the child of a picture family.

I took the test, along with another test that I'd made of BB, to a meeting I was having with everybody and his boys in the Tower. (I wanted to play a dirty little trick on Mark—embarrass him in front of everybody. I was going to show the ten-minute test I had of BB, trying to pass it off as "this great new discovery of acting talent." I was sure, you see, that Mark was the only one among the group who'd never seen BB's "acting ability" except on television commercials, which tends to be Mark's frame of reference anyway. I wondered if Mark would fall for it.)

I moved the group into their chairs for the

projection. The screen came down from the wall in the conference room. The show began.

There was BB in a series of shots of various television commercials. BB selling toothpaste. BB putting on "Covering" makeup. BB washing herself in a steaming hot bath. BB talking about milk and how much it meant to her sex life. BB drinking Coca-Cola and playing volleyball on the beach. BB shaking her ass for a new kind of bubble gum. BB using mouthwash. BB spraying herself in a men's locker room. BB washing dishes with a man on a white horse in her kitchen.

"She's perfect!" said Fowler.

"I like her looks," said the Twitch.

"What an ass!" one of Mark's boys yelled from the back.

"Stop the projector," commanded Jake.

There was a half-dead silence.

"Ha, ha," Jake said, in his most unfunny voice. "Ver-r-ry fun-nee."

Lights came on and the Suits in the room began to stare at each other with half-embarrassed looks on their faces. A nervous laugh.

(The trick had, indeed, worked. Mark had fallen for it.)

"Just thought you needed some amusement," I said to Jake.

"Well, I don't. So hurry up! I'm a busy man."

"Yes, sir."

"For Christ's sake, everybody knows that woman can't act." He sat down, followed by all the boys in the room. I could feel I'd made Mark smaller—reduced him.

"Okay, Charlie. Roll it," I yelled.

Now came the clip of Jacqueline. Jacqueline in front of that make-up mirror, framed with light bulbs. Jacqueline looking like a woman of eighty, face wrinkled, gray, hair white, jowls sagging, eyes blackened. Jacqueline peeling off makeup. Long strips of foam latex. Jacqueline looking ten, fifteen, twenty years younger. Peeling off more makeup. Looking thirty years younger. Looking like a . . . what else? Child of the movies.

"She's beautiful," said Jake, in a voice of his that I'd never heard in all the years I'd known him. The voice was filled with vulnerability. Seeing this woman grow young and beautiful had obviously moved him in some way—I wasn't sure how, but it had. He stubbed out his cigar, the screening was over.

On the way out he asked me, "When do you think you can start shooting?"

"Eight weeks."

"Try four."

That would put us precisely on the first day of summer, as we'd originally calculated.

"It's not enough time, Jake."

"Do it, Schwartz."

Everybody filed out. I don't think Mark and his boys were too pleased with my dirty trick. They smirked at me. In the past, looks like that were enough to kill me, ruin my whole day and make me cynical and malcontent. Today I was delighted.

The next four weeks were frantic as hell. A whole army of people—set designers, art directors, costume makers—went to work. Johnny rehearsed intensively with Jacqueline, fleshing out her part, adding nuance and detail to her character: This woman who is willing to betray everybody to get what she wants, to become a star. I knew how difficult a part it was, much more demanding than the "indicating," as it's called, that most actresses get away with, where they point to an emotion rather than experiencing it.

Johnny worked long hours with her, but the results were astounding. She began to pick up certain attributes of the woman whom I'd created in my original treatment. A crazed look. A strange way of walking. A tossing of the head. A haughtiness. (Contrary to the impression she made when we first met, she *had* studied acting; she'd learned from her mother, who was an old stage actress. She'd lived on the road for the first dozen years of her life.)

During this period, Johnny kept the rehearsals private; he didn't want me around. I understood. Deirdre was with me most of the time, fending off reporters begging for interviews. Every reporter and columnist in town wanted to know who this "mystery woman" was. Jacqueline-what's-her-name? She'd become hot copy. I was curious about the "true story" of Jacqueline myself.

So one night I got Deirdre to tell me. She and Jacqueline grew up as the only children of an old picture family. Their father was a famous producer; he worked, in fact, in Max Schumacher's stable at the studio. Max had him juggling dozens of projects. Until one day he had a nervous breakdown. That lasted for a couple of months, and Max had him producing again. He collapsed on the set of a picture. Another nervous breakdown. This process repeated itself until Uncle Max fired him for good. The man didn't want anything to do with the picture business after that. So he fled to New York, which resulted in the breakup of his marriage to his stage actress wife who wanted to stay out West for a career in movies—she couldn't stand going back to New York. So the daughters stayed with their mother, while the old man packed his bags and left for New York. He abandoned his relatives and friends, all of whom were in one way or another part of the picture business. The daughters went back and forth from here to New York, seeing their father every few months. (He'd tried to change his life completely and become somebody else. He was now a traveling salesman.)

Yet somehow, through it all, they survived, Deirdre and Jacqueline. They survived their father's complete breakdown and near-death at an early age, they survived all the pain of growing up with a mother for an actress, an actress for a mother —especially since their mother (who'd done so well on Broadway) failed miserably in her screen debut. They held together and survived.

Which was their story and maybe, in a way, the story of the Industry itself.

The next morning I woke up completely blank. Blank. All I could remember was the title of the picture—but nothing else. I didn't know who was in it, or what it was about. In fact, the harder I tried to remember who I was and what I was doing, the worse it got. On the phone I dialed the operator. What day was it?

"It's not my job to release such information," she said.

I thought I'd better call my secretary, but I couldn't remember *her* name, either. The only name I could remember was Jill McCorkle. I called Information.

"There's no Jill McCorkle listed," said the steely voice at the other end. "Sorry."

"There must be some mistake."

"Sorry, buster."

"Okay, okay." And I hung up. My routine had mysteriously broken down. I couldn't remember what I was supposed to do in the morning. Read the paper first? Eat breakfast later? Have a cup of coffee and run?

Suddenly the phone rang. Jacqueline. She called to say that she and Johnny needed more rehearsal time for the picture. She jolted me back to life.

I became clear again.

"I can give you a few days, but no more."

"Well, okay."

"You can do it."

"Why don't you come down sometime and watch?"

I was delighted, for I'd wanted very badly to watch a couple of rehearsals. I got to see how Johnny was working with her, getting her into the part.

Evidently he was exploiting her ambivalence toward the Industry. "Your father is calling on the phone," I heard him tell her. "Imagine that. You see it now. What does it feel like when the phone rings? What do you feel? Now your father, he's a very powerful man. Yes. For no reason at all he wants you to sell your body. He tells you that on the phone. He tells you that, but you resist. How do you resist?" I could see Jacqueline going through all kinds of facial and bodily changes.

Then Johnny rehearsed with Jake. He worked on the motivations of the Studio Chief. Why was the Chief doing this? Why was he sacrificing so much for this woman? How would he fight the Opposition Forces? To a large extent, of course, it was melodrama, yet I liked the way Johnny worked. He *allowed* both Jake and Jacqueline to develop the parts themselves, rather than trying to impose a character on them. He brought in De Niro and rehearsed them all together. I could see the complex ways in which he was shaping each performance, each nuance of character.

Meanwhile, I was shaping my own performance, and growing extremely fond of Jacqueline. I wanted to see more of her, spend time with her. . . . But suddenly, we hit the starting date. And the picture was ready to roll.

Day One of Shooting, June 21: I'm on the set at the crack of dawn, just as the sun is coming up over the Hill. I have on an outfit of jeans and jean jacket, faded very, very light blue. I'm here earlier than Johnny or the cameraman or any members of the crew (which, incidentally, I handpicked; all the fellows I've worked with in the past, loyal and professional—well, above all, loyal). I'm ready to shoot.

The cameraman arrives. He's Vilmos Zsigmond —"Ziggy," as he's called—and he's one of the best. Hungarian, soft-spoken, with long hair and equally long beard. He, along with Bob Altman, developed the technique of overexposing Kodak film, so that the colors look more faded, almost washed out. For this picture, I want a soft pink coloring, plus lots of gold in the background. Anyway, we were lucky to get Ziggy—one of the pictures he was supposed to shoot this summer fell through. He was, essentially, Johnny's choice. (I'd suggested other names: Gordy Willis, Connie Hall, Owen Roizman, Laszlo Kovacs, Haskell Wexler, John Alonzo, among others.)

It feels like a scorcher. Johnny and the crew arrive, and I go to the gaffer, the sound man, the camera operator, the two assistant directors, to every man on the crew and talk to them about the picture. I want to get their input, I want them to come up with suggestions. I want the best ideas we can get from them. (Most of the fellows are rather surprised when I say this; I guess they're conditioned to work differently. . . .) "I'm glad it's this hot," I tell the cameraman, "because then we'll get a real smoldering look to the shots of the studio. Like burning coals."

Johnny is busy looking over the script, which, in this version, is written on pink paper. (One version was on blue, another yellow, and now—pink.) "How can anything be scary that's written on pink?" he jokes.

"Where's Jacqueline?"

"Haven't seen her."

"Ciao."

Jacqueline still has time before we're ready. I walk over to her dressing room in the second big sound stage. Knock on the door.

She's not ready yet. I talk to the first assistant director and tell him that I want to make sure that everybody working on the picture starts out happy and stays happy. "Got any complaints?" I look at him sternly. "Tell 'em to me and not Johnny. But don't keep 'em to yourself. I want to know if somebody's not happy—or if we've got trouble. You understand?" He nods, smiles.

I wink 'n' sneer. Pretty soon he picks it up and passes it on to the second assistant director, who passes it on to the sound man, who passes it on to the gaffer, who passes it on to . . .

I turn around and the entire crew is winking and sneering, winking and sneering. Winking, sneering. Sneering.

Ready.

"Roll the cameras."

"Rolling."

"Speed."

"Action!"

The first shot is of Jacqueline pulling into the studio lot just after she's learned that Jake is going to shelve the film he was going to have her star in, because of pressure from the Opposition Forces. The look on her face? She's seething. Car pulls in at high speed, wheels screaming. She tells the security guard (played by the real guard Benny) she wants in. He refuses. She crashes the main gate. He goes after her. She storms inside the Tower.

Next shot she's on the top floor. Inside Jake's office, livid, ready to tear his eyes out. But Jake isn't there.

Day Three of Shooting: Jake is there, in his office. He's all made-up, with thick mask of foam latex that ages him considerably. He looks like this powerful patriarchal figure—which of course he is. He and Jacqueline are supposed to quarrel violently at this point in the picture. And Jake looks as though he's ready to do it. Jacqueline, in makeup that accentuates her dark side, should match him blow for blow.

Johnny has rehearsed this scene for almost half a day and now wants to shoot it.

Day Four of Shooting: He shoots it and it works out fine. The rushes look very good, indeed. Yet the whole time spent up in the Tower, on the top floor shooting, has been a colossal pain in the ass. I don't know why, but it just has been this . . .

The atmosphere is all wrong on the top floor. The offices are too cold, sterile. The green leather chairs hideous. I'm not convinced that the Suits up there see very clearly.

But the rushes—they were good. There's one scene in which Jacqueline is terrific. She confronts Jake for reneging on his commitment to her picture, her vehicle. "It's me they want to see," she snorts. "Me, me, me." And that rage suddenly makes Jake look smaller. You can see it on film. Jake Steinman reduced. I don't think I'm as afraid of him anymore.

Day Six: Wide-angle shots of the studio. The Tower. The Sound Stages. The Producers' Building. The camera work is fluid, almost lyrical. I see, in the rushes, all that pink and white and gold and black, especially the black of the Tower's exterior.

Day Eight: I think we're now about two days behind schedule and I'm just a bit worried. When we were shooting in the Tower, I noticed that Mark's door was shut the whole time. I bet he's waiting for us to fall a few days more behind and then . . .

Well, what could he do? *Jake is in the picture.* Yet just when you think there's nothing he can do, and you let down your guard, you get . . . *zapped!*

I can see a certain change already. People are beginning to relate to Jake . . . not as the real Jake Steinman, but as . . . an actor playing the part of Jake Steinman. It's weird.

Nine: De Niro appears for the first time. So far, we've just shot scenes between Jake and Jacqueline. Bobby has on jeans and a T-shirt with STUDIO stenciled in bold letters. He meets the crew and shakes everybody's hand. Disappears into his dressing room until he's called.

Johnny wants him to float through the backlot, as anonymously as possible, just this punk kid who could be anybody. A kook. A space cadet. A struggling young actor. An "unofficial observer," as Johnny himself was at one time. Johnny wants to see him go through changes. . . .

Bobby is easy to work with; he listens attentively, makes a few comments and then . . . goes in there and *does it*. You can't believe the transformation from this puny little guy into . . . the Actor. Off-camera, he keeps to himself, very private. He works hard to concentrate. He reminds me not a little of the young James Dean: the same quick movements, intensely focused eyes, skinny build. Jimmy was kind of a loner, too, as I remember him. Kept to himself until the cameras began to roll . . . suddenly, he was *there!* And you couldn't take your eyes off him.

Twelve: We're shooting all over town, in bars, the Lounge of the Pink Hotel, on the freeway, down palm-lined streets, in shopping centers, malls, drive-in theaters . . . It feels like we're everywhere and nowhere, it feels like we're in the bloodstream of the city. And suddenly everywhere we travel with the crew and cast . . . we see Warren. I have never seen Warren so many times in one day. Either he's following us around, or we're following him. Warren in the Pink Hotel, Warren in the supermarket, Warren on a bicycle, Warren in a bar picking up another chick, Warren cruising the freeway, cruising the Strip . . . I'm beginning to think that Warren is in our movie. He's certainly in everybody else's movie in town.

*　　*　　*

Thirteen: Warren must've inspired both cast and crew, because now . . . the script girl is screwing the gaffer, though the gaffer is more interested in the best boy. . . . The sound man, meanwhile, is *shtupping* the cutter (a woman fresh out of film school), but trying to keep it a secret. Jake's wife is on the set now to make sure that Jake isn't really falling in love with Jacqueline. . . . Johnny isn't sleeping with, screwing, or *shtupping* anybody— which surprises me, though I did see him drive off one night with Daphne Jones. All I seem to be doing today is keeping track of who's screwing whom. (Usually it's the *director* who's supposed to do that, because he or she has got to know *everything* happening on the set.) And Deirdre's watching me to see that I'm not . . . distracted in my task. The conventional wisdom (as Cinnamon tells me): "If you leave the set with a man, everybody will think that you slept with him."

Seventeen: There is, as always, an incredible amount of waiting. . . . Either you're working in a frenzy—or waiting. Today, we've gone back to shoot in the Tower. Jake's office is being used as a makeshift dressing room. I see Bob Goldsby on the set, and say hello to him.

"You seen Jackie?" He wants to know immediately.

"Nope."

And leaves in a huff.

(Bob's been acting so strangely toward me the past couple of days; I wonder if he's been having problems with his wife again.)

Shots of De Niro eating in the commissary. Shots of Jake working in his office. Shots of Hitchcock's "backless" house.

Hitch appears in person, for the first time. The moment the crew sees him, this wonderful roly-poly man in the black suit, this genius of the cinema . . . they *applaud.* A standing ovation. Hitch bows politely, then confers with Johnny.

Bob suddenly reappears, but says, "I can't talk. Here." And hands me a script to read. "It's an untitled love story." I look at the author's name: Joseph C. Gillis.

Never heard of him.

Eighteen: I'm still puzzled about Bob. Oh, well . . . How do we sell *Studio?* I've been thinking about it for a long time when I get a flash: The way to sell it is to say it's *not* a film about filmmaking (which also implies that it is). Call it an action-adventure-romantic thriller with class.

"What's class?" One of the assistant directors jokes with me.

"Cary Grant."

"He's class?"

"The very definition of it."

Twenty-one: Johnny's five days behind schedule, and I'm starting to worry. I can't imagine anybody trying to replace him, but who knows? I don't think Mark's forces are strong enough to fire him, even under the pretext that we need to have a more "disciplined" director (in other words, a hack) on the shoot. Jake wouldn't buy it, though what would make Jake look bigger than firing the director of his own picture? In any case, I won't allow it to happen. I'll fight Mark, or Jake, if necessary, to keep Johnny.

Johnny's getting goddam good performances from *everybody*, including I suppose . . . *me*.

Twenty-four: That woman reporter suddenly appears. What's her name? Barbara. Yes. She's here, though no one to my knowledge has authorized her on the set. Besides, Industry etiquette says that the set belongs to the director. He (or she) decides who can be here, and who can't.

I ask her to leave. (I'm still very pissed about her piece on the Suits, and she knows it.)

She refuses: "I have permission from Mr. Fowler to interview anybody I please, including De Niro. So where is he?"

"Bitch," I mutter and walk away.

She finds Bobby between takes, sitting out in the sun, wearing that STUDIO T-shirt, drinking the last bottle of Coke from the machine in my office. And whips out her tape recorder and sticks the mike in his face. And *demands* an interview. (Bobby is a "bad interview" in the Press. Purposely so: he doesn't like people digging into his private life, or needling him with pointless questions about what he ate for breakfast and whether he sleeps in the nude—he doesn't.) Yet Barbara is aggressive as hell—I suppose she has to be, it's her job.

Bobby looks over in my direction as if to say, "How the fuck did *she* get in here?"

She batters him with questions, poor guy.

"I really can't talk about it. I mean, I just never really know what's going to work. I just do the best I can for every role."

Thirty-three: There's a spy on the set now—one of Mark's boys. He's watching us now from a distance to see if we fall any farther behind schedule.

The spy is very well dressed: black Battaglia moc-casins, shirt by Arthur Gluck, suit by Christino.

"You got to be kidding!" Johnny is irate.

"No," I tell him, "it's for real."

"Get the son of a bitch off my back."

I tell Jake, but Jake only says quietly, "It's out of my hands."

I confront the spy face to face. He's a bit taller than I am, larger in build, with a hideous scar running down his left cheek.

"You authorized to be here?" I demand.

"Yeah."

"By whom?"

"I'm an unofficial observer." He growls.

"Well," I ask him to come closer, "take a look at *this*." And suddenly I punch him in the mouth with all the force I can muster. He reels off to one side, cupping his jaw, as blood spills out all over his Christino suit.

I turn and walk away.

Suddenly the spy jumps me from behind, wrestling me to the ground. He throws a couple of punches but fails to connect. I punch back—but also miss. The crew is cheering us on; they're not about to break this one up.

Then, as I'm getting to my feet, staggering a little, the spy belts me one in the mouth. And I go crash-ing into the sound equipment, microphones and cables flying in the air.

Suddenly Johnny appears, wearing his Cowboy hat. Takes one look at what's going on and goes after the spy. The spy confronts him. And they circle each other, like boxers in the ring. The crew is goading them on. And I catch a glimpse of Jake, watching passively, taking it all in.

Johnny throws off his hat and I catch it.

With incredible speed, he delivers a combination of karate chops and punches to the man's neck and stomach. The spy keels over, obviously in pain.

Several of the crew help him up, but the man pushes them away and suddenly runs off. Out of sight.

"You okay?" Johnny comes over to me.

"Yeah, sure." I toss back his Cowboy hat. "Popped my jaw, I think. But aside from that, I'll be all right."

He puts on the hat, tilting it to one side.

"Thanks, Johnny."

"Sure, man." He pats me on the back. Then winks 'n' sneers. Then the whole crew begins winking and sneering, winking and sneering at each other.

And we start to laugh.

"You'd think we were shooting a Western, or something," Johnny jokes lamely.

"We are." I walk off to find Jacqueline, feeling my jaw swelling like a balloon.

Thirty-eight: For the past couple of days, I haven't seen Jacqueline at all. I don't know where she is. Most of the time, she keeps to herself. "She tries to *believe* in the part she's playing," Deirdre tells me. I can't seem to get close to the leading lady —she keeps repelling me for some reason.

Johnny is now getting worried that he has a disaster on his hands. He says he can't sleep at night, he keeps seeing this disaster over and over again. I try to calm him down. I call a doctor I know to prescribe sleeping pills.

Thirty-nine: Johnny's feeling better this morning. I'm convinced that we're being watched. All day long I hear the radio playing while we're shooting on the freeway—the radio in my Chevy. Music, news, weather reports, jive, commercials. The station is a new one in town: KSIX.

I know the way Mark wants to sell this picture: as a "microcosm of American life." That's the way he sells every picture we make starring a machine.

It's getting harder and harder to shoot on the backlot now because crowds of onlookers have started to gather around our set. People want to catch a glimpse of Jacqueline, mainly, this "talented new actress," as the trades have been calling her.

Irv Steingart is back from his extended trip to Europe, and he looks even *younger* than after he got his face-lift. In some way, he's changed—but I don't have the time right now to figure it out.

BB has a minor part—and contrary to what I expected, she's been terrific.

Michael Steinman, I feel, is drifting more and more into our movie. He hangs out with Johnny after we rap for the day, and they talk about old movies together. At one level they're both film buffs. Maybe Michael will help us out, if we have to confront Mark and his spying boys again.

Johnny, meanwhile, has been having these long phone conversations with—I think—Daphne.

It's getting really hot now. Cinnamon has brought me that cologne she keeps for me in the icebox.

At least we're eating well. I've made a point of having the best caterers in the business serve us lunch. And I've ordered two kinds of wine with lunch, just as Francis Coppola does when he's shooting a picture.

Forty-one: Jacqueline doesn't want to do a love scene in bed with Jake.

"He could be my father."

"Haven't you," Johnny interjects, "felt anything sexual toward your father before?"

"But do I have to play it in the nude?"

"Yes."

"I don't understand why."

"It's not convincing any other way."

"No."

"Jacqueline, it'll be all right."

"Welllllll . . ."

"Come on. You can do it."

She agrees. And suddenly, out of nowhere, the crew chimes loudly: "Awwwwwwwwwwwwwwww riiiiiiiiiii-ght!"

Forty-nine: We're about seven days behind, yet oddly enough . . . not a word from Mark and his boys. It's a mystery. . . .

Fifty: I spoke too soon: Mark is suddenly on our asses again. He's sent the Twitch to watch over us, and the man has made the entire crew nervous as hell. They're starting to pick up his twitching. . . .

I told Johnny.

He said, "Don't worry, man. I'll take care of it."

I see him on the phone again—I'm sure—to Daphne. It's a plot.

I told Deirdre. And she said, "You see, Johnny's in cahoots with Jacqueline, while Daphne and Mark try to ruin the picture for Jake. But Jake is really in love with Jacqueline and doesn't want any competition from Johnny. He just wants to complete the picture so that he can go out in a blaze of glory —and leave his wife. Mark wants to get Jake out of the way, so that he can take over the studio empire. It's simple."

"That's the trouble with you readers, Deirdre," I smiled. "You know all the plots."

Fifty-one: Jake is standing at the top of the Tower, stark naked. "What am I doing here?" he wants to know.

Fifty-two: Boom, boom, boom. Sniperfire echoes across the lot.

Fifty-three: In the rushes, De Niro is so convincing, so believable . . . that it's frightening.

Fifty-four: Bob Goldsby is back again, watching Jacqueline on the set. I wonder . . .

Fifty-five: No sign of Mark or his boys now for five days. I'm relieved. Johnny's a real *mensch,* a good guy. Frank Shelby, the Suede Man, showed up late in the afternoon, accompanied by Al Lucky, and Johnny kicked them both off the set.

Fifty-six: We're coming down the home stretch, only four more days to go.

"Keep 'em askin' for more," whispers an old-timer to me. He looks like my uncle Saul, only much taller. "That's the secret of show business."

Fifty-seven: I realize that I've got the best tan I've had in years. Solid brown. I start looking and comparing my tan with others. The cameraman? Solid, very dark. The director? No tan. The writers? No tans, or else pink and peeling. The stars? No tans—except when they've completed their work on the picture. Then they burn themselves black.

Agents? Sometimes white, other times very dark. The Suits? They work on their tans, with calculation (will I impress more people? Will I get better results?)

I buy a T-shirt, with the lettering: HAVE A VERY BROWN DAY.

Fifty-eight: I'd like to make love to Jacqueline, I really would. But I can't seem to find her.

Fifty-nine: I bought another T-shirt, with lettering: ACTION IS NOT CHARACTER. I sneaked away this afternoon to eye Jake's Staggerwing. Jake is very big in the Democratic Party. Maybe I ought to be.

Sixty: We struck the set. The crew kept some of the flats and drops for scenery inventory. The other stuff was bulldozed and dumped in the Valley somewhere.

"I *am* big," I remember Norma Desmond saying. "It's the pictures that got small."

PART 4

Shortly after we wrapped the picture, a double-page announcement appeared in the trades. PRINCIPAL PHOTOGRAPHY COMPLETED ON STUDIO. CHRISTMAS RELEASE PLANNED. MR. STEINMAN WISHES TO THANK, PERSONALLY, ALL THOSE INVOLVED FOR THEIR OUTSTANDING WORK. And it looked as though we would beat out Harry Cohn and his boys. (Their competing film, according to inside reports, was hopelessly behind schedule, though I wasn't quite ready to write them off—because they had Francis Ford Coppola directing it.) Despite the fact that we'd gone seven million over budget by extending our shooting schedule (and including, surreptitiously, the very last sequence with the "twisted ones," as Johnny called them), Jake was very pleased with the results. He had to be—he was the star of the picture, just as much as his studio.

And he threw a grand party to celebrate wrapping the picture. He invited, as the society columnists put it so wonderfully, "four hundred of his dearest and closest friends." It was held on a Friday, on the backlot, and for once, in honor of the occasion, all the production machinery at "the factory" ground to a halt. Sound stages were opened up. Fireworks went off next to the Tower, explosions of all kinds in the glittery sunset—sparklers and cherry bombs, a rain of Roman candles. Thousands of people invaded the studio. The entire Industry press corps was here to dutifully record the event. I'd never seen so many people here at the same time.

The commissary was open to all, serving a dozen varieties of food: everything from the exotic to the junky. There were black tables, with fine white linen, just covered with food. The tables looked as though they stretched out beyond the studio lot, almost to infinity. I saw pâté and cold seafood (Florida crabs and Nova Scotia lobsters), roast tenderloin of beef, sweetbreads sautéed with cream and mushrooms, broiled salmon with aquavit, Chinese peapods, cold Senegalese soup, Sercial with Camembert, Belon oysters, Perrier water by the truckload, chili and lemon mousse, Grand Marnier soufflés, Beluga caviar, scampi, antipasto, lasagna (Johnny was delighted), as well as hot dogs and hamburgers, cole slaw and tuna, french fries, grits, yogurt, ice cream sundaes, banana splits, egg salad, beans, turkey sandwiches, and the worst Mexican food I'd ever eaten.

Wine and beer flowed freely. A rock group called The Dreamers (they were also doing the score for the picture; I was lucky to find them) performed live on the front steps of the Tower. People were dancing. Traffic leading up to the main gate was backed up for miles. Everybody in the Valley must've wondered what "those crazy people" at the studio were up to again. . . .

Bobby's '57 Chevy (now painted every color of the rainbow) was hauled out for everybody to get a closer look. I figured we might turn it into one of the attractions on the studio tour.

I'd arrived with Deirdre but had quickly lost her

in the crowd circling the Tower. I went looking for her, but instead found BB, wearing a kimono top over black velvet pants. She was standing next to Irv, and Irv was puffing madly on a cigar, enveloped in his own smoke. I said hello. They were talking about Europe and Irv's trip. Irv was a different person now (maybe the trip had done him a lot of good); more concerned with making quality Product than concept films. He took me aside: Did I need any help in my war against Mark and his forces? What could he, Irv Steingart, do for my cause? I mentioned a few things. He said, "I'll get right on it." (I wanted him to make sure Mark and his boys didn't interfere with the cutting of the picture.) We rejoined BB, who'd spilled wine on her black velvet pants. "It won't show," she said.

By the dinner tables that stretched to infinity, I saw the Swedish Shtupper in the company of many beautiful women. I walked up to him and said, "You don't know me, but I want to thank you for something that you once did for me. And I want to offer you a deal to make pictures at our studio." He agreed to meet with me, to talk about it. Suddenly Billy and Roy came out of nowhere (which was also their story as writers) and slapped me on the back. I nearly spilled my drink (which was a huge bottle of Coke). I was genuinely proud of the Kids (they brought out the father in me) and looked forward to their producing and directing their first feature with us. Deirdre magically reappeared, this time accompanied by her mother, the once-famous Broadway stage actress. We'd seen each other before but hadn't met formally.

"Mother, this is Mr. Schwartz. He's a producer. Tony, this is Mother. She hates producers."

Deirdre smiled, then left us standing there. "See you," she said.

And we got along famously, almost as though we'd known each other all our lives. "Two very lovely daughters you have," I said.

"Well, they're *different,* aren't they?"

"They're both very talented."

"I'd like to see Jacqueline make it in pictures."

"When *Studio* is released, she'll be a star."

Speaking about stars, I caught a glimpse of the Hairdresser and the Born Star. They both looked like they were sulking. He'd shaved off his beard, and her hair was cut short, no longer a frizzy natural.

And where *was* the star of this show? I don't mean Jake, who was preparing to deliver a little speech. I mean Jacqueline.

I went looking for her. And ran into Johnny. He hadn't seen her either, didn't even know if she'd shown up. Then I ran into the woman reporter, Barbara, whom I didn't want to see. She needled me for a quote. Finally I said, "This party is the end of the dream—and its beginning."

I excused myself and left.

"There you are!" shouted Cinnamon, bumping into me. "I've been looking all over. I want you to see who I brought along for a surprise."

With her was my little old landlady from years ago, frail and wrinkled, with huge bulging eyes and white hair. "Nice to see you, Mr. Warts." I didn't know what to say.

I excused myself again.

Still no Jacqueline. I saw Bobby, in his blue flight jacket and mirror shades, almost unrecognizable in the crowd. He thought he'd seen her in a chocolate-brown German car but . . . "Thanks, anyway," I said. "And thanks for the good work on the picture." We shook hands.

They were wheeling in Max Schumacher! I forgot about Jacqueline for a moment and went to greet Uncle Max. He looked terrific, this wonderful caricature of himself, wearing a brown derby, spats, a tuxedo with tails, white shirt. He stood up slowly with the help of his cane. And the Press was there, along with the photographers, clicking away to immortalize the occasion. Somebody suggested a few shots of Max with that bust of him that sits in the Tower lobby. I went to fetch the bust and immédiately flashed on my uncle Saul—who'd tried to take it home with him as a souvenir of his trip to fantasyland.

Jake saw me carrying the bust out of the Tower and yelled, "Hey, what are you doing, Tony?"

I told him, and he laughed. I think that was the first time I'd ever heard him laugh.

Jake joined Uncle Max for the photo session. It seemed like old times. The music. The good food. The excitement in the air. The fireworks. And nowhere to be seen was either Jacqueline or, for that matter, Mark and his boys. . . .

Days later the party was all but forgotten. Johnny and I were in the cutting room. We'd shot at a ratio of about thirty to one, meaning that we had almost three hundred thousand feet of film—to be pared down to twelve thousand. And we didn't have much time if we were going to make the Christmas release date. Four teams of editors were working day and night now. In the cutting, the picture once again takes on another life: You have so many choices, so many ways of engineering sequences, so many details to remember. . . .

One night we felt we had a winner. A cutter new to the picture suddenly *jumped* in his chair after seeing the footage from the very end of the picture. The reasoning was, other people would jump, too. And word of mouth would spread *within the Industry* that we had a terrific picture. Before we'd even have a release to the Public, everybody would know that *Studio* had a couple of scenes that made you jump. People, I hate to say this, will *pay* to jump in their seats. (Is fear a way of connecting people, allowing them to experience something, feel something collectively? Who knows what truly passes through the psyches of hundreds of people in a darkened room . . .)

Johnny and I squabbled over a cut here, a cut there: minor things, really. (We were both so close to the picture that I'm sure by now we'd lost all semblance of objectivity.) "Every cut has to have a purpose," I told Johnny.

"Hey, there are no rules," he came back at me.

Of course he was right. So I tried to get out of his way until he had a four- or five-hour assemblage of the whole bloody thing. Then I could make suggestions in terms of what should go where, which scenes played and which didn't.

I spent a lot of time with Gray Cooper and the Protégé. (We were going to use that vision the Protégé had had as the basis of our advertising campaign.) We worked on different marketing concepts, different "mixes" for each region of the country. Should we use radio and TV here? Newspapers and just radio there? But word of mouth would make or break this picture, just as it does with every picture. And word of mouth isn't something you can manipulate very easily. (You can create an awareness about a picture, but as the Protégé said,

"You can't get them off their asses to see it.") Gray came up with a number of intriguing approaches. Hold down the advance publicity on the picture, especially from the newsmagazines. (Too much exposure could kill it before it had a chance to find its audience.) Open the picture without any sneak previews. Open it in multiples. Allow people to discover it on their own. (Meaning that we shouldn't spend all of our advertising budget right away.) The Protégé thought we should do something to get the critics all excited. Perhaps open in New York with a big studio-type party for all the media heavies —local and national critics. If we could get them *talking,* that was the important thing. I agreed. And I thought we could promote Johnny Lombardo as this "hot new kid" that everybody's saying is a bloody genius. We could send Johnny, along with Jake and Jacqueline, on a national tour (hitting all the talk shows), and because they were all unknown to the Public, the Public might have a chance to "discover" them.

Before the publicity reversed. Which happens every time on a picture. Four weeks after opening people are lining up around the block and you're getting a lot of attention in the Press and people are talking, the word of mouth is spreading . . . when, suddenly, a pressure group of some kind says your picture causes brain damage . . . and the Press reports the accusations . . . and people start to hate your picture. "Oh, it's not as good as everybody says it is," they say . . . and you don't know whether to pump in more advertising dollars or what . . . because after four weeks you look in the trades and read that your picture doesn't have "legs" . . .

But it's fun. So, I met with Gray and his Protégé, and we worked our asses off to find the right way to sell *Studio*. We had Plan A, Plan B, Plan C . . . and we'd try them all, if one didn't work. . . . For the longest period of time, I just remember going into these . . . *rooms*. I mean, cutting rooms and conference rooms. . . . They were rooms in which you went crazy. One tiny piece of film lost in the cutting room and you'd go nuts trying to find it. One small mistake in the marketing and the picture would die before it had a chance to connect with an audience.

Still no Jacqueline. I thought she'd disappeared after wrapping the picture. Nobody knew where she was. I called her actress-mother and she told me, "Oh, don't worry. She does that." But I did worry—I felt rejected. And Deirdre worried and felt rejected by me. (I didn't know what to do about Deirdre—right now I had to find her sister.) I looked *every*where for her. I talked to the last person who'd seen her after we'd finished shooting. "New York, something about going back East," said the makeup artist who'd done Jacqueline on the last day of the picture. I called New York, I called her boyfriend, the would-be screenwriter with the new car, but his phone was disconnected, with no new number. I called her father in New York, now a retired traveling salesman. "Nope. Haven't seen her. She never writes. I never send birthday cards." I called Bobby, asking him again, thinking he'd know—because, after all, he'd worked with her. Bobby had no idea. "Weird lady. Yeah, she's weird. Never said much between setups. I like her, man. *Class*. Lots of it, you know?" I called London, Chicago, San Francisco—talking to people I knew in those cities who were part of the acting community, where, conceivably, Jacqueline might be hanging out. No luck.

I got worried, thinking something must've happened to her. Hitchhiking she gets picked up by a gang of hoodlums called the Black Cats, the street gang I once belonged to. They rape her. In a bar she's kidnapped by men in dark suits. Held for ransom. A note is passed to Jake. Why would she be gone so long? More than just a few weeks? I didn't want to go to the police, and both Deirdre and her mother thought I was insane to do so. "Oh, Jackie's just cooling out," her sister said. And her mother agreed. "She just wants to get away from all the publicity," said the actress-mother. At the studio Cinnamon told me, "You said you wanted a woman of mystery in the lead. Well?" One of the Suits who knew her (I remembered him from the lunch at the commissary) said, "Forget it. She's probably taking a vacation at the beach. Said she always liked the ocean." That was a lead. I called Michael Steinman, who was living out by the ocean, and asked if he'd seen her. No. Was he sure? Yes. "When you fixin' to come out an' run again?" he wanted to know. "Soon as I can, Michael." I called BB next, and she got mad at me for calling. Especially about another woman. Wasn't I interested in her *at all?* In *BB?* "Of course, I am. But you don't understand, BB. I've got to find this woman. I'm worried."

Meanwhile, I was noticing that we weren't getting any interference from Mark and his boys on the cutting of the picture. I chalked it up to Irv's good work. But I soon discovered that other forces were at play. . . .

Where was Daphne Jones? I hadn't seen her at the wrap party and began to wonder if her affair with Mark had gotten serious. . . . I asked Johnny. At first he wouldn't tell me anything, and I knew he was holding something back. He and Daphne had had some kind of a fling (knowing Johnny, I'm sure it wasn't anything very involved), and then suddenly, Daphne had disappeared from his life. What had happened? Had she gone straight to Mark Fowler, as part of a power-fucking trip, or what? Finally I told Johnny I was trying to figure out why Mark was leaving us alone, and if Daphne had anything to do with it?

"Yes."

That's all he would say.

I asked him again.

"I can't tell you."

I wanted to know why, at least.

"It's heavy."

"Tell me."

"No."

"Listen, I want to know everything that's going on at this studio."

He told me.

The story was that he and Daphne had become *very* close friends, very involved. And they both knew that making this picture right would mean a lot to their respective careers. They also knew that they needed me to make the picture right. And if Mark interfered in some way, or got me fired, things would get very fucked up. So they conspired, in their words, "to subdue Mark" by whatever means necessary. The means were quite simple: Daphne. Already having a reputation as a bit of a *shtupper* in the Industry, it was easy for her to gain entrée to Mark's private life. They calculated that Mark would think, "Hey, everybody else in town is *shtupping* her—what's the harm if I join in?" But little would he know that Daphne would make wild demands on his time. Call him at three in the morning. See him at the top of the Tower, interrupting meetings. Demand instant gratification. Needle him on the phone. Nag. Gossip to the columnists about him. *Threaten* to gossip. Until Mark was indeed "subdued" and the making of *Studio* was completed.

And all along I'd thought that both Johnny and Daphne were just out for themselves. They'd saved my ass from Mark—and I was grateful, though I couldn't bring myself to thank them.

"You did that for me?" I shook my head.

"Yeah. Sure." Johnny didn't think anything of it.

"I don't know whether to thank you or punch you in the mouth."

The next day I found Jacqueline. BB called and said she'd seen her walking along the Beach. "Now you're sure?" I demanded.

"Sure I'm sure."

"Sure it's not Deirdre?"

"Yes."

"Remember I told you about seeing Deirdre walking along the Beach?"

I drove out in my German car (the first one, since the second was now with Michael Steinman, permanently) and really sped on the freeway. By the time I got there, it was early evening. BB said that she'd seen Jacqueline go into one of the old houses at the far end of the Beach. I took off my only pair of black shoes and walked barefoot down to the old houses. The sun was setting, I could feel the chill of the night air. I had a hunch . . . that house, up ahead, she's in there. I went up to the front door of this huge old ranch-style house. Bob Goldsby, my lawyer and best friend, answered the door.

"What are you doing here, Schwartz?"

"Looking for Jacqueline."

"Well," he lied to me. "She's not here."

"It's all right, honey," came a voice from another room. It was Jacqueline's voice.

"Can I come in?"

Reluctantly, Bob let me in. It was hard to believe: Bob and Jacqueline. They'd both been at the tennis club, they must've known each other for some time. . . . Yet why all the mystery? Why keep their relationship private all during shooting? Even Deirdre didn't know. . . .

"Simple. Bob's getting a divorce and we wanted some time in private before the film's released."

She offered me a Coke. "I know you like Coke," she said.

"No, thanks," I heard myself saying.

"Jacqueline, can we have some time together alone?"

"Bob knows everything about you," she said. "He knows and understands your plans for *Studio*. You told him, he said. You told him how you were going to use the film to make a personal statement about the Industry."

"My plans were a fantasy."

She didn't look convinced.

"Okay, okay."

Bob looked pleased, but I didn't know why.

The next thing I knew Jacqueline and I were walking alone together on the Beach. Seeing the last rays of the setting sun. But it didn't feel very romantic. How could it? She was serious about Bob, and he was willing to leave his wife of many years for her. I suppose he'd become her personal manager. Not a bad arrangement, I figured. Yes, Bob knew too much about me, and that made me feel vulnerable, especially if he ever misused what he knew. . . . How much romance could there be?

"I must mean something to you, Tony."

"Well . . ."

"Symbolically, you know?"

"You do."

"I sensed it the first time we met. I didn't want to get too close to you."

I told her about the strange pictures I see at night —the men in the conference room—which I can't resolve, which I try to resolve, because I'm not sure if I'm for the system or against the system, if I'm the friend or foe, the winner or loser. . . .

"You know," she says, "all the people in your dream are you. That conference table is you. That room. Those green leather chairs. The men standing around the table are you. The men who say, 'We must control,' are *you*."

"How do you know?"

"I just know, Tony. They're you. They're your invention. And that window you look for? It's you. The window in the shape of a big screen . . ."

"Yes?"

". . . you know what that is?"

"What?" I felt stupid, being unable to figure out what I'd been seeing.

"It's a movie screen. It's your way out. The movie you've just made—you're free."

"And what about that woman in white. Was it you?"

A long pause.

"It was me," she said.

Another pause.

"I was in your dream, I remember it," she confessed.

"Come again?"

"I'm in a lot of people's dreams. Deirdre knows, she knows it. She can't be, but I can. It started when we were children. We discovered we were in each other's dreams. And sometimes we were in other people's dreams, too. But then something happened. She lost it. So now she collects them in the form of all those movie scripts, you know?"

"Yes, I've seen them."

"I'm in a lot of dreams because I'm a lot of different women. People tell me that. Johnny told me that's why I'm a good actress. To you, I'm Jill—"

"McCorkle."

"I'm sorry if I've caused you pain. Let's go back."

It was getting dark, the sun dying in the ocean.

"Jacqueline, I don't believe you but I want to hear more."

"Okay."

"Tonight."

"Okay, we'll meet in your dream tonight, Tony."

I expressed skepticism.

"I've never done it."

"Oh sure you have. You probably meet people you know all the time in your dreams, Tony."

"I don't know."

"You just don't remember, that's all."

We were at the door of the huge old house.

"At midnight," she said, kissing me on the cheek before disappearing inside.

"Let's do it," she said, pulling my hand.

I drove back to my house in the Canyon. All my lights were on for some reason. A malfunction in the timers? I didn't remember leaving them on. And my security alarm system was turned off. I didn't remember that, either. It felt kind of eerie to be there, as though people were watching my every move.

I fixed a light dinner. Ate slowly. Read the news

magazines. Watched the Eye. Fell asleep in bed at midnight, *wanting* to see what I'd seen so many times before.

And sure enough, I did. The conference room in the Tower. The green leather. The long table. The faces with masks of simulated flesh. The window.

She's there. Jacqueline. Just as she promised. Somehow, I'm not afraid, knowing that she's there, on my side. She looks stunning, wearing white, dressed in expensive gold jewelry. Everything is so clear, lucid. We exchange knowing smiles. And I confront the black Suits in the room, telling them: "We don't need to control. There are other ways." They look at her. She agrees with me. Saying nothing but agreeing. The window dissolves into a movie screen.

Studio is playing.

"It's not the truth, gentlemen," I say, my tongue at last uncurling. "It's not who you are, it's who you *think* you are."

I take Jacqueline by the hand and we leave the room together. I stub out Jake's cigar. And we fly. We soar and dive, we bank and turn. We land on the Beach and I carefully, delicately strip her of her clothes and her layers of makeup . . . until she is naked, young again, and I am naked, and young again. I make love to her with no passion, yet with great passion. I plunge and rise, plunge and rise. . . . I go deeper, climb higher. I reach for other worlds, other ways of knowing. I keep climbing and climbing, seeing more . . . knowing more . . . feeling . . . climbing, soaring . . .

Until I'm free and let go.

Until I have no fear and wake up.

* * *

The next morning she called me. "That was *sensational*," she began. "You make love very, very well."

The picture was released on Christmas Eve (without sneak previews). Yet word of mouth had apparently spread (through our Industry and among the Public), because there were lines around the block in every major city. On the basis of those lines, experts in the business, like Ted Mann, could predict *how much* of a hit *Studio* was going to be —and the predictions were good indeed. The critics, of course, saw the picture, talked about it, and reviewed it. Sarris liked it, Kael didn't. Kael didn't like it because she wanted another picture to win the New York Film Festival competition. Simon liked it because of Jacqueline's pretty face. Farber both liked and disliked it. Reed liked it but *not* because Kael didn't. He was genuinely moved by Jacqueline's performance (I was too, for that matter). Canby liked it but qualified his review with all the reasons why you were *not* supposed to like it. Champlin liked it and waxed eloquently for thousands of words, more than was really necessary on his liking of it. Cocks panned it, but the next week Schickel, in an unprecedented move, said that *he* liked it even if Cocks didn't. Wasserman neither liked nor disliked it; in his absurdist view of the world, he couldn't take it seriously. Ebert hated it but it was never clear why. In the trade papers, "Murf" thought it was a winner, with good potential at the box office. He congratulated everybody connected with the project—and made us all feel very good. Knight liked it and thought that Jake Steinman would become a star.

Which happened. Jake began getting offers from

other studios to make various appearances in their films. He turned most of them down but still didn't mind all the attention. Meanwhile, gossip spread that Jacqueline and Bob Goldsby were living together and Bob was in the process of getting a divorce from his wife, so that he and Jacqueline could get married very soon. Reporters and photographers discovered their private retreat on the Beach and hounded them for confirmation of the gossip. They held a press conference not long after the film was released—and announced their engagement. In passing, Bob said that I was "the brains behind the picture" and "should take credit for its success." Well, that sent some shock waves through the Industry, especially the top floor of the Tower—where Mark and his boys were situated.

Not only was Mark mad about that, but he was also mad as hell about Daphne. (Johnny and Daphne were now a "steady couple about town," as the gossip sheets say; seen at all the right spots.) She had broken up with Mark once the project was completed, and Mark knew he'd been used and thought *I was behind it*.

So my stock at the studio was at an all-time high. Mark was gnashing his teeth because he'd had nothing to do with the success of the picture, and everybody knew it. Rumors were still in the air about who would be first in line to succeed Jake. One day I asked Johnny.

"Well, who is it today? Mark? Irv? Michael Steinman?"

He smiled at me, "You're not even warm."

Nevertheless, while *Studio* was grossing big bucks, I was plagued with the feeling, once again, that nothing truly belonged to me. Bob Goldsby referred my case to gain custody of Jason to somebody else in his law firm. And the word was that my second wife Sandra had broken up with her actor-boyfriend—meaning that it would be increasingly difficult to get Jason away from her. I felt deeply hurt.

And I couldn't figure out why the picture was such a hit. From my point of view, it was just a series of battles over a period of many months. All I could remember from the making of the picture were . . . these *fights*. "Not a happy day on the set," I told myself. Yet the damned thing was taking off, soaring into the stratosphere. . . .

One night I drove out to the tacky part of town, where I used to live, and found the same movie theater—the local bijou—I went to years ago. I stood in line (it was raining), like everybody else, and bought my ticket and went in. Eating popcorn from a huge tub, I sat in the same seat I used to sit in years ago. The seat was nine rows from the screen, dead center. I sat in my film buff's slouch, head back, feet up, body curled. I ate popcorn and watched. Most of all I watched how the people around me were watching. I noticed how they were responding. I saw their eyes, their faces mesmerized by what was on the screen. For what was on the screen (in the guise of the actors) was everything we knew and felt about the Industry—every dream we'd had, every passion. It was all there, and they were taking it away from us. They identified with De Niro, they identified with Jake and Jacqueline. They saw our studio for what it was: this dream factory with all its greed and ambition, success and failure, all its winners and losers, princes and paupers, warriors and kings . . . this last fairy-tale kingdom, where everybody was fighting, as everybody

tends to do in such a kingdom, over . . . a woman
of beauty . . . and mystery.

One morning not long after that I bolted out of
bed suddenly awake. I knew I was awake because I
could see things so clearly. Looking in the mirror,
I saw a person who was trying to be too many different people. I saw a person who was trying to
look young all the time. I noticed that underneath
those layers and layers of looks that weren't me,
there was another person. That person had a deep,
dark tan. That person had lines of character. That
person *knew* things. . . . All of a sudden I found
myself shaving this moustache I'd grown because
everybody else had also been growing one. (·Beards
last year, moustaches this.) In the process I cut myself a lot and remember licking the cuts. (The blood
wasn't so bad, and for some reason I wasn't afraid
to taste it.))

I found myself throwing out of my closet all my
old clothes—clothes I'd bought year after year for
the sake of being with it, being in fashion. The only
thing I left was a white suit. I liked white suits—
not because they were at one time trendy, but because I looked like myself in one. The cut was right,
I felt good wearing one.

The doorbell rang—my gardener. He wanted to
know if he could come three times a week now. I
found myself saying, "Sorry, but I'm selling the
house." The phone rang. Cinnamon. There was a
writer at the office waiting to see me. He had a
script that "I had to read." What's it about? I asked.
A machine, she said. "I don't wanna see it," I told
her.

I stopped lying to myself. I knew that my boy
Jason couldn't belong to me now and that maybe

it was better *for him* that he lived with his mother. But I still hated Sandra for it, hated her for keeping him from me.

All of a sudden I began moving pieces of furniture out of the house, dumping them on the front steps. They were pieces I never really needed or had much use for, stuff chosen to impress people with my style and taste and class. Why did I need to do that? Couldn't I find a more authentic way of doing that?

I called Jake and said that I wanted to see him this morning. He said, "Could we make it later in the week?" I said no.

I met with Jake a little while later in his office. He looked surprised that I'd demanded to see him. "What can I do for you?" He asked. I flicked a speck of dirt off my white suit.

"Jake, I'm taking over this studio. I want you to call a meeting of the board of directors tomorrow and announce to them that you've picked your successor. Then I want you to hold a press conference and announce the same thing." The Press, I told him, will report the event as follows: "A new studio chief and president of the largest motion picture company was named yesterday in a surprise move that left in doubt the fate of the company's head of Film, Mark Fowler, who had been rumored at one time to be next in line of succession to Jake Steinman."

Mark's fate, however, would not be in any doubt, as far as I was concerned. "I want you to inform Fowler that as of nine o'clock tomorrow, he is no longer an employee of this company. He is to speak to no one, lock his office door, go down into the underground lot, get into his car, and drive off the lot.

That's all. His personal effects will be sent to him at a future date."

By week's end, I told Jake I wanted the resignations of Mark's boys, his twitchy assistant, and Roger Dalton. I said, "Let Harry Cohn the Third or the Fourth or the Fifth, whatever he is, hire them."

Jake said nothing.

I said that as studio chief, I wanted to build my own management group. I wanted a position for Michael Steinman, either as head of Film, or as a company vice-president. I wanted Irv Steingart to head the television division. I wanted Johnny to have a seven-year contract with us, giving him "total freedom" to do as he chose on various film projects. I wanted to start a low-budget feature division, with Daphne Jones coming aboard as an executive producer. I wanted Gray Cooper and his Protégé to be "given their heads" to devise new marketing strategies, so that we could bring to bear the greatest amount of intelligence in the selling of studio Product. (Every picture deserved an equal chance to find its most receptive audience.) I wanted Jacqueline to sign an exclusive contract with us, and, in return, for us to find properties especially suited to her talent. I wanted Hitchcock to start work immediately on a new picture. I wanted to set up a writer's building—by converting that motel across the street from the Tower into a workable space—and hire teams of writers to develop new material. I wanted to attract new talent, fresh blood from the outside. And I wanted to do it in a different way than we'd done before.

He said nothing.

"Our whole system," I told Jake, "is based on the buying and selling of people. And the currency is money. Instead of using money, why can't we buy people, if indeed that's what we have to do in order to survive, with freedom? After all, it's a lot cheaper."

He said nothing.

I wanted us to attract signature producers and directors: men and women who made projects they really *believed* in—and we could believe in. Projects that had a strong reason for being made. And I wanted to start a fourth television network—one that was different in both content and programming from the other three—where we could excel in quality Product.

He said nothing.

I wanted Jake's Staggerwing. I had to have it.